EMBRACING THE WILD

D.V. WILLIAMS

Published by Claw Mark Publishing

www.dominic-williams.co.uk

Typeset in Palatino Linotype

Photography by Brian J. Davies

ISBN: 978 0 9957715 2 9

For everyone who has ever discovered their dreams come at a price, and often one they never expected to pay.

To Yasmin,

Dom W,
xx

CONTENTS

INTO THE WILD
(A Tigers Tale)

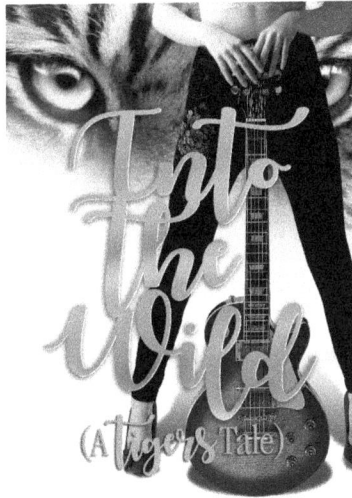

D.V. WILLIAMS

Every dream has a cost.

A lifelong ambition. A secret affair.
Something has to give.

Tigers Book One

ACKNOWLEDGEMENTS

Without the talents of some important people, Rebecca's story would still be a manuscript languishing on a digital shelf, a story waiting to be told, instead of a growing series of books. While I couldn't possibly thank you all by name because if I did it would need its own volume, there are those who really do deserve a special mention.

My thanks go out to MD once again for his stunning cover design, to Brian Davies for his wonderful photography, Rhys Williams for his help with tattoo designs, and to Kate Davies for her keen editorial eye. It really is a family affair.

Those who have read early drafts and whose invaluable feedback has continued to refine and shape the finer points of these books include Alex Bryant-Evans, Lynsey Rogers, Karen Bailes, Simon Blake and Kate Davies. A reader's eye view is so important. I know Rebecca and her unfolding story so well, it's easy to imagine everyone sees things the same way.

A big thank you and hello to the writers and authors both locally and around the world, some well known and established, some not, whose community spirit, support, advice, and friendship means such a great deal. There are far too many of you to list, and despite the temptation to name-drop, I shall resist. Particular thanks go to all at the LWC and the ALLi.

Finally, I would like to thank you, the readers who have already delved into Rebecca's world and wanted to know more. It is your enjoyment which helps to make writing such an immensely satisfying thing to do. To all those who are about to take the plunge for the first time: welcome. Rebecca's story so far has already shocked and delighted many, and I promise you there is plenty more of the same to come before her tale is complete. Enjoy. Sometimes guilty pleasures are the best of all.

Dominic

'And though she be but little, she is fierce.'

William Shakespeare

CHAPTER ONE

'Oh, Rebecca! Oh, sweetie!'

Linda's voice soothed me, but for once she didn't seem to know what else to say. Sitting on the edge of her bed, I stared disconsolately at the floor and played with my fingers.

'I never set out to fall in love with him. I just couldn't help it.'

'I know. Why do you think I was so keen to warn you about emotional attachment? I knew what you'd be like and there was always a chance he'd patch things up with his wife. Besides, what was not to fall in love with?'

'I didn't think you even liked him very much, not until recently,' I said, looking up at her through watery eyes.

Linda seemed surprised.

'It wasn't that I didn't like him, I just didn't see the appeal at first. I came to see him in a different light, that's all. I think he loved you too, that's why it broke his heart to have to make that choice, but what's done is done. He treated you well, didn't he?'

I sniffed and nodded.

'He was always such a gentleman, perhaps even too

much of a gentleman sometimes.'

Linda's mouth broke into a sneer. She adopted a sing-song playground voice and nudged me on the shoulder.

'Becca likes it rou-ugh! So who's the kinky bitch no-ow?'

She had a point. It was nice to play rough sometimes. What I'd never expected before Steve was that sex could cover the whole spectrum from tender and emotional to wild and savage via some unexpected detours along the way. It could be anything and everything: a whole previously undiscovered world. There were endless vistas of thought, emotion, and sensation to explore; rivalled only by the magic I felt when I made music. In a sense they were one and the same; they both had the ability to make me feel so totally alive.

I couldn't help smiling, even if it felt like my face was going to crack.

'There, that's better!' Linda chimed. 'Now the sun can come out again.' For the moment, though, it was still raining outside. 'Look on the bright side; you've had the kind of introduction to sex that wet dreams are made of. You've overtaken me in quite a few areas I can tell you. To be honest, I've got some catching up to do. I mean, you went into it wanting to know about sex and relationships, and look at you now! You can't say you've got nothing to write songs about anymore can you, 'Little Miss Experienced'?'

'I guess not, and I know all that, but it just hurts so much. It's like an empty ache all over. It's like . . .'

'Grieving?'

I nodded.

'Yes. I suppose it must be.' Thankfully, I'd never lost

anybody that close to me.

'You have got it bad.' She thought for a moment. 'It's kind of like riding a horse, though.'

'What do you mean?'

'Think about it, right: you've broken it in and learned to ride it; you get knocked off and take a fall, so what do you do?'

I shrugged my shoulders

'I don't know.'

'You dust yourself down, get back in the saddle and take the reins, baby! Ride that sucker! I'm not saying right this minute, but my offer still stands: you like Scott, he likes you and I'm happy to share him. I don't think Dean would be your cup of tea. You're a straight down the line, fifty/fifty kind of gal, and with him, it's more like seventy-five/twenty-five if you catch my drift.'

I didn't.

She sighed heavily and took a moment to choose her words, perhaps regretting her unguarded moment.

'Dean likes me to be in charge and I like being in charge with him. It's a different kind of dynamic. It's . . . complicated. Scott's more straightforward.'

'You mean dominance and submission?'

'If that's what you want to call it, yes. That's definitely part of it. I'm glad you used that term, though, rather than S and M; they're not the same thing. It's something we're exploring. I know you kind of played around with that a bit, but to you, it was a game you played, role playing if you will. With us, it's something that runs a bit deeper than that. I'm still trying to work it out as I go.'

This was surprisingly candid for her. I didn't want to interrupt, but that seemed to be about as far as she would go by way of explanation.

'Anyway, stop changing the subject. Get your exams out of the way and then you can let your hair down. Help yourself. You have my permission.'

I shook my head.

'But what if he's not interested in me?'

'You haven't actually listened to a word I've said, have you?' She rolled her eyes in exasperation. 'Take it from me. I've seen the way he looks at you.' Now she raised her eyes and her hands skywards in an earnest gesture and putting on a dramatic voice like a ham actor. 'O! She doth teach the torches to burn bright.'

'What?' I couldn't help genuinely laughing this time.

'Shakespeare, sweetie: *Romeo and Juliet* I think! Basically, it was Shakespeare's way of saying Juliet was a hot bit of stuff. Trust me; Scott won't say no. Just think about it, will you?'

'Alright, alright!' At that point, I would have said anything to pacify her. 'I'll think about it. Jeez! I can see why Dean prefers to give in to you; it makes for an easier life.'

Linda seemed satisfied with her victory.

'Listen, back to the subject of Steve and I know you probably don't want to talk about it, but this is important. You were friends long before it became something more, right?'

'Yes.'

'And there's no animosity there?'

'No. As much as I'm hurting right now, I can't blame him for the way things have turned out.'

'Good. And your paths are going to keep on crossing, aren't they?'

'Yes, of course. He's around a lot of the time. I can hardly avoid him when he's working in the studio with my stepdad, can I?'

'Exactly! So you're going to have to dry your eyes, man up, and deal with that on a daily basis.'

I puffed out my cheeks.

'I know. I mean, I can rationalise all that. It's just going to be hard emotionally, especially because I can't let any of it show at home. One part of me wants to hate him for the way I'm feeling, but I can't.' I looked up into Linda's eyes which were watching me with their familiar cool detachment. 'When I think about it, though, it's going to be just as hard for Steve. He's going to be seeing me too and he'll have to keep it under wraps as well, plus he's trying to rebuild his marriage at the same time. What I don't understand is how it got so bad between them that she let him go in the first place. He's such a sweet guy. She must have been mad.'

Linda reached for a tissue and held it out to me.

'Relationships can be complicated, that's for sure. Come on, blow your nose and tidy yourself up. We'll take a walk into town when the rain stops and go catch a movie or something. There's got to be something worth watching and there's bugger all else open on a Sunday.'

Thankfully the weather was starting to ease off already. Linda was right. I needed to get out and change the scenery, if only for a few hours.

My period had started the day before, so I was relieved the pill had done its job. Being pregnant now just didn't bear thinking about. The three weeks of tablets had finished on Friday, so next week it would start over again. I decided to keep it going. At least I'd be prepared for all eventualities.

Just as Linda had predicted, it was hard for me when I saw Steve over the next few weeks. We both had to act like nothing had happened, but we made our excuses not to work together in the studio on Saturday mornings. He was finding it just as difficult as me. I couldn't have stood being alone together and not being able to touch him. When I closed my eyes I could still smell his clean hair and taste his skin. Images of our lovemaking haunted my dreams. If I tried hard enough when I lay in bed at night and closed my eyes, I could still feel him inside me and the warmth of his body pressed close to mine.

I lost count of the number of times I played back the video clip on my phone. I knew every moment, every gesture; my coyness as I lay there with my hands tied above my head, Steve's hand tracing the line of my body down to my underwear, his delight at my readiness for what was to come, his teasing fingers inside me before he put the camera down.

What he'd forgotten to do was to stop the recording, so even though there was no picture, it had captured every muffled noise and eventually every last unbridled cry as we gave ourselves to each other and to the moment. Jesus, I was loud! No wonder Steve had tried to keep me quiet. It went on for a long time too. The poor woman next door can't have been able to hear the telly over the noise we made! I assumed she was on her own if she was living in a one bedroom flat. It was hardly surprising she'd stared at us when we both turned up again the following weekend.

Sometimes when I was alone I would play the video back, my fingers straying to the moist valley between my thighs. I missed him. I missed us. I missed the sex. God, how I missed the sex! It was so tactile and exciting and wonderfully messy. That's something romantic fiction always forgets to mention, but the mess is half the fun. There's something delightfully instinctive and organic about what happens when human beings physically connect. I had Steve to thank for that particular eye-opener; the things we'd done and the experiences we had shared would colour my world forever. The idea of Scott started to become more and more appealing as time went on.

Linda even caught me watching the footage on my phone a couple of times.

'Why do you keep torturing yourself with that video over and over? I know you probably enjoy a bit of homemade porn but give it a rest. Move on!'

I couldn't bring myself to delete it, though. It felt like all I had left of him. But it wasn't: I had a little chain of gold stars around my ankle and my star in the night sky . . . and a song.

CHAPTER TWO

In the weeks that followed, work began on the extension to the house. There had been a delay with the start date but now work was underway in earnest and a team of people was busy digging out the foundations.

Before long the exams were upon us too. I spent long hours in the exam room, looking up at the clock for inspiration before putting pen to paper again in a flurry of writing. Each time I would breathe a sigh of relief when I got to the end and put my pen down. Linda barely broke into a sweat. One by one I ticked them off my list as the days rolled by. I needed to let off some steam and I had a good idea how.

I found Scott in the sixth form study room. I could see him through the window and knocked on the glass. Half a dozen faces looked up from their work, including Scott's. He put down his textbook and came out to meet me.

'Hey, Rebecca! What's up?'

'Have you got a minute?'

'Sure.' He looked puzzled.

I led him away from the door and down the corridor slightly.

'How are your exams going?' I asked.

'Oh, not too bad, nearly done. I've got one on Friday then one on Tuesday next week and that's it. What about you?'

'There's one more to go. I'll be finished this Wednesday and I'll be so glad when they're over. Fancy doing something to celebrate the end of my exams?'

'Yeah, that sounds good to me. I'll check what Linda's up to.'

This was it: the crunch moment.

'Actually, I was thinking just you and me,' I said. He opened his mouth as if he was about to say something then closed it again. 'Don't worry, Linda's fine about it.'

'Oh?' Realisation dawned. 'Oh!' A little smile began to creep into the corners of his mouth. 'So where would you like to go?' He still wasn't making any assumptions.

'How about back to your place first and we can decide what we want to do? Ours is crawling with builders and machinery right now. They're concreting in the foundations and laying the floor for the new gym. I'll meet you after school.'

'Wednesday then.' He brushed his fringe to one side and smiled.

Oh yes! Mentally, I gave myself a high five. *Mission accomplished. Phase one complete!* I still couldn't believe I was doing this, but Sadie could. My inner tiger definitely owned the better part of my confidence.

Ten minutes later, I caught up with Linda on her way out of the door. My brother Rob was still in lessons.

'Oh, there you are. I was wondering where you'd got to,' she said.

'I was just talking to Scott.'

'And?' That had aroused her interest.

'I'm seeing him on Wednesday. Are you sure you're alright with this?'

'Of course! It was my idea, wasn't it? That's what friends do; they share.'

I wasn't too sure that was the kind of sharing that went on in a typical friendship, but then Linda wasn't a typical friend. I decided to keep my own counsel on that one.

'As long as you're sure.'

She winked.

'Knock yourself out, sweetie. Just be gentle with him, okay? He's no virgin but . . . well, let's just say he hasn't had the Sadie treatment yet.'

I giggled.

'That's better!' she said. 'It's been a while since I heard that sound.'

-0-

If the clock could have gone any slower for my final exam, it would have been going backwards. I finished with about twenty minutes to spare and sat, twiddling my thumbs and shifting in my seat while most of the people around me still had their heads buried in their papers, drowsy with the heat. As the instruction to finish writing was given, Linda looked across at me, smiling. I took a deep breath.

I found Scott by the door of the study room, fanning himself with an exercise book. He had loosened his tie and undone the top button of his shirt in an attempt to keep cool.

'How did the exam go?' he asked. 'You still look fresh as a daisy. Everyone else is melting.'

'It was fine. I'm looking forward to getting out of here, though. How far is it to your place?'

'It's about ten minutes walk, but in the opposite direction to you and Linda. The shop's on the way, though. Do you fancy an ice cream?'

'Now that sounds like a plan.'

I fancied something. Images of him licking ice cream off my naked body flashed through my mind, followed by a familiar tingling dampness between my legs.

Let's not get ahead of ourselves.

Sadie was pacing. She would have to contain herself until we knew where we stood.

'Great!' he said. 'I'll get my stuff. I don't have any lessons last thing.'

We stopped off at the shop and emerged with a couple of strawberry cornets, diving into them quickly before they melted. As we were walking, we laughed and talked and licked away the drips that ran over our fingers. My mind ran riot while the rest of me tried to remain cool. I wanted to lick more than just ice cream.

'What's your family like?' I asked, making conversation.

'My sister Suzie's away at university. She'll be back for the summer soon. Mum and Dad, well, they're alright.' He shrugged his shoulders. 'They're both at work at the moment.'

Oh good. We'll have the house to ourselves for a couple of hours.

By now I had reached the cone. I could feel Scott's eyes on me as I scooped out the remaining ice cream with my tongue.

'What?' I asked, knowing full well the effect I was having.

'Oh, nothing.' He swallowed. It clearly wasn't 'nothing'.

I pressed my advantage, probing to the bottom of the cone with the tip of my tongue then licking my lips slowly.

'Mm, I needed that.'

I smiled inwardly. Now I had him going.

Scott's home was a modern semi-detached house, modest and unpretentious.

'After you,' he said, opening the front door.

I stepped into the hallway and turned to face him. As soon as the door had closed, Sadie seized her moment and pounced. I pressed my lips to his and pinned him to the wall. At first, he didn't respond.

Shit! I've got it wrong. He doesn't want me.

In a moment or two, however, he recovered from the shock and pressed back urgently, his tongue seeking mine. One hand found its way down to my behind and pulled me in close.

Game on!

We untangled our tongues and pulled away, breathless.

Scott grinned.

'So that's the kind of celebration you had in mind. I wasn't sure.'

'I'm not trying to take you away from Linda. I'm not looking for romance. It's just a bit of fun if you want to.'

'Why wouldn't I? You're smart. You're funny. You're gorgeous. I'll tell you what, though; you and Linda are one hell of a double act. I can't work your relationship out.'

'Nor me, sometimes. Linda has that effect on everyone around her. Anyway, we can talk later,' I said, steering him through the lounge door and backing him towards the sofa. 'Right now,' I reached for the belt of his trousers, 'we've got other priorities.'

He grinned.

'Well alright then, if you put it like that!'

I could already feel the stiffness of his erection through his trousers. He clearly wasn't against the idea. Slipping his trousers and briefs down, I freed his cock and wrapped my fingers around him, stroking gently. It was slimmer than Steve's, more boyish, but nice, though.

'You don't mess about, do you?' said Scott, incredulous.

'No, I don't,' I shot him my most heated look; it felt good to be using it again, 'and you haven't seen anything yet.'

I pushed him back onto the sofa, dropped to my knees and wrapped my lips around him. It felt good. It tasted good. Before long, though, I reined myself in and instead, licked slowly upwards from the base then teased the end with my tongue, holding his gaze with mine. I wasn't going to unleash my party trick too soon. Besides, I had needs to satisfy; it had been too long. There were condoms in my schoolbag, but fuck it; I couldn't wait. We were safe anyway.

Hoisting my skirt over my waist I straddled him and with one hand pulled my knickers aside. With the other I guided him, brushing the head of his cock against me. He sat transfixed, like a rabbit in the headlights of an oncoming car, not even sure what to do with his hands. I sank myself down onto him and ground my hips. He groaned, opening and closing his mouth wordlessly.

'How's that? Nice?' I asked.

He nodded dumbly, enjoying the view.

'You can touch me, you know. In fact, I'd like that,' I added, rocking myself in his lap. The shallow motion was quite enough. I had a feeling this could be a short rodeo if I went too hard or too fast.

He eased my blouse out of the waistband of my skirt and skimmed his hands up my body, caressing my breasts through the material of my bra, and I let go of my skirt so I could undo my buttons. Although I hadn't felt it too much up until now, things were suddenly getting a bit warmer. I quickly shed the tie and blouse, unclipped my bra and dropped it to the floor then took his hands, placing his outstretched palms over my exposed breasts.

'Do you like it when I do that?' he asked, massaging my tits.

I nodded, settling myself into his lap with my hands against his shirt. He was still mostly dressed.

'You can do it harder if you want,' I told him.

I leant forwards and began to lift my whole body up and down on him, deepening the strokes, settling into a rhythm. God, I'd missed this. I was beginning to enjoy the prospect of corrupting him too; it was going to be fun. Scott squeezed my breasts in his hands and drawing me close, reached out with his tongue to flick it against my stiffened nipples.

'Oh yes, that's it.' I lifted my hips until he was only just inside me then sank down hard on him again.

He gasped then redoubled his attention on my right

nipple, sucking even more ardently than before and swirling around the areola with his tongue. Now I was coming down on him harder, pushing him deeper into me, intensifying the pace. He wouldn't be long now, but I knew exactly what I was going to do.

'Oh Rebecca, I'm going to come.'

I thought so.

Quick as a flash, I lifted myself up and descended on him. I only just made it. The first jet exploded from the tip as my lips closed around him, hitting the roof of my mouth. I took him to the back of my throat as the eruption continued, only easing back once his frantic climax had abated, then swallowed, licked a droplet of semen from my top lip, and grinned at him.

'There! Isn't that better? Aren't you glad we came back to your place now?'

'Yes!' he squeaked.

'One thing, though: you owe me.'

'Huh?'

'An orgasm,' I explained.

He bit his lip, looking self-conscious.

'What would you like me to do?'

I ran my tongue across the arch of my top lip. He got the message. Standing up, I slid my briefs down over my ankles and tossed them aside. They draped themselves decorously over the back of a chair. I positioned myself on the sofa, making sure my skirt was still underneath me while he moved around to face me again. In my mind's eye, I could see him trying to explain damp tide marks on the furniture to his mother.

'What's so funny?' he asked.

'Oh, nothing!' I reached out my left hand to take hold

of his tie and draw him towards me, raising the front of my skirt and slipping two fingers inside myself with the other. 'Now get that tongue over here, Scott Maybury.' I lifted my knees and stroked myself gently while he brushed his lips up my inner thigh towards their goal.

He certainly wasn't complaining about my request. His willing tongue made contact and travelled up towards my clitoris. In fact, Linda had trained him quite well. Scott wasn't at Steve's level but he was off to a damned good start. Perhaps, with a few pointers, I'd make an expert of him yet. Images of Linda with her fingers in his dark brown, wavy hair, her head thrown back and her mouth agape, invaded my mind. To my surprise, they intensified my already heightened arousal.

'Oh, yes Scott. Fuck me with your tongue.'

For a moment he looked up at me, startled. Maybe I'd gone too far. Maybe Linda wasn't as outspoken as me when it came to these things. I found it hard to believe she wouldn't be direct with him about what she wanted. Maybe it was the way I'd said it. Whatever the reason was, after only a brief hesitation he complied with my request, plunging his tongue in and out of me, rocking his head backwards and forwards. Grabbing his hair, I pressed hard against my clitoris with my fingers and without warning my orgasm overtook me, racking me from head to toe. Scott continued the movements of his tongue inside me, more gently now, until my muscles finally released their tension and the flood of sensations subsided.

I sank back onto the sofa, still trembling and panting. Beads of perspiration were trickling into my eyes. Scott looked pleased with himself. His fringe clung to his forehead and the area around his mouth glistened wetly.

I found my voice again.

'Thank you. You have no idea how much I needed that.'

'I think I'm beginning to work it out.'

'Come here you!' I insisted, pulling him close and kissing him, licking the moisture from around his lips and drawing them into my mouth before releasing them again. 'I don't know about you, but I'm thirsty.'

Scott nodded.

'Yeah, me too! Fancy a cold drink? There should be some cans in the fridge.'

'Sounds good.' I leant forward and peeled my back away from the sofa. 'What time are your folks coming home?'

He glanced at the clock on the wall.

'My mum should be here in just over an hour. Fancy taking this upstairs along with the cold drinks?'

'Now you're talking.'

In the end, we left to take the walk back to my place with only about five minutes to spare before Scott's mother was due back. Having hurriedly dressed, we spilt out of the front door into the afternoon heat, still giggling and laughing together.

'Take a good look,' I said. 'This is probably the last time you'll see me in school uniform.'

Scott looked worried.

'Of course, you'll still see me, just not in the uniform,' I assured him.

Now he looked relieved.

'I thought for a minute you weren't interested in seeing me again.'

'Don't be daft. I've had a great afternoon and Linda and I have an understanding about this. Just don't go crowing about it to your mates, okay? This is just between the three of us.'

'Don't worry. I won't say anything.'

'If you're good and keep your word, then next time . . .' I leant forward to whisper into his ear and told him exactly what he could do to me. Judging by the reaction I could feel lower down when my hand brushed against him, it met with approval even if he did look a little shocked. I assumed he intended to keep his promise; I had every intention of keeping mine.

-0-

Linda was a bundle of excitement when I saw her the following day. Even though she still had one more exam on the Friday, she'd had more than enough of revising and was keen to hear the latest.

'Come on then,' she said, sitting down on the edge of my bed and patting the space beside her. 'Spill the beans!'

'Have you talked to Scott?' I asked, sitting down beside her.

'Yes I have, but I want to hear it from you.'

'It was fun.'

Linda grinned.

'Fun? You scared the bejeezus out of him. I think you must have had a lot of pent up frustration to unleash because at first, I think he was terrified. You nearly traumatised the poor wee boy.' Every now and then, like now, for instance, the County Antrim in her accent would resurface, even though her family hadn't lived in

Northern Ireland for years.

I shrugged my shoulders.

'Would it help if I said Sadie made me do it? You encouraged me to make my peace with her, remember?'

'I'm only teasing you.' She lay back on the bed, resting her legs on my lap and her hands across her stomach. 'He had the time of his life, but I think you wore him out. I'll find out next time I see him if he's learned anything new.'

'Oh, I think he might have,' I said with a hint of smugness. 'Just you wait; you'll be in for a few pleasant surprises.'

Linda looked intrigued.

'We'll have to come up with some sort of time share agreement or he'll be no good to either of us. He's got nothing to complain about, though. How many guys get to butter their bread both sides without lying or pretending to anybody?'

'I guess it's easier for me too, knowing I share him with you,' I said. 'There's actually less emotional entanglement, not more.'

'Now you're getting it. Have your fun but be open about it. Your immediate future won't leave much space for relationships. To be honest, they'd be a distraction, but it doesn't mean missing out on life's little pleasures, does it?' She winked. 'If you want hearts and flowers and commitment then there'll be time enough for that later.'

'Sometimes I don't think there's a romantic bone in your body, but I actually think you're right. Why shouldn't I enjoy myself? This way nobody gets hurt: least of all, me. I don't think I could cope with that again.'

'How are things with Steve, by the way?'

I sighed.

'Getting easier I suppose. At least we're talking and everything's friendly, although I still avoid spending too much time alone with him.' My mood became a bit more sombre. 'The trouble is, I still miss him. I loved him more than I ever admitted to myself at the time. I won't be making the same mistake again in a hurry.'

Linda was sitting up again now, propped up on her hands.

'That's my girl. The past is the past. Carpe diem, baby! Carpe diem!'

CHAPTER THREE

The car pulled up outside the railway station.

'Thanks, Mum.' I leant across to peck her on the cheek and picked up my bag. 'I'll see you later.'

'Good luck, sweetheart.'

'It's only a meeting, Mum.'

'I know, but I'm not used to you going into London on your own. You've grown up so fast I wonder where my daughter went sometimes.'

'She's still right here, Mum. She always will be.'

She looked across at me and gave a little sigh.

'Don't mind me; I'm just being a bit sentimental. One of the hardest things about being a parent is letting go. It makes me proud and sad, both at the same time.'

I opened the car door and stepped out into the morning rush.

'I'll see you later. I'm not sure when; it just depends on how long the meeting takes. There's probably a lot to discuss and as we all know, Mitchell can talk.'

'You know where you're going don't you?'

I leant back in through the open door.

'Of course I do. I've been there with Jeff a couple of times now but it's time to stand on my own two feet. He's busy and I've got my own career to work on.'

'Just give me a call when you're on your way back. I'll meet you here.'

'Okay, Mum.' I smiled, closed the car door and waved her off.

London was waiting. The rest of my life was waiting. Slinging my bag over my shoulder I strolled through the station entrance.

Three trains and one hour twenty-eight minutes later I was being buzzed up to the reception at Sacker Management. There was a young girl on reception I hadn't seen before.

'Please take a seat, Miss Taylor. Mr Sacker should be with you soon.'

I thanked her and made myself comfortable on the sofa. A couple of minutes later the door opened and Mitchell's PA, Penny, appeared. Her hair had changed a bit since the first time we met. As well as still standing up like an angry porcupine, it now had blue streaks in it. I would have placed her in her mid-twenties, even though she tended to dress younger, displaying a curious mismatch of professional efficiency with quirky individualism.

'Would you like to come through? Mitchell's a bit held up at the moment. Join me in my office until he's ready. I've made some coffee.'

She led the way through the double doors. The sound of conversations and telephones ringing came from every room, and periodically someone would emerge from a door and disappear through another one. It was a hive of activity, a far cry from the hushed atmosphere of the first time I had seen this place.

Penny took me into the office next to Mitchell's and poured us both a coffee. I could hear Mitchell's raised voice on the other side of the connecting door but I couldn't make out what he was saying. I hadn't heard the normally urbane Mitchell Sacker shout before.

'Cream, one sugar, right?' Penny's voice yanked my attention back into the room.

'Yes. Thank you.' She was right. 'What's happening? Why is Mitchell upset?'

'Between you, me, and the gatepost he's a bit annoyed with one of the artists. They've given an interview that was nothing to do with us, said some things they shouldn't have, and now they're being misquoted all over the papers. You have to be careful where the press is concerned; you can't take them at face value.'

'It sounds like a minefield.'

'It is, but you'll get used to it. All that's a way off for you yet, I expect.'

She handed me the coffee and I thanked her.

'Mitchell runs a tight ship,' she continued. 'He doesn't like nasty surprises, but his heart's in the right place, though.' Penny looked wistful for a moment.

'Speaking of hearts: how's your boyfriend?' I asked.

She rolled her eyes skywards.

'Still being a dick. I don't think I'll be putting up with this one for long. How did your exams go?'

'Alright, I think. Now they're out of the way I'm just looking forward to getting on with the music.'

'Good. Well, I'm sure Mitchell will have plenty to say about what the next moves are. Just don't forget to have your say about things. I know what he can be like.'

'Thanks. I'll bear that in mind.' I took a sip of my

coffee.

Mitchell poked his head round the door.

'Penny, I think Rebecca's still waiting in reception and . . . Oh hello, Rebecca. Okay, strike whatever I was about to say. Come on in and take a seat.'

I smiled at Penny and took my coffee through with me.

'Thanks for coming, and sorry to keep you waiting. We've had a bit of a panic on this morning. There are a few things I wanted to discuss with you today.' He gestured me towards a seat by the coffee table. 'Firstly, are you still sure you want to stick with being put forward to the public using your full name?'

'Yes.' I remained resolute. 'I know you're keen to separate the private from the public, but I can still do that and use my own name. I still need to be me, just a public version of me.'

'Then that's fair enough. What the public sees is never the whole person. You won't want them to either. What gets marketed is not just the music, but you. You're part of the package, part of the product, and you need to keep some things back for yourself otherwise the whole of you ends up becoming public property. On the work side too, you'll have to get used to the fact that all they'll ever get to see is the tip of the iceberg and not the years of hard work that go in before you ever get your music out there. You're lucky that you started young and Jeff has steered you very wisely.'

He looked reflective.

'Do you know why I have all these tribal masks around the walls?'

I glanced around me.

'Because you like them? I remember you saying that everything in this office meant something to you.'

'Yes, but it's more than just that, though. They interest me because they represent the masks that we all wear. We put on a different mask, a different persona for every situation. Whenever you're in the public eye you're on duty. You'll come to value your privacy when you're not on show. If you can balance those, that's one of the keys to a long and successful career. I've just had to try and clear up the mess caused by someone who forgot about the dividing line between their private life and their public one.'

'What about the motorbike?'

'That? That's a promise to myself. I'm married to my work. There isn't room for much else in my life, but one day when my job is done here, I'll hand this business on to someone worthy of it and ride off into the sunset on my Harley. Everybody needs a dream, Rebecca, and that's mine; it's what sustains me.'

All of a sudden, he seemed less like a walking computer and more like a human being. Perhaps I was beginning to see the man that lived behind his own mask. I had a feeling I wasn't the only one who did.

Mitchell reached for a glass of water and took a sip.

'On the contract front, Pristeen Records is still looking like the front runner. They're going to want a showcase gig before they commit, though, so we need to recruit a band, at least for the short term. It will also be a good way to sound musicians out with a view to keeping the right people involved as things progress. I've shortlisted a few. They're all quite young, but you'll need a group of musicians who can grow with you and are hungry for success. Better that than a bunch of jaded old pros who won't go the extra mile or stick with a longer-term project like this.'

He got up and handed me a file from his desk.

'These are all up and coming musicians with real potential, so I want you to take away the info and have a good look through. See if any of them grab your attention as possible band members. I've got my own favourites but I want to see what you think. Ultimately, it's going to be you who is working with them, day in, day out, and it will undoubtedly have an impact on your creative direction.'

'Okay. Have they done demos?'

'Yes there are demos in there, plus some of them have put stuff up on websites. Check them out. Also,' he regarded me coolly, 'assuming everything goes to plan, once the contract situation is settled and we're ready to start recording, there is the matter of a record producer.'

'Oh!' I was surprised. 'I thought Jeff would be doing that.' I'd never recorded with anyone else apart from Steve and Jeff.

'He's a good producer, but he's too closely involved to be objective. He knows that too. He'd be the first to admit it. What's needed is a fresh perspective from someone who can pull all the elements of what you do into something with the kind of cohesive identity we were talking about before. Again, I've got some people in mind but we'll cross that bridge closer to the time. It depends who's available to take on the project too, and we don't know yet when that's going to be.'

He was probably right. He usually was.

'Did you bring any more demos with you?' he asked.

'Yes. There are five more songs, well, maybe six.'

Mitchell gave me an odd look.

'One of them I'm not sure about,' I qualified.

'Well, play me the five first.'

I handed him the disk and he put it into the sound system. Mitchell listened carefully all the way through then pressed his hands together before speaking. When he did that, he reminded me of a vicar about to lead a prayer.

'Well, it seems to be gelling into a style that's all your own now. Pop with an edge I suppose you could call it, although there is still a bit of everything in there. It's up to date but with shades of the familiar, kind of retro with a modern twist. By my reckoning, you've got a couple of album tracks in amongst these, plus maybe one that is single material. That's batting a pretty good average.'

I could still sense the hint of reservation in his voice.

'But none of it really blows your socks off, though, right?'

He nodded, pressing his lips together.

'If I'm totally honest they're good songs but they don't have the impact needed to break you out there in the marketplace. What it takes is that one single that will really get you noticed.'

I took a deep breath. If Jeff wasn't going to be producing then what the hell! I had nothing to lose.

'Well, then there's this.' I reached into my bag and handed Mitchell another disk.

He put it on and played it through, listening carefully but giving nothing away. I squirmed in my seat. When I listened to it like this, I couldn't believe I'd actually put some of that stuff in the lyrics. I'd gone too far this time; I knew it.

His face remained dispassionate. There was no hint of any emotion.

'Do you mind if I put that one on again?'

I swallowed.

'No, carry on,' I said.

He seemed to be brewing up to something. He was going to have a go at me for wasting my time on something nobody would release; I could see it coming. When the song had finished for the second time, he gathered his thoughts then fixed me with a look that went right through me, choosing his words carefully.

'That's it.'

'What?'

'That's it.' His eyes lit up. 'That's what we've been looking for. You wouldn't be the first female artist to make her mark with a very sexual record and you won't be the last but this . . . this has the impact we're after. We might have to tone down a few of the lyrics for radio airplay but otherwise, this has 'hit' written all over it.'

He paused for a moment, running something through his mind.

'It's a pretty major departure of style and, um,' he waved his hands about, for once lost for the right words, ' . . . subject matter, shall we call it? If this ends up being the song that makes your name then I hope you're ready for the attention you'll get, both good and bad. When did you write this?'

'Actually, I co-wrote it a while ago.'

'Who with? Surely not Jeff!'

'No. With Steve, his engineer.'

'I see. And has Jeff heard this?'

'God, no! Why do you think I kept it under wraps?'
This all felt like it was going south fast. Mitchell could
probably see the terror in my eyes.

'Let me make one thing really clear. Your private life is
just that as far as I'm concerned. It's obvious a song like
this didn't come from nowhere, but how it came about is
none of my business. If it does become a single and it's a
big 'if' because record companies are the ones with the
final say in this, then that's some way off in the future. I
won't be saying anything to Jeff. Okay?'

I began to relax a little again. Mitchell still looked
quietly excited.

'No more second guessing yourself. Don't hold back.
If there's one song of yours I've heard so far that's going
to make your name, then this is it.'

-0-

Mum's car was waiting for me when I emerged from
the station entrance.

'Hey Mum!' I said, clambering in and flopping down
on the seat.

'Good meeting?'

'Yes, very! I've got lots to think about.'

On the way home I told her about the plans to recruit a
band and the change of producer. She didn't seem
surprised.

'I thought that would happen. It's quite usual to
change producers for a fresh approach. It shakes things
up a bit.'

I omitted to tell her about the song. By the time that
came to light, enough time would have elapsed to

provide an alternative explanation.

We were still busily talking as we came through the front door and made our way to the kitchen. Mum put the kettle on.

'Oh, I've got some news for you too.'

'Oh yes? What?' I asked, reaching for the biscuit jar.

'Steve and Valentina are officially together again. He's moving back in. Isn't that wonderful?'

Mum regarded me impassively even though she was smiling. Inside my head, a maelstrom of emotions fought each other for control. I took a chocolate digestive and closed the lid of the jar again, although I no longer felt very hungry.

'That's good. I'm happy for them.' It wasn't a lie. I did wish them well; I just felt sad for me.

'Have you and Steve had a falling out? You don't seem to have spent as much time in the studio with him lately.'

'No. It's just that I've had the exams to focus on and let's face it, he's had other things on his mind too.'

Mum seemed to accept my explanation.

'Anyway, I've made a lasagne for dinner. I know it's one of your favourites.'

'Thanks, Mum.' I was glad she'd changed the subject again.

I resolved once more to speak to Steve. I needed to let him know I wished them happiness. The thing that bothered me was that he hadn't told me himself. I'd had to hear it from Mum and face her armour-piercing gaze unprepared. That rankled.

-0-

Come Saturday, everybody was at home, and with the album project in London nearly finished, Steve was busy preparing the studio to see action again. I'd had it all to myself to practice and write for a while, which meant I could plug my favourite guitar into the Marshall and make as much noise as I liked. Thanks to all the time I'd spent around Steve and Jeff, I knew my way around the studio these days. I even miked up the speaker cabinet, running it via the mixing desk and out through the control room monitors as well, just for effect, even when I wasn't recording new ideas. It felt good to go in there and get everything out of my system. Some days my ears would still be ringing when I closed the door behind me and came back into the house.

I made everyone tea and took a tray with two steaming mugs across the courtyard. The weather was nowhere near as hot as it had been only the week before, so we were back on the teas again. Steve was tidying cables and hanging them on their hooks in the store room when I entered. He saw me out of the corner of his eye, looked around and came through to meet me.

'Good morning.' I handed him the tea. My tone was probably a little curt.

'Thank you,' he said while I looked at him reproachfully.

'Why didn't you tell me you were moving back in? It would have been nice to know.'

He sighed and put the mug down on the coffee table.

'Firstly, I've hardly seen you and secondly, I didn't know how to say it. I've caused you enough heartache already.'

'Steve, you were never the cause of the heartache. Life

got in our way.' Try as I might, I couldn't stay angry with him for long. 'I'm glad for you both. Just don't run away from me, please. I still value your friendship and the time that we had together will always be special to me. You know that, don't you?'

He pinched his lips together and nodded, closing his eyes for a moment in the way that he did when he was trying to process his emotions.

'How's Valentina?' I asked.

'She's fine. Oh towards you, you mean? We don't really talk about that. We're trying to focus on the present and the future rather than looking back. I'm so sorry things turned out the way they did.'

'I know. And I know you cared.' I wasn't sure what else I could say about it. Why linger? I'd done my best to move on. 'Listen, you know that song we wrote?'

'Yes.'

'I've played it to Mitchell and he thinks it's got real potential. I don't know when and if it's going to go anywhere, but I'll make sure you get credit for writing it with me. It's half yours.'

He shook his head.

'I didn't do it for the money.'

'I know that. You wrote it for the love of making music; don't we all? But what's rightfully yours is yours, and if it ever makes any royalties, then a share of that is due to you.'

'Well, you deserve success. There's still a lot of work to be done between now and then, I guess.' He smiled and took a gulp of his tea.

'And I could use your help with some of it. We make a good team, we always have!' I assured him.

He looked relieved.

'I'm so glad we're talking freely now. It would kill me for things to be difficult between us.'

'Yes.' It was like the weight of the world being lifted from my shoulders. 'Me too.' I had an idea for an ice-breaker. 'I'll tell you what you could help me with. I've been looking through the profiles of potential band members. Would you take a look? I'd appreciate your views.'

'Sure.'

'Stay right there. I'll get the file.'

-0-

In the days that followed, the frame and wall panels of the gym went up, along with the roof trusses. Work began almost immediately on tiling the roof before the red brick skin of the walls could be built. Jeff said that it would blend in with the rest of the house when it was finished.

The weather warmed back up again and I felt so much happier now that Steve and I had got past our awkwardness. The summer was an open book in which I could begin to write my own story. I felt truly carefree and at ease with myself for the first time since things with Steve had come to an end.

It was a sweltering day and it must have been hot work for the two lads up on the roof. Mum handed me a couple of cold drinks on a tray to take to them. I could hear them talking as I made my way along the front of the house and it was only when I rounded the corner that I heard my name being mentioned. I ducked back around the wall and listened.

'What did you say the daughter's name was? Rebecca is it?' He gave a low whistle. 'Fuck me! I could do some damage there.'

'I know what you mean. Even her mother's hot. Talk about a Milf! You can see where she gets it from.'

'Out of our league, though. Way too posh!'

I wasn't posh. Just because we had money behind us these days, it didn't mean I was stuck up. I felt quite irritated about that. And what did he think he could do to me? He wouldn't be quite so confident once he'd been mauled by Sadie. She'd leave nothing but bones behind and have fun doing it.

I rounded the corner with the tray of drinks, striding confidently over the gravel. They both fell awkwardly silent. Perhaps they were wondering if I had overheard any of their comments. I couldn't be sure who had said what, though. They were both in their early to mid-twenties and stripped to the waist, their muscles taut beneath their glistening skin which dripped with perspiration in the afternoon sun. Sadie licked her lips.

'I brought you some cold drinks. You both look like you need them.'

'Thank you. We'll be right down,' said the taller of the two, still looking a little sheepish.

'I'll leave the tray here and pick it up later.'

There was nothing Sadie could do right now. She would have to bide her time. Rob hadn't broken up from school for the summer yet but Mum was still here. Besides which, Sadie had yet to select her prey and I had no idea which of them might become a lamb to the slaughter. Stalking them could be as much fun as the kill.

I was suddenly aware of the effect the way I was dressed could have on them. When I'd dressed myself that morning, I was thinking only of keeping cool in the heat but I was wearing only the shortest of denim shorts that made the most of my legs and a crop top that exposed plenty of the rest of me. I could feel their heated stares burning into my back when I sauntered off again, swaying my hips slightly.

Try and cool down now, boys.

Mum was in the kitchen, doing something on her tablet when I came back in.

'Have they got their drinks?'

'Yes. They were just coming down off the roof to get them when I left. What are their names again?'

'Tim and Julian I think. Tim's the shorter one of the two.'

The trouble was there wasn't much to choose between them. I liked the look of them both, in their different ways. A thought was forming that just wouldn't go away; it just kept playing over and over in my mind.

After all, if I couldn't choose, who said I had to?

CHAPTER FOUR

I woke up to a clear blue sky interrupted by only the occasional white fluffy cloud; the start of what was hopefully going to be another beautiful day. It would be the perfect excuse to wear my new backless, floral print, cotton summer dress with a skirt just long enough to be modest but short enough to catch the eye. I selected a pair of blue sneakers to go with it. Hopefully, that little ensemble would catch the workmen's attention.

I washed, dressed and went down to breakfast.

Mum was bustling around; making sure Rob had a packed lunch with him before he went off to cricket training. He was pretty useless at anything like that. If he had to fend for himself I was sure he'd either starve or live on takeaways, neither of which was ideal for a budding sportsman.

Mum looked round at me as I came into the room.

'Are you planning to get out there in the sun today?'

'Yes. I figured a bit of fresh air might do me good. Linda's coming over this afternoon to join me. It is the start of the summer holidays after all.'

'Good idea, just don't forget to put some sunscreen on.'

To while away some time, I took another look through the musician's profiles. Several of them looked promising. I shortlisted a few drummers, bass players and keyboard players, and it seemed like a toss-up between two guitarists; Alex Carter and Richard Fossey. Since I wasn't sure who would be the better fit musically, I'd have to meet them and hear them play to be sure.

It was at least the sixth time I'd been through the information and Mitchell was expecting me to report back at the end of the week before we arranged auditions, but I was already fairly decided. I phoned him to let him know my thoughts.

That killed about an hour.

After that, I donned a pair of sunglasses and took Rolo for a walk. Half way along the main road towards the park, a cyclist wolf-whistled as he pedalled past and I allowed myself a little smile of satisfaction. At least my choice of outfit for the day was meeting with approval. My smile became a smirk when he almost veered into the kerb, only recovering himself at the last moment.

That'll teach him not to look where he's going.

On my return, I waved to Julian and Tim who were working away on the roof of the gym. They waved back.

After that, I didn't really know what to do with myself. I paced my room, agitated, unable to get the two roofers out of my head. The creature within me demanded to be fed, but what was I going to do about it, throw myself at them? And besides, Mum was still around.

Feeling listless with the heat, I poured myself a cool bath, stripping off then easing into the fragrant water with a sigh. I splashed some of it over my skin and closing my eyes, laid my head against the side of the bath, allowing my thoughts to wander. They didn't have to wander very far.

Heart in mouth, I walk along the front of the house with a tray of cloudy lemonade and a plate of neatly arranged biscuits. I still can't believe I'm doing this. Somewhere way overhead skylarks are warbling loudly, celebrating the summer. I stop, take a deep breath and round the corner of the house. Julian and Tim look over from the stack of tiles they are preparing to hoist up to the roof.

'I brought you some refreshments,' I say in as matter-of-fact a voice as I can manage.

'Thanks. We could use a break right now,' Julian says, rubbing the back of his hand against his forehead. 'It just keeps getting hotter and hotter out here.'

'Just you wait!' says my inner voice.

I sank a little lower in the enveloping water, my hands brushing lightly across my skin.

They pick up their drinks from the proffered tray and I hold out the plate of biscuits. This could still go horribly wrong but it's too late to back down now.

'Try one of the chocolate ones before they melt,' I encourage.

'Thanks.'

They each take one and stare at the plate. They look at me then back to the plate again.

'Something up, boys?'

Underneath the biscuits, I've carefully hidden a layer of condoms. Now they are peeking out from beneath the chocolate hobnobs.

'I wouldn't try to eat those ones if I were you. They're a bit chewy.' I'm enjoying this. The slack-jawed look of disbelief on their faces is priceless. 'You do know what they're for, don't you?'

They both nod.

'Oh, good! I did wonder.' I look from one to the other, then back. 'After all, you both seem to reckon you know how to handle me but here's the thing; I think it's probably just a load of talk unless you can prove otherwise.'

'What? Both of us?' asks Tim.

'Well, unless you've got somebody else hidden behind the gym I guess it'll just have to be the two of you. That is if you're up to it!'

They look at each other and grin. Still, they hesitate.

'Don't worry; there aren't any hidden cameras,' I continue. 'This isn't a wind-up, but it's a one-time offer: take it or leave it.'

They look at each other again and seem to reach an unspoken consensus.

'We'll take it!' they both reply.

'Good. I was hoping you'd say that.'

'Who do you want first?' asks Julian.

'First?' I snort. 'I don't think you quite understand. You think you could handle me one at a time? I meant together.'

Their jaws drop even further than they have already. I wish I had a camera to capture their expressions. It's worth all the tea in China.

I place the tray and plate on a stack of roof tiles, scoop up a handful of condoms and lead the way through the doorway into the shade of the unfinished gym. My hands float on unseen wafts of air and I feel light on my feet.

Still, the boys remain rooted to the spot.

I turn to look at them over my shoulder.

'Well, come on then!'

They move as one like sprinters out of the blocks.

Within moments there are rough hands all over my body. They aren't the smooth, students' hands of Scott or the deft, musicians' hands of Steve. These ones, which roam their way up my thighs and grab at my breasts through the thin cotton of the summer dress, are work-hardened and calloused despite their young age.

My hands traversed my wet skin. In my mind at least, they belonged to Tim and Julian. With my fingertips gently tracing around the areola of my left breast, my right hand slid down my body and into the water to caress my inner thigh. My breath began to sigh as my body tensed in anticipation.

One hand sweeps my hair back and I can feel Tim's lips brushing against the back of my neck. Julian kisses me hard on the lips and slips the straps of my dress off my shoulders allowing it to fall to my waist then clamps his hot mouth over one stiffened nipple.

Tim has clearly taken my words to heart. His hands find their way under the skirt of my dress and roughly pull my underwear down to my knees. Then his voice appears in my ear, full of dark intent.

'Bend forwards. I hope you're ready for this.'

I reach behind my head to pull him in closer.

'Bring it on. Do your worst!' I sneer, arching my top lip, my voice laden with challenge.

In fact, after calling their manhood into question, neither of them is likely to go easy on me. It's no more than I expect and no less than I deserve. By now, I figure I'll be lucky to escape without bruises.

Julian takes hold of my hands as I lean towards him and holds me in position with his fingers locked around my wrists, while Tim ditches his shorts and quickly rolls on a condom. His fingers reach between my thighs, testing my opening then suddenly he's inside me, filling me with sharp, urgent strokes. I guess I hadn't expected much concession to foreplay.

'You like that? Is that what you wanted?'

I turn my head to look at him over my shoulder.

'It's a start, I suppose.' If they wanted posh bitch, I'll give them posh bitch.

Julian keeps my wrists trapped between the fingers of one hand and undoes his jean shorts with the other, easing them down just far enough to free his cock. It's a nice one, although to be honest, I've yet to meet one I haven't liked.

'Suck it!' he says, steering it towards my already parted lips. 'I bet you've never had one in your mouth while you were being fucked before.'

He tastes salty from the heat and I suck him greedily while his mate slams into me from behind, his hands grasping my hips. He's right of course; it is a new experience. I'm not going to tell him that, though, and besides at this very moment, I can't very well say anything. The best I can manage is the occasional spluttering noise while he steadies my head with his shovel-like hands and uses me for his own satisfaction.

Just when I'm getting used to it, Julian pulls out of my mouth and begins rolling on a condom. I take a deep, welcome breath and wipe away a trail of saliva from my lower lip.

'My turn!' he insists, nursing his erection.

Tim withdraws from me and I step out of my knickers which have now fallen to the floor. Julian's strong arms lift me off my feet. *Supporting my weight with his hands underneath my upper thighs he lowers me slowly onto himself and begins lifting my whole body up and down on his cock.*

With two fingers I parted my labia, resting the middle finger of my other hand between them and slowly rubbing it up and down with the water lapping at my hands, moaning softly.

Not to be left out, Tim takes up position behind me again, rubbing saliva over his erection. He lifts the skirt of my dress and eases my buttocks apart, nudging against my tender opening with the head of his cock. Julian stills his movements, sensing what Tim is about to do. I have no doubt either and do my best to relax, which isn't easy with my muscles already clamped tightly around his friend. Ever so slowly, he eases himself into my back passage until he has buried himself inside me.

'You asked for it, and now you're gonna get it!' says a voice in my ear, half threat, half promise. I can't argue with that.

I rest my head on Julian's shoulder, whimpering as the startling sensation overwhelms me, but Sadie isn't ready to show any sign of weakness. Having laid down the gauntlet in the way that I have, there is little choice but to accept the consequences.

I lift my head, resolute.

'Fuck me, both of you. Do it.'

It takes them a few moments to find their stride. I don't think they've done this before either; we are all venturing into unknown territory. They settle into slightly different rhythms. Sometimes their movements alternate so that as one of them pushes himself into me the other pulls back, then they are in concert with each other again, filling me in unison.

Now my hands worked earnestly beneath the water, the movements of my fingers increasing in their urgency. I could hear water lapping against the sides of the bath.

The sweat pours off them, dripping like bullets onto my skin as they continue; pistoning in and out of me in a rocking motion. Tim bites softly into my shoulder and I cling to Julian with my arms around his neck, rolling my hips in time with the two of them. Now we are beginning to move like a well-oiled machine, a great industrial engine that rocks back and forth, working smoothly and with unity of purpose towards our common goal.

I arrive first, fragmenting into shards while the rest of the mechanism powers on.

The feeling was rising within me too. I pressed harder, allowing it to build until my breath exploded between my lips as I came, my fingertips still working around my clit in circles. I dissolved into the water, sliding the back of my head down the side of the bath until I could feel my hair fanning out around me. My movements slowed as the moment passed and I recovered my equilibrium, opening my eyes, but the movie in my mind hadn't yet run its course. I closed them again, allowing the scene to play out.

I know they won't be too far behind me now, and I'm ready to reclaim the power in our see-sawing battle of wills. Perhaps I can make them an offer they won't be able to refuse.

'Come on my face, both of you!' I entreat. 'Cover me.'

That seems to do the trick.

They release me and my feet find the floor again while they tear off the condoms. I slide to my knees, taking them both in hand and working them with long, firm strokes, squeezing them hard and teasing the sensitive heads of their cocks with my thumbs. Tim can't take it any longer, letting go with a sudden exhalation.

I look up at him and laugh in delight as a long arc of come explodes from the end of his cock and lands in a line that stretches from my forehead down to my chin. Closing my lips around the end I suck hard, torturing him with my tongue until he can't stand it any longer and pulls away, just in time for Julian, pumping his fist around his aching hardness to erupt, spattering my face with his come. I lick away the semen that clings to my lips.

They give each other an astonished look when I scoop up their ejaculate with my fingertips and feed it eagerly into my open mouth. Mopping up a drip that has fallen onto my breast, I massage it into my nipples. I know I have them captivated. They'll be unlikely to forget this little performance in a hurry.

I stand up and in one movement peel my dress up over my head before wiping myself down with one of the tee-shirts they discarded when they started work.

'Well guys, I hope you're up for round two because I'm not finished with you yet. You can't say I didn't warn you.'

'You want more?' asks Julian, still not quite believing what he hears and sees.

I look them both up and down.

'Oh, I'm just getting started.'

The image faded and I opened my eyes, my circling fingers slowing to a halt.

Jesus! That was a good one.

Perhaps I would pluck up the courage to try that out for real some day. The idea of it certainly turned me on but I doubted I actually had it in me to be so brazen. I stood up, the water running in little streams down my body, and reached for a towel before stepping carefully out of the bath.

While I was drying myself, my phone caught my eye. I still needed to get some remaining frustration out of my system.

Fuck it! Why not!

I picked it up and dialled.

'Hi, Scott! It's Rebecca. How are you?'

'Good, thanks. I'm down by the river at the moment, enjoying the sunshine with a couple of mates. How about you? You don't fancy joining us, do you?'

'I'm expecting Linda soon, but listen, what are you up to this evening? Mind if I come over later?'

There was a moment's silence. He was trying to play it cool but I could almost hear him punching the air on the other end of the line.

'Not at all! Sounds good to me.'

'Who's that?' asked a male voice somewhere in the background.

'Oh, it's just my sister with a bit of family news,' he said, dismissively.

Good boy! He'd obviously kept his end of the bargain.

I didn't think he'd be too disappointed with the evening ahead. After all, I still had a promise to keep. It seemed only fair.

CHAPTER FIVE

'Both of them at once; now there's a thought!' Linda pouted, relishing the idea.

'Shh! Keep your voice down; they might hear you.'

We had already set out a couple of sun-loungers in the front garden and were lying out in our bikinis, watching the boys at work and sipping iced drinks through straws. Linda seemed quietly pleased with what she saw.

'So, are we talking about one there and one there?' She pointed up and down to the appropriate areas.

'Well, there are a few permutations and combinations. You do the maths. I did manage to work my way through a number of the possibilities but that was definitely one of them.'

She slid her sunglasses down her nose and looked at me.

'Why don't you make your fantasy a reality and go for it when your Mum goes out?'

My mouth dropped open.

'No. I couldn't.'

'Yes, you could! Why not? I reckon talking them into it would be like taking candy from a baby!'

'No!' I insisted.

'I'll join you. We could take them on together.'

Now it was my turn to look at her over my sunglasses.

'I can't believe you're actually serious.'

'Of course I am. Come on; it'll be fun.'

'No! Absolutely not!'

Fantasising about having the two of them was one thing, but when it came to it I just couldn't bring myself to take the plunge. It seemed like a step too far.

'Besides, I'm seeing Scott later. The way I'm feeling, I don't think he'll know what hit him, but I'm not sure he'd be into sloppy seconds . . . or thirds for that matter.'

'I still think you're missing out on a golden opportunity. Well, I'm going to go for it! Sure you won't join me?'

'You haven't got the bottle!'

Pouting, she paused and looked at me with an enigmatic smile.

'Are you daring me? I do love a challenge.'

I thought about it for a moment.

'Go on then. I dare you.'

'If you don't mind me muscling in on your fantasies then challenge accepted. You're on! It's definitely one worth chalking up to experience.'

I shook my head.

'Of course I don't mind! They don't belong to me. Just because I'm not going to, it doesn't mean you can't step in and have your slice of the fun. I seem to remember somebody saying that's what good friends do; they share, remember? Besides, there's no guarantee they'll go for it anyway.'

We lay back on the loungers, enjoying the sunshine and sipping our drinks until Mum came out and got into her car. She pulled slowly up the driveway, opening the car window as she pulled to a halt again.

'I'm off to meet Sandra for a coffee and do the shopping before picking Rob up. Will you two be alright here?'

'We'll be fine, Mum,' I said.

Bingo!

Once she'd disappeared out of the gate, I nipped back to my bedroom for some condoms and tucked them into Linda's bikini top with a gentle pat.

'There you are. Better safe than sorry!'

'Wish me luck,' she drawled before getting up off the lounger and sauntering over in the direction of the gym, swaying her hips.

Go, Linda! Work it, girl!

Tim and Julian stopped what they were doing when they saw her coming over.

'Hi!' she called out, waving as she approached.

'Hello,' said Julian, sounding a little unsure what she was up to.

I could see them both looking Linda up and down while they talked. She looked amazing in a bikini. Her breasts may have been smaller than mine but her legs went on forever. I couldn't hear everything they were saying, though. Snatches of the conversation that carried across the lawn went missing whenever the breeze picked up, but there was no mistaking the look of surprise on the young men's faces.

'I see,' said Julian, glancing across in my direction. 'If I didn't know better I'd say you were just using us for your own entertainment.'

I sipped my drink and hid behind my shades, doing

my best to look nonchalant.

'Well, if you're not interested . . .' Linda knew she had them wriggling on the hook and now she was reeling them in.

Julian held up one palm towards Linda.

'Let's not be hasty. That's not what I was saying.' He was clearly the spokesman of the two.

Linda seemed to be thoroughly enjoying the banter. She made it look effortless.

'So do you think you'll be able to help me out? Some itches just aren't as much fun when you scratch them for yourself. A bit of assistance comes in handy from time to time.'

Tim seemed to be more a man of action than words.

'I think we should be able to help,' he said bluntly.

'Then lead on,' Linda encouraged.

They took her by her offered hands and she followed them into the gym. Crossing the threshold she turned her head to me, wide-eyed and drop-jawed, exaggeratedly mouthing in my direction.

'That was so easy!' she seemed to be saying, just before they disappeared from view.

I took another long sip of my drink and settled back on the recliner to soak up the rays and listen. It wasn't more than a few minutes before the mingled sounds of what the three of them were doing echoed off the nearby line of trees, so maybe it was a good job nobody else lived too close to us. I smiled to myself as I tried to picture what was happening. It didn't require too big a leap of the imagination; I could still hear some of the things Linda was saying.

I don't think she realises how far her voice carries when she raises it. And she still has the cheek to accuse me of owning a filthy mouth!

I was both impressed and surprised.

It was almost an hour before Linda appeared in the doorway, closely followed by the two grinning lads, still wobbling slightly as she retied her bikini bottoms. She squinted in the bright sunlight and replaced her sunglasses.

'Thanks, boys. I needed that.'

'Glad we could help,' said Julian, doing up his shorts. 'Do come again.'

Tim was still grinning from ear to ear. She turned towards them, droll as ever and cool as a cucumber.

'I think I've already come enough for now, but thanks for the offer.'

Linda sashayed across the lawn towards me, kicked off her flip-flops and sank down onto the sun-lounger.

'Well?' I asked, handing her a drink.

'Fucking brilliant, but I think I'm going to be out of action for about a week while I recover! I told you they'd go for it, though. There's probably still time before they finish the roof if you change your mind.' She shifted position slightly. 'I must say, that Tim's a well-built lad. If I died today, they'd have to bury me in a Y-shaped coffin. I really need to work on my stamina if I'm going to make a habit of it.'

I was still laughing at her previous comment.

'Well, there's always the gym once it's finished. If I could peel Rob off the equipment then I'd probably use it to keep in shape myself, but the trouble is I don't think I'd bother if it was just me on my own.'

'Then why don't I come over sometimes and we can

make the most of it together?'

'You know what?' I said. 'You're on!'

We poured some more iced lemonade, clinked our glasses together and settled back to watch Tim and Julian working away as if nothing had happened. The only clue was the occasional smile in our direction, which we returned with a wave.

CHAPTER SIX

After Tim and Julian had finished the roof and gone on their way, the bricklayers arrived. By then I was too busy to pay them much notice and besides, none of them really appealed. Some part of me regretted never plucking up the courage to go for it myself and I resolved not to let Sadie down again. Why should Linda have all the fun?

I still saw Scott on and off. Both he and Linda seemed perfectly happy with the arrangement and we all made the most of it because when autumn came he would be off to university. Dean was in the same year as us, so Linda would still have her plaything for a while yet; that is if she didn't tire of him first. I never could tell.

As it turned out, Mitchell had similar ideas to me regarding who would be a good fit for the band. He took on board what I said about the guitarists and we invited them both to audition. Even though Richard was really good, Alex got the job. It just felt right. Everything clicked with Alex on board. He could write songs, good ones too, but he didn't see himself as a singer and would never have pushed himself forward as a front man; he was too unassuming for that. Once rehearsals were underway, we included a couple of his songs in our set. Although we had to change the key of one of them to suit my vocal range, that was straightforward enough.

Initially, Mitchell had suggested hiring a rehearsal venue in London, but for much of the time Jeff and Steve were away working again, so we did a lot of our rehearsing in Jeff's studio. During the week, the rest of the band stayed in a house down the road that Mitchell had rented. It worked out a lot cheaper than putting the band up in London too. Mitchell was relieved to keep the overheads down. It would be a long time before any of his investment paid dividends if indeed it ever did.

As he was fond of saying: 'There are too many unknowns and no guarantees but you've got to speculate to accumulate.'

It almost passed me by when the exam results arrived in August. Despite forgetting the date they came out because I was so wrapped up in the band, my results were better than I thought they would be. Linda did exactly as expected with top grades across the board. She made it look so easy. We still spent time together when we could, and sent each other affectionately insulting texts when we couldn't.

At first, most of the band would spend time with family and friends at weekends. A couple of them had girlfriends or in the case of Helena the keyboard player, boyfriend. The others remained single. Before long we would find ourselves busy at weekends and many evenings too.

One by one their relationships would falter as we got busier and busier. There was one lineup change towards the end of the summer when our original drummer had to be replaced, but the new guy, Daniel, was pretty quick on the uptake and it didn't take him long to settle in. They were good times, though, filled with the hope and expectation of things to come but for now, at least, the band members were as poor as church mice even though they were each paid a basic retainer. I was no different, but at least I had the support of my family and they could afford to look after me. I offered to give half my retainer to Mum out of principle, even though she said it wasn't necessary.

The band was becoming like a little family too, but we were more like brothers and sisters. Even though they were a bit older than me, none of the band was over twenty. I was never tempted to get involved with any of them; things would have become too complicated. I found my fun elsewhere when I could, which wasn't nearly as often as I would have liked. Thank heavens for Linda's little birthday present. It was on its third set of batteries.

Once the gym had been completed, Linda and I kept our promise to each other to make the most of it when Rob wasn't in there. It gave us the perfect excuse to get together and catch up on the latest news. She was back in school and underway with the final year of her A-level studies. As I'd suspected, there was no point in my going back; the band was taking up all my time and energy. The sixth form seemed to provide Linda with rich pickings when it came to the opposite sex. In a way, I envied her freedom.

Sometimes when I was on the walking machine, I mused that it felt like my whole life was on a treadmill. I could console myself that it was one of my own choosing and there was something worthwhile at the end of it.

Eventually. Maybe.

After a couple of months of rehearsals, Mitchell began arranging gigs. We played pubs, small clubs, anywhere that would have us just for the experience. To start with the gigs were even free just to get a few people through the door, but word began to spread and our audiences grew modestly but steadily as we travelled further afield. We began to play clubs in London and some of the other major cities. It seemed like we spent our lives going backwards and forwards in the van.

Our only concession to luxury was Mick, our driver and roadie. One of Mitchell's handpicked people, I reckoned he was in his early-to-mid fifties. He didn't have much hair and had even less of a neck. Every available inch of space down his arms was covered in tattoos. Despite appearances, though, he had a heart of gold. If we had a mascot, it was him.

Some of the other band members could drive but it would have been unfair to expect them to do all the driving as well as everything else, and the insurance would have been astronomical. We even got quite adept at power napping on the move, heads lolling against each other's shoulders on our way back from gigs in the small hours of the night.

It was just before one of our London gigs towards the end of the year that Mitchell gathered us in his office. Unusually for him, he stayed behind his desk.

'Right, ladies and gentlemen, this is it; the moment we've all been waiting for.'

He slowly peeled off his glasses. I was pretty sure it was just for effect because I had my suspicions he was blind as a bat without them.

'You've been honing your stage act for a while, long enough at least for Pristeen Records to decide whether to take the plunge or not. They're sending representatives along to Friday's gig. I don't think I need to remind you all how important this is. If they come away impressed and decide to offer the contract then we can start working towards an album. If they don't, well . . . we've got a lot of rethinking to do.'

He replaced his glasses and looked at each of the band in turn, then finally at me.

'You've all worked very hard to get things together as quickly as you have and to gain as much experience of working together as possible. The important thing to remember is that you are going out there to enjoy doing what you already do night after night. Show them that, and you'll be ready to move on to the next stage. I'll be there to do the necessary schmoozing. You just concentrate on giving it your all. Good luck. I have every confidence in you.'

Everybody visibly relaxed at his parting words. Up until then, it had been like being summoned to the headmaster's office, although that wasn't something that happened too many times in my school career.

As they filed out of his office, Mitchell called me back.

'Rebecca, can I have a quick word?' He waited until the others left the room and the door had closed behind them. 'I know you're keen to include that certain song of yours but I want to keep it under wraps for now. It might be seen as a bit controversial in places, so let's not make them too jittery. We don't want to play all our cards too soon. There will be a right time to unveil that one, to the record company and the public, but not yet. Timing is everything.'

I nodded my agreement.

'That's okay. We've got more than enough good songs for now.'

'We're almost there, Rebecca. Then we can get started on the real work of getting your music out to a wider audience.'

CHAPTER SEVEN

The Banana Club was one of those venues that everybody played on their way up. Some made it, some didn't, but the list of artists that had performed there was like a 'Who's Who' of the music business.

Despite its legendary status, when we arrived in daylight it looked uninspiring, to say the least. Its grey brickwork, which would have been drab enough to start with, was stained with years of London grime and steel shutters had been drawn over the doors. It looked more like a prison than a palace of entertainment, except that the protection was there to keep unruly individuals out, not in.

Inside, it was a bit more inviting. They had a good in-house PA and lighting system with a control booth at the back of the auditorium, and it would be a luxury to have a stage big enough for us not to have to jostle shoulder to shoulder when we played. There was actually a proper backstage dressing room too, albeit cramped. We wouldn't have to get changed in the toilets this time. There was still only one dressing room for us so it was a good job Helena and I had overcome any false modesty about changing in front of the guys some time ago.

We all brought our equipment in from the van and set up, aided and abetted by the ever-present Mick. Having been around the block with a few bands he was always ready with some down to earth advice if we asked him, and being almost as wide as he was tall had its uses too. He was remarkably efficient at extracting payment from venues that might otherwise have been less forthcoming. We didn't ask him how he did it; we were just grateful that he did.

At least we didn't have to use our own smaller PA this time; that was one less thing to hump around. The sound check went well after we'd replaced some dodgy leads. Gigging always seemed to have its casualties as far as equipment was concerned. Two songs in, and with a bit of fiddling to get the vocal sound right, the sound man at the mixer raised his thumb in the air and we were good to go. From here on in it was a waiting game.

The support act would have to set up their equipment in front of ours, which left them even less space. They had only just arrived but were still in plenty of time. Maybe I should have left a shoehorn to help them get on and off the stage with. I chuckled at the thought as we made our way out through the stage door into the side alley and headed towards the main street in search of food. I was hungry now. I'd been too nervous to eat lunch.

After a brief band meeting, we decided on pizza. It was a toss-up between that or going to the burger bar a few doors further down. Mick left us to it and settled down with his sandwiches to keep an eye on the van.

I was glad we'd managed to set up early. Singing on too full a stomach is never good and I always avoided fizzy drinks before going on stage. Tea and coffee weren't recommended either. I stuck to water; in fact, I usually took a bottle on stage with me.

It's funny how quickly such little rituals develop. Linda bought me some tiger-striped underwear as a joke, which she presented to me when she came to see us on stage for the first time. Sadie approved. One evening when I'd been wearing them we had a particularly good gig. From that point on they became my lucky pants. I was wearing them today too; it would have been tempting fate not to.

Tonight we were going to be supported by another of Mitchell's up and coming bands, so from his point of view, his artists were getting double the exposure. His people had done a good job promoting the gig because, by the time we got back from the pizza restaurant, there was already a queue forming at the doors of the club. The doors were due to open at seven-thirty, the support would begin at eight, and hopefully we would hit the stage by nine.

It was almost dark now and the signs at the entrance to the club had been lit up. It never ceased to amaze me how much better venues looked by night; they acquired a glamour they didn't possess in the daytime.

Nobody noticed us slipping past the line of people and in through the stage door at the side of the building. Despite our having set up a website with biographies, photos and news of upcoming gigs, most of the audience probably still had no idea what we looked like.

As well as a website, Mitchell had insisted that I started making more use of social networking. I'd never bothered much with it before, preferring instead to communicate the old-fashioned way, but he was adamant that it was an important point of contact with the fans. That meant I'd have about a hundred followers if I was lucky. Nevertheless, I took his advice.

We flashed our backstage passes at the bouncer on our way in. I don't think I heard him speak once all night and he certainly didn't smile; he just nodded silently to each of us as we went past. He was even bigger than Mick.

I had decided to wear a short dress, coupled with black, calf-length boots. The 'kooky chick' look ought to work. Mitchell had been in agreement.

'We can go more down the road of wardrobe and styling later, but it's a good look; it suits you.'

After changing, we watched from our hidden positions at the side of the stage while the audience filed in. Most of them headed straight for the bar at the rear corner of the venue for their plastic glasses of overpriced beer. Someone was making money tonight, but it certainly wasn't us; not yet anyway. Most of what we got paid for the gig would be swallowed up by Mitchell's costs.

Where was he anyway? I hadn't seen him. We just had to trust that he was somewhere in the building and get on with it.

The support act was good. I watched them from the side of the stage for much of their set but eventually I had to go backstage to finish preparing. I liked their music. The audience warmed to them eventually but they seemed a little nervous at first. Perhaps they still lacked the confidence and panache that we had worked so hard to acquire.

When they had finished their set, the stage was cleared of their equipment. We had fifteen minutes while the bar got busy again before it was our turn. The butterflies in my stomach decided to throw a party.

Backstage I could see that Helena was in a similar state. Daniel the drummer was pacing up and down. Alex and Rafael the bass player sat quietly, looking pensive.

'Come on guys,' I said, 'gather round.'

We put our heads together in a circle, arms around each other's shoulders.

'This is it. I've been waiting for this all my life and I'm sure you have too, but you know what? What's meant to be will be, whatever happens. I only know one thing: I'm going to go out there and give it everything I've got because I don't want to get to the end of tonight and think I could have done more. I'd never forgive myself for that. This is our moment. Let's just fucking go for it!'

We were still hugging each other when the stage manager put his head round the door of the dressing room.

'You're up. Let's go, people.'

We followed him out of the dressing room and down the dimly-lit corridor which twisted and turned until we passed through another doorway and reached the steps at the side of the stage. We collected our instruments from their stands. Daniel twiddled his drumsticks nervously between his fingers.

The auditorium lights went down.

In the dim glow from the equipment, I could make out Mick's outline at the side of the stage. He had already been round checking everything was still in tune. By now, he knew the music as well as we did. We would be opening with 'Cross My Heart', one of our more energetic numbers; something that would get the crowd on our side.

I lifted the strap of the Les Paul over my head, plugged it in and slipped a plectrum between my fingers. We took our places and waited in the near-darkness, listening to the occasional whistle from the expectant crowd.

Checking the patch number on the effects board, I rocked my foot forward on the volume pedal. Daniel counted us in with a click of the drumsticks.

One, two, three, four . . .

We struck the opening chord and the lights came up in a flash of blinding white. There was no long introduction; we just launched. Instinct took over. Five short lifetimes of preparation had led us here and we weren't going to let ourselves or each other down. I let rip into the opening lines in a kaleidoscope of sound and coloured light. By the end of our first number I could feel the audience warming to us, so we rolled up our proverbial sleeves and dived headlong into the set without pausing for breath.

For the next few songs, I left my guitar in the care of Mick and concentrated on the singing, stalking the stage and working the crowd as if my life depended on it, occasionally pausing between numbers for a short introduction or a little bit of banter with the audience. Often when we played I would catch Sadie out of the corner of my mind's eye, sitting at the side of the stage, but tonight she was on stage with me, rubbing up against my legs while I poured my life and my soul into the microphone.

Over the course of the next hour and a half, we gave the audience everything we had, stripping the music back to the acoustic simplicity of 'Drifting' in the middle of the set before building everything back up again. By the end of our last number, the audience were baying for more like a pack of hounds.

We took to the wings, panting, clothes clinging to our damp skin with whistles, cries of 'more' and the stamping of feet ringing in our ears. My heart was still pounding. A slow handclap got underway, building to a rapid crescendo and we looked at each other, knowing we still had two more songs in hand. We kept them waiting just long enough then came on again to a round of applause and more whistles.

Ten minutes later we left the stage for the final time and the house lights came up. I was still tingling from the adrenaline coursing through my blood, giddy with laughter, heart thumping. The others were the same, jumping up and down on the spot and hugging each other with cheesy great grins across their faces.

Back in the dressing room the rest of the band cracked open the complimentary beers. I settled for a can of coke but I was feeling the same rush that they were. I could understand where the old saying about sex, drugs and rock and roll came from; the feeling was addictive. I didn't want it to stop. Drugs were a slippery slope I had no intention of going down, but the sex and the rock and roll; I could live with those! I felt so turned on I could have gone all night.

There was a knock on the door of the dressing room. Mitchell poked his head around, smiling broadly. Everybody looked towards him.

'Well?' I asked. 'What did they say?'

'We should have confirmation on Monday morning

but I'm fully expecting them to come back with good news. They were blown away. You didn't just meet my expectations, you exceeded them; all of you. And you, Rebecca . . . I'm speechless. There was something magnetic about you tonight. I'm so glad I put my faith in you. You're rapidly becoming the performer I knew you had the potential to be.'

My lucky pants had done their job again, and Sadie . . . enough said.

None of us could quite believe it was really happening, looking at each other then back to Mitchell, trying to take it in.

'Listen, I've got to go and see the record company people off,' he continued. 'I just wanted to let you know the lie of the land. Believe me when I say you rocked out there. Hopefully, I'll be speaking to you all on Monday when I've heard from them.'

With that, he disappeared round the door again and the party really got going. The rest of the band let their hair down celebrating and I joined them for a while but I still felt so agitated, so restless. I didn't know quite what to do with myself. Maybe some fresh air would help. When everybody was busily engaged in conversation I slipped away unnoticed, making towards the stage door. A young stagehand in a pair of overalls was walking the other way, heading for the labyrinth of corridors backstage.

'Great gig,' he said as he passed me. 'You've got one hell of a voice.'

'Thanks.'

Cute!

I stopped.

Maybe there was a way to burn off some of that excess energy. Sadie seemed ready to hunt the urban jungle. I turned on my heels and followed him around the corner.

After a few wrong turns, I eventually caught up with him somewhere deep in the bowels of the building, just outside the boiler room. I wasn't going to let Sadie or myself down this time. He looked surprised to see me when I rounded the corner and marched right up to him, and even more shocked when I planted a passionate kiss on his mouth, delving in with my tongue.

'What was that for?' he asked, grinning.

Just come out with it!

'I guess gigging gets me all worked up sometimes, and today's your lucky day. How'd you fancy a fuck?' I asked him.

For a moment he just stared.

'Is that a trick question?' He still looked like he couldn't believe his good fortune.

'No, just a direct one.'

'Then yes.'

Kissing him again while his fingers glided across my skin and found their way under the straps of my dress, I unzipped the front of his overalls and reached inside. My fingers found his growing stiffness and wrapped themselves around him.

Mm! Promising!

I peeled his overalls off his shoulders then with one hand I backed him up against the wall and brushing my lips down his firm, young torso, sank ever so slowly to my knees.

-0-

When I returned to the dressing room, Helena was waiting by the door.

'Where did you get to? I've been looking all over for you. We were starting to worry. Mick and a couple of the other staff have cleared the stage. The van's round by the stage door and we're about ready to load up. Are you alright? You look a bit flushed.'

'Never better!'

The stagehand passed us in the corridor, zipping up his overalls and trying to suppress a smile. I hadn't even asked him his name, not that it particularly mattered; I'd still made his night.

'I just needed to get my head round things, that's all. Come on then; let's get packed up. It's late and the only thing keeping me upright is nervous energy. I think we're all going to crash and burn tomorrow.'

CHAPTER EIGHT

Linda looked up at me from the bench while I adjusted the weights machine.

'Hanging from the overhead pipes? Really?'

'Well they were quite low, and I did test them first to see if they'd take my weight. I couldn't help myself; I was so pumped up after the gig.'

'Well, you're certainly getting quite inventive. You're rather orally fixated too, aren't you?'

'I'm what?'

'Orally fixated. I mean, you sing for a living, you enjoy your food even though you never put on an ounce, and you seem to, um . . . rather enjoy putting things in your mouth.'

I chuckled.

'You make me sound like a dog. They do everything with their mouths too.'

Linda snorted.

'Trust me, honey; you're anything but a dog.' She sat up and reached for a towel. 'Didn't anybody notice you'd gone missing?'

'Yes, they did. The trouble is there's no such thing as privacy in a band situation. Everyone knows everybody else's business.'

Linda shuddered.

'I couldn't deal with that. It would drive me mental. So when do you find out for sure about the contract?'

I puffed out my cheeks.

'Tomorrow morning, hopefully. Mitchell seems confident.'

-0-

The call finally came through on Monday at ten thirty-three. I was pacing the kitchen, waiting for news. Mitchell phoned me first before ringing the rest of the band.

'Rebecca, we're in. They want to give us a two album deal. There will be a meeting in my office tomorrow at ten to go through the fine print with everybody. My legal guy will be there to help translate the contracts into language human beings can actually understand. Once that's done, and assuming everything's agreed, we can officially sign at their offices later this week. Congratulations.'

'Thank you, Mitchell. We couldn't have got this far without you.'

'Just doing my job, Rebecca. Now we've got an album to record. You'd better clear your schedule because this is where it gets interesting.'

'Don't worry. I'm on it. See you tomorrow.'

After rushing through to tell Mum, I got straight on the phone to Linda.

-0-

Despite the good news about the recording contract, it

was just another Thursday evening at home. The weekend was going to be a busy one. The signing was all set for the morning and we still had gigs booked for both the Friday and Saturday nights, so I was making the most of the family time. Rob was helping Jeff set up a new television in the lounge. I was helping Mum clear up after dinner and was just about to put a saucepan in the dishwasher when she dropped the bombshell.

I had no idea I would feel the way about it that I did. In fact, I didn't see it coming at all.

'Oh, by the way,' she said, 'I heard some wonderful news today. Jeff rang me as soon as Steve told him. Valentina's pregnant. They're expecting a baby next May.'

I dropped the pan with a clatter, suddenly fighting for breath. It was like a hammer blow to the chest. The last piece of hope I had for any future with Steve had just been taken away from me. It really was over. I put my hand over my mouth and burst out crying; there was no stopping it.

Mum stared at me while the penny dropped.

'Oh, Rebecca!' she sighed. 'Oh, you didn't! I had a nagging feeling there was something between the two of you. I couldn't be sure, though, otherwise I would have said something.'

She wrapped her arms around me.

'You fell for him hard too, didn't you? And you've been bottling it up all this time.'

'How did you know?' I sobbed, barely able to see through the tears.

'I didn't until now.' She looked suddenly concerned and a momentary flash of anger crossed her face. 'Did he .

. . did he take advantage of you?'

'If you mean did he start it, then no.' I had to put her straight for Steve's sake. 'That was down to me. Don't go blaming him. It's not his fault.'

She wiped away the drips that were running down my cheeks and was close to tears herself but she tried to make light of it.

'Mind you, when I think about it you left a trail of clues a mile wide; all that sneaking around and acting strangely and then moping around the house like a bear with a sore head for a good month after they got back together.'

My face cracked into a stiff smile. I was trembling.

'What about Jeff? Do you think he knows?'

She shook her head.

'Blissfully unaware, darling, and that's the way it'll stay. As much as I love him he's a man, dear. They're not exactly fabled for their powers of observation. There's no point him knowing about any of it now; it would only make things awkward between him and Steve.'

'What must you think of me? He was married.'

'Separated, sweetheart, so don't go beating yourself up about it, and I could see how close you'd become; I just didn't realise it was that close. Besides, I can understand the appeal. He's not exactly hard on the eye is he?'

This was too weird.

'When I was your age he'd have been exactly the kind of man I went for,' she continued. 'In fact, if I was a few years younger I'd . . .'

'Mum!'

Now it was my turn to pull back and stare at her. I'd never heard her talk like this.

'What? You think I've lived like a nun all my life? Things got pretty wild in my teens I can tell you, so I'm in no position to preach,' she said.

I didn't speak straight away. I wasn't about to make any more confessions of my own and Mum's revelations were messing with my head.

'I didn't think they could have children,' I said, finally.

'They just had problems conceiving, that's all. It's amazing what happens when couples relax and stop trying too hard sometimes; nature takes over.'

Mum seemed ready to change the subject again. Maybe she could see how much it hurt me to talk about them.

'While we're sort of on the subject, I suppose you think those movies you found were Jeff's little secret, don't you?'

'What?' This change of tack wasn't much better.

'And it's 'pardon', not 'what'!' She gave me a look of exasperation. 'The films belong to both of us. There's nothing wrong with a bit of grown-up entertainment.'

Mentally I was sticking my fingers in my ears and chanting 'La, la, la, la, la. Not listening!'

'Look, I know nobody likes to think of their parents as having a sex life. Just because every generation pretty much discovers sex for itself they think they invented it. I was the same.' She softened. 'The point I'm trying to make is you don't have to hide things from me. If you need to talk, I'm here. I couldn't open up to Nanna and Pappy when I needed to. They belong to a very different generation. I don't want you to have to feel as alone as I did. I made a lot of mistakes: your father for one.'

'Huh?' *What's she going to hit me with now?*

'Don't get me wrong. You and Rob are the best thing that ever happened to me. You were never mistakes, but your father was a different story. I don't think I'd have ended up with him if I wasn't rebelling against your grandfather. Things might have been different if I felt like I could talk to them. I don't want you to feel like that.'

'What could I say?' I lamented. 'Steve's like . . . Jeff's best mate, and I didn't know how you'd react either.'

Mum shrugged her shoulders.

'We're more alike than you think. In fact, I probably started younger than you did. That's teenage rebellion for you. Your Pappy could be a bit . . . controlling.'

Whether I liked it or not, I was starting to see Mum in a whole new light. She sat me down at the breakfast bar and made two mugs of tea.

'Here you are. The cure for all the world's ills!'

'Thank you.' I took the steaming mug and wrapped my hands around it. Sensing my mood, our poodle, Rolo, came over and nudged my arm with his nose. I looked down and stroked his head, grateful for all the unconditional love I had in my life.

Maybe I could finally put Steve behind me. I hadn't realised how much I'd still been holding on to him despite all my efforts to get him out of my system. Now my whole adult life stretched away into the distance in front of me.

Some of those adventures and misadventures had been a lot of fun, though, even if they were failed attempts to purge me of the past. They weren't going to be my last; I knew that much.

CHAPTER NINE

'Well? What do you think?' Mitchell asked, peering at me through his round glasses.

I had already taken the time to read through the file a couple of times but I still felt like I was flying by the seat of my pants.

'Two, maybe three producers stand out for me. What about this one?' I tapped his picture on the page in front of me. 'He's done a lot of different stuff and he's really well known, but wouldn't he be a bit 'trendy' for what we do?'

'I don't think so. He's got his finger on the pulse of what reaches an audience and he has a good reputation but he wouldn't be too urban for you. Why did you pick on him?'

'I don't know. Gut feeling, I suppose.'

'There's nothing wrong with that. You've got good instincts. Underneath that fashionable exterior beats the heart of an honest artist like you. He's had his share of the limelight and knows what it feels like. In fact, he's still releasing records under his own name from time to time. Being American, he might inject a more international appeal too. Getting him involved would be a real catch.'

He leant back in his chair and looked at me for a moment.

'If he stands out then why don't we set up a meeting? We wouldn't be committing to anything and neither would he at this stage. We're also fortunate that he's over here putting the finishing touches to someone's album at the moment and enjoys working with British artists. He's quite the anglophile really.'

I nodded.

'Okay. Go for it!' I had a good feeling about this, although I was quite surprised that someone with his profile would consider producing an unknown newcomer like me.

-0-

On the day of the meeting, I was already in Mitchell's office when Penny ushered him in. Despite being a similar age to Jeff, Doug Prentiss looked lean and handsome with well-defined features and what would have been a shock of curly black hair if it hadn't been cut quite short. If it wasn't for his hair I wouldn't have been sure whether he was of mixed race or just had a really good suntan. He had the relaxed confidence of a man who had achieved success early in life and wore it well, along with his close-fitting designer jeans, collarless shirt and a burgundy leather jacket.

Doug gave us both an easy smile and shook first my hand, then Mitchell's.

'Thanks for coming, Doug. Please, take a seat. Can I offer you a coffee?'

'Not for me thank you, but I would like a mineral

water if you have one. It's the caffeine; it doesn't agree with me.'

'Sparkling or still?'

'Sparkling please.'

Mitchell stepped over to the desk and buzzed the request through to Penny before we took our seats around the coffee table.

'So,' he said, 'the reason we're here is to examine the possibility of you coming on board as producer for Rebecca's first album. Have you had the chance to listen to the demos I sent you?'

'Yes, I have. In fact, I had them on again in the car on my way here.' He turned to me. 'Rebecca, you're writing some good songs. I can see a lot of potential there. I've already got some ideas that would help to make the most of them.'

'So you'd be interested?' I asked.

'Yes, I would. I don't normally work with new artists, but in your case, I'd be prepared to make an exception. I can't quite put my finger on it but there's something soul-deep about your music. I like that.'

I was warming to him already.

Penny appeared with a glass and a fancy looking bottle of, no doubt, expensive water and placed it on the table in front of him. He looked up and thanked her, smiling. Nervously, she smiled back. It was a rare crack in her hyper-efficient but quirky exterior. She must have seen a lot of famous and powerful people come through this office and it was unusual to see her flustered. Maybe Penny liked older men but who was I to be critical of that? Even though Doug was comfortably in his forties, he was still an extremely attractive man and in amazing shape. He oozed sexuality and confidence.

Mitchell looked momentarily agitated, shifting uneasily in his seat and replacing his cup of coffee back on its saucer before his impassive mask returned. No one else seemed to have noticed, except for me. Penny retreated to the adjacent office.

'So,' said Mitchell, 'what would be your overall vision for Rebecca's music.'

Doug poured himself a glass of the water and took a sip then placed it on the table.

'Well, it's like this . . .'

We spent the next hour throwing ideas back and forth. I liked what he had to say and he seemed enthusiastic. In fact, I was disappointed when he had to go.

'I'm sorry I've got to leave you so soon. Time is money and we're in the middle of mixing an album. I've left my cell number with Mitchell. I'm looking forward to the chance of getting more involved once the current thing is all finished, so call me if you want to talk some more.'

'Thanks. I will.'

'Thank you for coming, Doug.' Mitchell was unusually radiant.

'It's been a pleasure. Nice to meet you, Rebecca. You too, Mitchell. Your reputation precedes you. It's good to put a face to the name.'

We shook hands again then Penny magically reappeared to see him out.

'Well, what do you think?' asked Mitchell when Doug had gone.

'I can't believe Doug Prentiss might be producing my first album.' I was grinning from ear to ear and trying to contain my desire to jump up and down on the spot.

'That's so awesome.'

-0-

Linda was, as always, ready to hear the latest.

'So is he as much of a hunk in real life as he is in his videos?'

'He does have a certain, relaxed charm, yes. I don't see him 'that way' though. I just think he'd be a great person to work with. He's already brought a fresh view on songs I thought I knew inside out.'

She stepped off the cross trainer and reached for a towel.

'So it's really happening then?'

'It certainly looks that way. We'll see.'

'You know, we're both very lucky really,' Linda mused. 'We both have the opportunity to do what we want with our lives. We're fortunate enough to be well supported and not to be held back by a lack of opportunity.'

She paused, thinking while she dried herself down.

'Making decisions about what happens in life is one thing, but not everybody gets to make real choices. There's a big difference between making your mind up between the lesser of evils and actually choosing what you want to do. Plenty of people have dreams but they don't all get the chance to realise them, no matter how hard they work, because doors are closed to them.'

'Go on,' I said. Linda was leading up to something. I could tell.

'If you think about it, we don't live in a fair society where everyone has equal opportunities. This is not a meritocracy. You've worked hard to reach this point and had a lot of help to even get this far, but hard work isn't the deciding factor between success and failure. All it does is help tip the scales in your favour, that's all. The world is full of the hard working poor, and at the other end of the scale, there are the wealthy, some of whom have never done anything to deserve their good fortune and often have little appreciation of it. Don't get me wrong; I'm not saying that everyone at the top is a parasite and that everyone at the bottom deserves better, far from it, but there is no inherent justice to how the world works.'

She marshalled her thoughts for a moment, overtaken by one of her more philosophical moods.

'I think there are two things that make the difference between worldly success and the lack of it.'

'Which are . . . ?'

'Luck and ruthlessness.'

'How so?'

Linda was on a roll this time. Letting her have it out seemed to be the best option. Besides, I wanted to see where she was going with this. It was at times such as these that I learned more about the workings of her mind than any other. The best thing for it was to light the blue touch paper and stand back.

'To get ahead in life you need one of those two things and more often than not, both. Good fortune doesn't necessarily go to the deserving; that's just a comfortable little lie we tell ourselves to make it easier to get through the day. Money always follows money and opportunity tends to gravitate towards better-looking people so it follows that on average, those who are fortunate enough to look good are also better off in other ways. That's just how it is. If you are fortunate, though, it's a gift. You need to acknowledge it, be grateful for it and make the most of it, and that's exactly what you're doing. You were born beautiful. You were born talented and there's no shame in that; the crime would be in wasting it.'

I stepped onto the running machine and set it to a programme that would start off at a walking pace.

'Let's not count any chickens before they've hatched. I haven't made a bean yet.'

'There's more to good fortune than just money. In fact, money's probably the least of it. You're getting the chance to do the thing you were born for, to live a life inspired by the things you love and you have the opportunity to share that inspiration with others. Not many people can truly say that. A lot of people go through life thinking they've made choices when they haven't; they've made decisions guided by necessity. They're steered and manipulated from cradle to grave believing they have free will when really they don't. They spend all their time surviving and none of it actually living.'

'Okay. So I get that I'm lucky. What about ruthlessness?'

'There are those who say you make your own luck. You don't; that's just a euphemism for ruthlessness. It's amazing how many people will lie, cheat, steal, and manipulate to get what they want. They're quite prepared to step over as many bodies as it takes to ensure they get to the top of the pile and stay there. It's the basis of capitalism. We're all living in one giant monopoly game dominated by self-interest.'

The machine began to pick up the pace and I broke

into a jog.

'Go on. I'm listening.'

'Entering into many walks of life is like stepping into a tank full of sharks and I'd include politics, law, large sections of the media and most of corporate business amongst them. I can't speak for the music industry but I'll bet it's got more than its fair share of sharks.' She snorted. 'I'm sure you'll meet them along the way. Once those sharks hit a critical mass there's no going back. No matter how pure your motives are when you climb into the tank, pretty soon you're faced with a dilemma: are you a shark or are you lunch? The only thing that survives in there for any length of time is the sharks and even then they'll attack the others if they're weak or wounded.'

'So what are you going to be, shark or lunch?'

She smiled enigmatically; clearly one step ahead of me.

'Neither! I choose door number three.'

'And what's that?'

'Stay out of the fucking tank! If you can't fix a crooked system from the inside, then subvert it from the outside. If that's what it takes to hold onto your soul, no matter what people think of you, no matter what taboos get broken and whether it's within the law or somewhere outside it then so be it. I won't be a slave to something that doesn't deserve my allegiance.'

'So what are you going to do once you've got all your qualifications?'

Now we were getting to it. She'd never given much of a clue as to what she was actually planning to do for a living.

'I've got some ideas for a business. It's early days yet.

We'll see.'

'Come on, you've got to give me a bit more to go on than that.'

'Just consider it wealth redistribution by giving the rich exactly what they want.'

That was it. I knew Linda well enough by now to recognise when I wouldn't get any more out of her. The shutters of her mind had come down again as suddenly as they had lifted.

-0-

Doug did come on board to make the album with us, exactly as I'd hoped. I enjoyed working with him. He brought a breath of fresh air, even to songs I already thought I'd tired of.

We squirrelled ourselves away in a residential studio on the Sussex coast to record. Due to budgetary limits, we had to work quickly. The days were long and tiring, but we had enthusiasm on our side. The band liked Doug too; his clarity of vision and easy-going efficiency got the best out of all of us.

The nice thing about living and working in the same place was that we were so focussed. We could fall out of bed in the morning, grab some breakfast in the communal kitchen and go straight into the studio to begin recording, tea in hand and toast in mouth. It was almost like working in the studio at home, except bigger and more luxurious. Most of the time, we all ate together in the evening. Quite often Doug joined us too. There was nothing of the big 'I am' about him.

Sometimes we weren't all needed in the studio at once.

Doug, Pete the resident engineer, and Alex would settle themselves down to cut his guitar parts in peace, leaving us with time on our hands. On occasion, we would walk the half mile down to the beach and stumble over the pebbles with our hands in our pockets, bracing ourselves against the stiff spring breeze that whipped in off the sea and breathing in the salty air with our hair flying behind us. I would stand at the water's edge, looking out over the waves as they rolled in and out, creeping further up the beach with the incoming tide, and trying to picture what lay beyond the horizon. There was a whole world out there waiting for us; it just didn't know it yet.

Sometimes I'd go down to the beach alone, or take the studio owner's Labrador with me, throwing pieces of driftwood for her to fetch while she bounded along the finer shingle and sand exposed by the low tide. I would return to the studio refreshed and with a clear head, ready to record again.

In just under a month we had recorded more than enough songs for the album, so we could afford to pick those that worked best as a collection and keep the others up our sleeve. We even recorded my special song, although at first, Doug raised his eyebrows when I played him the demo.

'Whoa, sister! You don't pull your punches, do you? Mitchell did mention there was one song that might rock the boat a bit. It's got 'single' written all over it but we might need to take the edge off a little.'

I dug my heels in.

'It would cut the heart out of it if it was too toned down. The whole point is that it's sexually honest. You can't make a song that's all about sex and not lay everything on the line.'

'Well, it certainly does that. I tell you what. We'll record two versions; one can be a little more radio friendly and the other version would be for the album.' He chuckled to himself. 'They'll have to put warnings on the album cover, though, and you'll probably have to fight your corner with the record company.'

He sat back in the control room chair, his brown eyes regarding me impassively.

'When it comes to stuff like this, what people do and what they're prepared to admit to are two different things. Attitudes are a lot more open than they used to be but if anything, mainstream record companies are more conservative than ever; they don't like taking risks. Our task will be in persuading Pristeen Records that stirring up controversy will be good for record sales. If we can get them to see it our way then you might get your wish.'

Doug paused for a moment, thinking.

'I love the way it builds, though,' he continued. 'I'd really want to play on that with the arrangement; increase the energy and tension as the song goes on. It's kind of like . . .' He caught me smirking at him and shook his head. 'Okay, yeah! I get it. Nice little musical joke. You're a one-off; I'll give you that.'

Once additional musicians had come in to add extra parts to a few of the songs and all the recording was done, we took a couple of weeks break before moving to another studio to mix everything.

Meanwhile, my eighteenth birthday was looming.

Linda had already learned to drive and at least the breathing space in our schedule gave me time to catch up with her and get behind the wheel myself. Mum and Jeff said they would help me look around for a reasonable second-hand car once I had passed my driving test. It would be such a relief to be independent and mobile.

Linda was on hand to catch up over a coffee in the local cafe after school.

'You're working too hard. All work and no play makes Jack a dull boy. You need a break; let your hair down a bit.'

I placed my coffee on the table in front of me and sagged into a chair.

'I know. It's just that it's all so near and yet so far. Mitchell's still trying to persuade them to release the one song we all believe in, the one I played you on my birthday last year, but they're obsessed with playing it safe. The album's hopefully coming out sometime towards the end of the year, but we really need a successful single to stimulate interest or we're beating our heads against a brick wall. Even if we get to make our second album, they might not bother to release it if the first one doesn't make enough money.'

'Can they even do that?'

I stared into my latte.

'Yes. Unfortunately, they can.'

'Listen. I know what'll cheer you up. It's your birthday the week after next. Keep the Saturday afterwards free.'

'I don't think there's anything in the diary for that day yet anyway. Why?'

'Let's just say I've got something planned that will help get all that frustration out of your system.'

'What are you up to?' I gave her a penetrating stare.

Linda lowered her voice.

'You want to blow off some steam, right?'

'Yes.'

'And you're still on the pill?'

I nodded. This was getting odd.

'And you're not going to be on your period?'

I quickly did the maths in my head.

'No, not till the following week. What's going on?'

'Well, I know what you like to do to relax, so dress up sexy and be prepared for a night to remember. Are you up for it or not?'

What did I have to lose? If she'd arranged some kind of double date then what the hell. Frustration had been getting the better of me lately and I had a feeling she hadn't been idle behind the scenes.

'Fuck it! You're on!'

Linda glowed with satisfaction.

'Good girl. You won't be disappointed. I can't tell you any more yet; you'll just have to see, but I promise you it'll be a night you won't forget in a hurry.' Something seemed to be running through her mind; a moment of doubt maybe. 'You do trust me, don't you?'

'With my life.'

She seemed reassured and took a deep breath.

'Good! As long as you're game for anything and I've got a pretty good idea that you are, then you're in for a treat.'

She sat back in her seat and tossed her hair over her shoulders, enjoying the mystery.

'I wish you'd tell me what's going on,' I said.

Linda shook her head.

'And spoil the surprise? No way. Not on your nelly!'

CHAPTER TEN

My eighteenth birthday passed relatively quietly. At my request, there was no party, no big fuss. I didn't really feel like it. I was just glad to have some time off work to catch up with my family and it was nice not to be living out of a suitcase for a few days.

Mum and Jeff took me out to a pub after lunch. Jeff called it a rite of passage. Although I had sneaked the occasional drink while out with the band, it wasn't a big thing for me and I didn't drink to excess, even after gigs. Sometimes, when the opportunity arose, there were better ways of getting things out of my system.

It was worth going just for the surprised look on Mum's face when I ordered a pint of beer. I was sure she expected me to be drinking a glass of wine instead. I shrugged my shoulders and took a sip. The quenching bitterness took me by surprise, but once my palate adjusted I discovered I quite liked it.

'It seemed like the thing to do,' I said. 'I'll try anything once. If I don't like it, at least I can say I gave it a go.'

And I usually come back for more.

It was nice to spend some time doing nothing in particular, just chatting and playing a few games of pool, even though I wasn't all that good at it. Mum was, though. Perhaps it was a sign of her misspent youth.

Once Rob had come home from school and we'd smartened ourselves up for the evening, we went out for a meal with Nanna and Pappy. It was lovely to see them too.

Although it was a deliberately low-key way to celebrate my eighteenth birthday, I had a feeling Saturday was going to be a big night. Linda remained tight-lipped about it. Despite my attempts to probe her for information, she was giving nothing away.

I didn't see her through the day on Saturday; she said she would be busy, although she did send me a text.

Linda
Don't forget to get your glad rags on. Dress sexy. Pick you up at 7pm sharp. Have something light to eat before you come out. There will be nibbles, but not till later.
Kinky Bitch ;-)
1:23 pm

Okay. So we're not going out for a meal; at least not straight away.

Her text struck me as a little odd. Maybe Linda was planning on skipping straight to dessert. It wouldn't have surprised me. Thankfully, I was prepared on the clothes front; I'd bought myself a new outfit especially.

Me
All in hand. Off to get my hair done at 4.
Slut / Sadie
1:27 pm

Linda
Excellent. See you later. I'm not sure who should
be more excited about tonight, you or me.
KB
1:29 pm

Rather than spoil my hair later, it seemed to be a good idea to shower early and shave my legs and other places while I had the time. Afterwards, I stood in front of the long mirror in the bathroom, running my hands over the smooth contours of my body and inspecting my handiwork. I'd do, I suppose. The new piercing in my navel added an extra twist. Whoever Linda had lined up for me wouldn't be too disappointed at the end of the evening if all went well. I moisturised all over and dressed in jeans and a tee-shirt before heading into town for my hair appointment.

By the time I returned, I was starting to feel nervous and excited about the evening. Whatever Linda had in store for me, it was bound to be good. Besides, Sadie hadn't been out to play in a while and she was getting restless.

I laid my new outfit on the bed. The clingy dress was made of a deep wine-red, lacy material with see-through, full-length sleeves and a skirt that maintained decorum, but only just. It was quite low-cut, so I didn't bother with a bra, but there were lacy knickers in the same colour and high-heeled shoes to match too. It ought to please, I thought.

I was pretty sure I hadn't made this much of an effort before going out for the night since the time Linda and I spent the whole afternoon preparing for my first big night with Steve, but somehow it just felt right. After all the hard work and long days of the last few months, I just wanted to let my hair down. I needed this. Besides, I would have my best friend for company too. What could be better? We didn't get to see enough of each other these days, between the demands of my work and her A-level finals looming on the horizon.

I made myself a sandwich and followed that with a peach from the fruit bowl. It was tasty but really ripe. The sweet flesh gave way as I bit into it, juice running down over my chin and onto my tee-shirt. It was a good job I hadn't already changed. I licked my fingers, put the plate in the dishwasher, and went upstairs to brush my teeth.

By half past six, I was dressed, made-up, and ready to go. Rob met me on the landing when I came out of my room in a waft of perfume.

'Okay, who are you and what have you done with my sister?'

I stuck out my tongue at him and crossed my eyes. I would have blown him a raspberry too but I didn't want to ruin my lipstick.

'No, seriously though: you look amazing,' he continued.

'Thank you. I've been told I scrub up well.'

'Has Mum seen you?'

'Not yet. I take it she's downstairs.'

'Just getting dinner ready, but if you're off out you won't want any, will you?'

I shook my head.

'Linda will be here in a few minutes. Can you save me some, just in case I'm hungry when I get back later? I don't really know what Linda's got planned.'

'Yeah, okay.'

Mum was impressed with the outfit when we got downstairs. She gave me a knowing look. I don't think it was the response Rob had been expecting. Jeff was more cautious.

'You're not seriously going out like that, are you? You'll die of cold.'

'I'm not walking; Linda's picking me up in her car. Anyway, it's what people wear to go out and I am eighteen now. It's my choice.'

He couldn't really argue with that. Instead, he went back to laying the table while Mum gave me a conspiratorial smile.

The front doorbell rang. I opened my clutch bag and checked my phone. Six fifty-one; Linda was early. I ran to the front door, or rather ran as best I could in heels, and opened it. Sure enough, it was Linda, looking resplendent in a silver evening gown.

An evening gown? Fuck!

I hadn't thought it would be that posh a night out. I didn't even own one.

'Hi there, Rebecca! Are you ready to . . . ? Wow! Oh yes! They're going to like you,' she said, looking me up and down.

'They?' I asked.

She chose to ignore my question.

'A Scarlet Woman, eh? Aleister Crowley would have been proud.'

'Who?'

'Oh, it's not important,' she said with a wave of the hand. 'He was some kind of ritual magician who the press used to call 'the wickedest man in the world'. He was nothing of the sort, though, not by modern standards, although he was a bit of a twisted old fruit. Anyway, there was a succession of women he involved in his rituals who he called his 'scarlet women'.'

Now I was feeling a bit uneasy but tried to make light of it.

'You're not dragging me off to be the sacrifice at some sort of Satanic Mass, are you?'

Linda seemed to find this highly amusing.

'Nothing like that,' she guffawed then lowered her voice, almost to a whisper. 'The only thing likely to be sacrificed tonight is your virtue on the altar of lurve.' She emphasised the last word, enjoying the sound of it.

'Since my virtue is long gone, I don't have anything to worry about then, do I?'

'Are you ready to go?' she chuckled.

'Ready as I'll ever be.'

'Then let's go. Your carriage awaits!'

'Are you sure I'm dressed properly for the occasion?'

'Don't worry. You're perfect. Come on, the night isn't getting any younger.'

I called back into the house.

'See you later.'

Don't wait up.

An assortment of muffled voices wished me well from the kitchen as I closed the front door.

Linda's white mini was nice. I was unlikely to be able to afford anything as new. Loretta and Brian hadn't thrown that sort of money at her brother Ryan either, so I wasn't too sure how she was able to afford it.

'So how long does it take to get where we're going?' I asked as we clambered into the front seats.

Linda was taking extra care not to crumple her evening dress and lifted the hem clear of her heels. Once she was satisfied her dress was safe, she turned to look at me.

'About half an hour.'

In my head, I tried to work out what towns lay within a half-hour drive from our house, but we seemed to be driving out into the countryside, away from more built-up areas.

She wouldn't say any more. I could tell she was excited, though. All the way there she was trying to suppress a wicked grin so I knew she was up to something, but still she gave nothing else away.

We turned into a driveway with a pair of large electric gates and pulled up. Linda lowered the window and spoke into an intercom on a post outside the gates.

'It's Linda Maloney. I'm here with the guest of honour.'

Guest of honour? What in blue blazes . . . ?

She remained oblivious to my stare as the gates swung smoothly open and pulled forwards onto a long, tarmacked drive. It was lined with an avenue of trees and shrubs, lit up by a combination of concealed lighting and old-fashioned, lantern style street lamps. In the gathering dusk I could make out immaculately kept lawns and at the end of the drive, an enormous, white house lit up from ground level by lights all along the front. A warm glow emanated from every one of its tall windows, only increasing the mystery of what lay within.

Linda eased the car towards the house while the gates closed behind us and parked up in the turning area out front. There were already at least twenty cars there, most of them expensive. Their owners were nowhere to be seen.

Linda led me through the unlocked front door and into a vast hallway with a central staircase that led up to a galleried landing and a great chandelier that commanded the centre of the ceiling. I looked up in awe.

'What are we doing here?'

'Follow me,' she said, leading me to the left of the stairs and through a door into a panelled drawing room which was lit by a number of lamps, lending it a subdued glow.

'What on earth is this place?' I whispered.

'Wild, isn't it? This house belongs to some old family friends.'

'Oh!'

That kind of 'friends'? What the hell was I getting into?

Linda could see that I was becoming nervous and took me by the hands.

'Listen, I know these people. You don't have to do anything you don't want to. You can back out if you don't want to go any further.' She fixed me with a steely gaze. 'I wouldn't ask you to do anything I wouldn't do myself. In fact, I already have and you know what? I had the time of my life. Like I said before, I can promise you a night you will never, ever forget.'

I kept my hands in hers, unsure whether to take the plunge or run a mile.

'I'll understand if you don't want to,' she continued. 'Nobody's forcing you to do anything, least of all me.'

Looking deep into those bottomless green eyes I shook my head.

'*Carpe diem, baby!*' I heard Linda's voice saying, but her lips never moved.

'There's no way I'd cop out now,' I told her. A well of resolve had sprung from somewhere inside and the words had left my mouth before my brain had time to intervene. 'I wimped out once before but you gladly went where I was too afraid to go. When I think about it now you were trying to make a point, weren't you?'

Linda pressed her lips together and nodded.

'Let's face it, everybody has fantasies, some of which can get pretty wild,' she said, 'but how many people have the balls to live them for real? If people were more open and honest with each other they'd realise that many of them secretly want the same things, but thanks to social pressures and expectations most people bottle it up and never let it out; they're too afraid of what others will think of them or too ashamed of what goes on in their own heads.'

She looked at me earnestly, gripping my fingers tight.

'You know, when I get to the end of my days, for better or for worse I'd rather be remembering the things I did rather than regretting the things I didn't do. I never wanted to be one of those people who didn't take chances when I had them and I don't think you do either. I wanted to give you the opportunity to go beyond even your wildest imaginings and this is it, sweetie. This is it.'

I took a deep breath.

'I must admit I regretted not going for it when I had the chance. Now it's my turn to take a leap of faith and I won't let you down.'

'Fair enough!' she said. Her voice became softer. 'Thank you for your trust in me. I won't let you down either.' She let go of my hands. 'Now, I need you to get undressed. You can leave your clothes here.' All of a sudden there was an air of authority in her voice again.

I just stared at her.

'Do you trust me?' she asked and I nodded. 'Then do as I tell you and you'll see.'

I slipped out of my dress and placed it over the back of a chair, along with my clutch bag. It was then that I noticed Linda wasn't joining me in taking her clothes off.

'What about you?' I asked.

'Oh no, sweetie! I had my turn a couple of months ago. Tonight is all about you.' She looked me up and down carefully. 'And there's no point keeping those on,' she said, pointing at my little, lacy underwear, 'they'll only get ruined.' Linda chewed the inside of her cheek, thinking. 'Keep the shoes on, though. They definitely add that extra something, and by the way, I'm loving the piercing; it's very you!'

I peeled off my underwear, lifting my feet to slide the flimsy material over my heels. I could have sworn for a moment that she was biting her lip.

'Oh, honey, you look great. You are going to be one popular girl tonight.'

Linda stepped over to a bureau by the wall and produced something made of soft, black cloth from the top drawer. I stood rooted to the spot while she stepped around behind me and tied it firmly but sensuously around my head. Now enveloped in darkness I stood still, my chest heaving with anticipation.

Her fingers gently brushed my neck, trailing down and over my collarbone, then without warning her hot mouth was pressed against mine. Without thinking I responded, despite the alarm bells going off in my head.

Linda! She really had caught me off guard, but then again I wasn't totally surprised. Perhaps if I was honest with myself, I already knew. I'd never been kissed that way by a girl before, let alone Linda, but I liked it. Our lips pressed tightly together, her tongue delving into my mouth and yet it was still somehow softer, more sensual than a man's kiss. I was tingling all over, especially when I felt her fingers brushing against the lips of my pussy, testing my wetness with her fingertip. Suddenly her lips were gone, leaving me open-mouthed and wanting.

'God, I'm . . . I'm so sorry!' she stammered. 'I just got carried away. I've wanted to do that for so long, but maybe now is not the time. We'll have to talk about this later.'

'Yes, we will.' My voice was calm, despite my inner turbulence.

'Self-control, Linda,' she muttered to herself before the confidence returned to her voice. 'I think we can say you're suitably in the mood, though. Do you always get that wet down there? Since you're obviously ready, let's go and meet your adoring public.'

She knocked slowly three times on a door to an adjacent room and the hubbub of voices on the other side suddenly stopped. Up until then, they had only been present on the edge of my consciousness but now their absence threw my situation into stark relief.

I could hear the key turn in the lock and the door swinging open on its hinges. I had no idea what I was about to walk into. My imagination ran amok, painting a jumble of scenarios in my mind's eye. All I knew for sure was that at that very moment I had never felt so dangerously alive, consumed by the dichotomy of my need to explore every dark, sensual corner of my desires and my fear of the unknown.

Carried on a tide of adrenaline and heart in mouth, I took the leap of faith and stepped forwards. Linda steadied me as trembling and naked except for the blindfold, a gold anklet and my high heeled shoes, I allowed her to lead me into the room that lay beyond. I could sense the people all around me and hear their breathing but I had no idea how many there were. The door behind me latched shut with a solid click.

Linda let go of my hands which fell to my sides and I stood, conscious only of my nakedness, the deafening sound of my own breathing, and the unseen eyes whose gaze burned into my skin.

I waited.

Gentle hands took the tips of my fingers and lifted them up until I was standing with my arms outstretched to the side, a defenceless but willing sacrifice. At first, I felt only the lightest touch on my arms, the merest kiss of something other than skin, but I couldn't place it. I had no sphere of reference. It felt soft, delicate. It tickled.

What is that? Silk? No, not silk.

It ran from my shoulders down the tops of both arms to my wrists then traced the line underneath back to my sides.

Satin? Lace? Neither of those; it had fronds which trailed against my skin, just touching me. One side moved around to my breasts, the other to my back, still making only the lightest of contact. My whole body tingled.

Feathers! That was it. It had to be some kind of feathers but they were soft, so soft.

They moved languidly down my body, my breath catching in my throat when they reached my most intimate areas and lingered there for a moment before carrying on down my legs.

Wandering in the shade of coconut palms on my own personal island paradise, I could hear the rolling of waves upon the shore, smell the hot, salty air, feel the gentle breeze on my skin. Happily lost, I drifted, awash with sensation.

Crack!

I gasped, flinching at the shock. The stinging blow across my buttocks jarred the senses, sensations of pleasure and pain mingling on their way to my brain followed by a wave of prickling heat as my skin reacted to the impact.

Of what? A riding crop? It was too wide for that. *A belt perhaps?*

The feathers continued their delicate teasing, traversing my skin at will; first here, then there. I had no idea where they would touch me next. I floated, weightless in the blackened void.

Crack!

Again there was the resounding smack of the leather across my behind and the multitude of sensations; a profusion of neurones firing simultaneously. I yielded to the rush of blood around my body, the stinging heat from my buttocks and the soft caress of the feathers everywhere else.

Unknown hands brushed lightly against me; first a breast, then a thigh, then my behind. I had no idea who or how many of them there were. Soon, gaining in confidence, they were everywhere: cupping, stroking, squeezing. I threw my head back, overwhelmed by the wave of sensations from every part of my body that threatened to engulf me. My head spun and my knees went weak as a pair of lips brushed against each of my breasts; each with its own warm, wet, teasing tongue. Teeth raked my stiffened nipples and the lips closed around them, sucking hard.

They broke away leaving me gasping, expectant.

Firmly but gently, I was moved further into the room and bent forwards until my hands rested on the back of something with quilted upholstering. My fingers brushed against the pile of the material. It felt like velvet to the touch. I thought it might be the back of a chair, but it was too low for that; I was bent too far forwards.

Fingers wrapped themselves around one of my ankles and lifted my foot off the floor slightly, steering it to one side until my feet were well apart with my legs straight, forming a V shape. From that position, with my weight pressing forwards on my hands and my behind in the air I was helplessly exposed; they could do what they wanted with me. They had me right where Sadie wanted them.

Two hands took hold of my right foot and a tongue began licking between my exposed toes and up towards my ankle, finding the spaces between the straps of my shoe. Another tongue followed suit with my left foot. Together they worked their way slowly up the backs of my calves and onwards up my thighs, kissing and licking and sucking by turns.

One of them positioned themselves underneath me, wrapping their hands around my thighs and reaching up with their tongue to tease the folds of my pussy. Two more hands gently parted the still stinging cheeks of my arse and a second tongue swirled and licked around the delicate pucker of my anus, gradually probing deeper. At the same time, the tongue beneath me found its way up to my clitoris, gently at first then pressing harder. I groaned in response, my knees threatening to buckle underneath me. My need was now all consuming; an ache that left every muscle clenched in anticipation.

Linda's half-whispered voice appeared in my ear, full of both promise and menace.

'Enough teasing: let's get you fucked, birthday girl!' Her words turned me to liquid.

Someone positioned himself behind me, brushing against the opening of my pussy with the swollen head of his cock and I sighed deep and low in my throat as he slid slowly, smoothly into the eager depths of my body. He laid his hands on my hips and set about his task, moving in and out of me while Linda rested her hands on top of mine, pressing them into the upholstery, keeping them in place.

Finally!

It was just what I needed to release the tension, the steady, rhythmic push that would feed my craving, satisfy my need. I was just beginning to relax into the hypnotic constancy of his movements when he eased himself out of me only to be replaced by another who continued where the first had left off. A couple of minutes later, yet another unseen lover followed on from the other two. A succession of men took their turn with me. I wasn't sure how many of them there were; it no longer mattered. All I knew was the urgency of my desire and my need for release. Keeping my legs straight and my bum in the air I pushed back against them, matching their strokes as each man had his fill.

They all felt different too; not just because every man was a different size and shape, but also because they varied in height which completely altered the sensations. I'd never really noticed that before. Then again, I'd never exactly been in the same situation!

The first one to take me anally caught me by surprise. I suppose I'd been lulled into a false sense of security, thinking I knew what was coming next. I didn't. He must have been well lubed up; because one moment I could feel him nudging against me and the next he was sliding effortlessly into the silky cocoon of my backside and ploughing me with deep, even strokes. I could feel two hands pulling my cheeks apart.

Oh, yes. Fuck me like the voyeur I'm sure you are!

Up until now, I'd said nothing, but Sadie couldn't keep her silence any longer.

'That's it. Fuck my arse. I bet you like watching your cock going in and out of me too, don't you? Well, take a good look then you kinky bastard.'

He growled and laid into me harder. I took that as a 'yes'.

After he'd had his turn, I never knew how I was going

to be taken, or how hard. I lost count of how many there were, but by then what difference did it make? I figured I might as well earn Linda's nickname for me, and besides, in a fair and equal society if a young, single man could be encouraged to sow his wild oats and practically receive a pat on the back for doing so, then why shouldn't a young, single woman do the same?

I was content to be the vessel for their lust, their fuck toy. On the one hand, I felt so dirty and used but on the other, I was the centre of attention, the object and focus of their desire, a goddess for the day.

'You . . . are . . . Venus,' said a voice in my head.

It felt so deliciously abandoned. I was embracing the role of concubine and loving every minute of it.

When the last of them withdrew and wasn't replaced straight away by another, I wondered what was happening. I felt almost cheated. Linda's voice appeared again, close to my ear but loud enough for the whole room to hear.

'Something tells me you've had it up the bum before, in fact I know you have, you naughty girl. You took all that much too easily for a first timer and you know what happens to naughty girls, don't you?'

I shook my head, still panting heavily.

'They get punished. Are you ready to be punished?'

I nodded, my lips parting silently in anticipation.

'Are you sure? Tell me . . . tell me!' she ordered. Her hands held me firmly on either side of my head and her voice was commanding now, insistent.

'Yes.'

'Then you're going to need this.'

A thick, leather belt slid between my parted lips. Its

uniquely sharp, earthy smell and taste filled my senses. Linda's whispered voice was close to my ear again.

'Bite down on it, sweetie.'

The moment I did so I was impaled anally by a thrust which pushed me down and forwards, crushing my breasts against the upholstery and forcing all the air out of my body. The unknown man's battering ram of a cock set about a savage pounding which turned my legs to jelly and reduced me to a whimpering wreck. He bunched my hair in his fist and pulled my head back as he fucked me mercilessly. I would have screamed or bitten my tongue if it weren't for the leather between my teeth. It was relentless.

He went on for much longer than any of the others but I was beyond caring. It wasn't even what I'd call a pleasant experience and yet I didn't want him to stop either. All the time, I gripped the back of the furniture and Linda held my face in her hands, whispering sweet words to me which mitigated the brutality of his thrusts.

'That's it, baby; my brave, brave Rebecca.'

I'd never felt more a woman than I did right then; no longer a girl but a woman: a woman who could fuck like her life depended on it, a woman who could take on anything and still come back for more.

'You can do it. You can take it all, you clever girl.'

I arched my back, gritted my teeth and came so hard I could feel my muscles spasm around his cock while it continued to ravage me. No one else had come yet, but I could tell he was not going to stop until he had emptied himself.

'Good girl. Nearly there now.'

He continued his relentless assault until I could feel

him beginning to tense behind me, his ragged breath catching in his throat. He pulled out, tugged off his condom and sandwiched his iron-hard erection between my buttocks, pumping between them until he shot out a long jet of come which I could feel running down my spine and collecting in the small of my back.

Long hair brushed against my shoulders and a woman's nails raked my skin. Her tongue ran down the length of my back until her mouth closed around the pool of creamy liquid.

Linda?

Then she was gone again, leaving no trace except for the cool wetness where her tongue had been.

My skin was beaded with sweat and my makeup would have been smudged and streaked where tears had run out from underneath the blindfold. I could feel my nose running too. I must have looked a mess, still sprawled across the furniture, sobbing and panting with exhaustion.

Linda wiped my face and cradled me.

'Have you had enough or do you want some more?' she asked.

I steeled myself. Most of the men in the room hadn't come yet. I felt somehow responsible. How could I stop now? I took a deep breath.

'I want more,' I whispered back, then finding my voice announced to the room, 'More!'

'Good girl!' cooed Linda. 'It seems to me that we've overlooked something. Our birthday girl has only come once yet and that just won't do. After all, it's our responsibility to make sure you're thoroughly fulfilled.' It must have been her tone of voice but somehow her words seemed loaded with meaning I had yet to fathom.

I was helped to my feet but was pleasantly surprised to discover that my legs could actually take my weight; at least *they* were beginning to recover. Without warning, I was lifted off my feet by hands underneath my arms and behind my knees, moved around to the end of the piece of furniture I had been leaning on, and lowered towards its flat surface.

Of course! It isn't a chair; it's a chaise longue.

I was aware of someone beneath me because I could hear his breathing and feel the warmth of his skin. My feet touched the floor and he guided himself into me while I lowered myself onto his lap with my legs astride him. His hands reached around to stroke my breasts and I ground myself onto his cock. Now it was my turn to call the shots . . . or so I thought. Despite the blackness that still enveloped me, I was just beginning to take back my share of control when I felt someone else position himself between my open legs, taking hold of my thighs and lifting my feet off the floor.

He isn't going to . . . Oh my God, he is!

With a little adjustment on my part, the second man began to ease into me alongside the first, filling and stretching me to my limits.

So, two into one will go! Your maths teachers were wrong.

Now I knew what Linda's veiled words meant; not only that, but it was now clear she was ring-leading everything. We would definitely have words later.

Once he was all the way inside me, the pair of them began to fuck me in tandem, carefully matching each other's movements, rocking in and out of me as one. I leant back a little, rolling my hips in time with them, and a pair of strong, young hands supported my shoulders, taking my weight. As we settled into a rhythm, I became more aware of what was going on around me. I could hear sighs and moans of pleasure; a chorus of ecstatic voices, many of them female, more than I'd imagined up until then.

Reaching down with one hand, I could feel myself stretched tight around the two men who were working me together and slid my fingers up towards my clitoris. I had no idea how balanced on the brink I'd been. I pressed hard and collapsed as I came, sagging backwards into the arms of the young man beneath me while his hands tenderly cupped my breasts. I could feel his breath moving my hair.

They hadn't finished with me yet, though. I was just regaining my equilibrium when the second cock was replaced by another, even fatter one.

Jesus! What next?

I lay back, tongue pressed against my top lip as they began moving once more. I don't think I'd ever had a workout like this . . . of any kind. By the time my latest anonymous lover withdrew again I was really getting back into my stride. Sadie wasn't ready for it to be over and neither was I. I leant forwards into a sitting position and repositioned myself over the tip of the young man's erection.

Let's give the boy a treat for all his hard work! Sadie agreed.

In one smooth movement and letting my own weight do the work, I slid my arse down onto him, enveloping him to the hilt. It was his turn to grunt in surprise and a gasp went round the room. I pulled up to tease the tip of his cock with my anus before plunging down on him again. Over and over I fucked him hard while the room went wild. Now they were *my* audience. Mine!

Once again, someone positioned himself between my open legs. Instinctively, I knew what was coming. It was now or never, not that I had much say in the matter.

Lifting my feet into the air with their hands around my calves they sank into me. Now we were on territory I knew and understood, at least in my head, although nothing in my imagination could have prepared me for the extraordinary feeling. This time, penetrating me both ways, the two of them set up a rocking motion where, as one pushed into me, the other pulled back.

When I leant back again, another cock brushed against my lips. I opened my mouth to receive him, sliding my tongue down his length until yet another tried to make its way alongside as well. Since I could only just get my lips around them I alternated between the two, stroking them both hard and bobbing my head back and forth until the rising feeling within took over and I tipped my head back, waiting for the moment. The two men at the other end of me kept up their see-saw motion until I couldn't hold back anymore. I almost passed out when I came again in a swirl of stars that illuminated the blackness like fireworks.

The others withdrew and I was left sitting on the young man beneath me, still impaled on his erection which had lost none of its stiffness. He still hadn't come yet. I was impressed by his self-control.

Linda's voice appeared in my ear again.

'I think it's time for you to see the light,' she said, slipping the blindfold from around my head.

Blinking in the harsh glare, I put my hand up to shield my eyes from the brightness as the room came slowly into focus. There must have been forty or so people in the huge, beautifully appointed reception room. They varied in age from twenty up to somewhere in their late forties or early fifties. Most of them were naked and there were a surprising number of women, some of whom were stroking the men's erections or engaged in various acts of pleasure. A few of the guests wore Venetian-style masks which covered the top half of their faces. It lent them an element of the bizarre, something otherworldly. Over to one side, two of the men were locked together in vigorous intercourse. I'd never seen that before. They seemed completely absorbed, oblivious to everything else.

When I dragged my eyes away from them and carried on scanning the room I could see one man with his face half obscured by an expensive-looking video camera. The bottom half of him was hidden by a woman with short, flame-red hair who knelt in front of him with her back to me, hands resting on his thighs. Her voluptuous figure and smooth, alabaster skin caught my eye but the most striking feature was a tattoo of a pair of angels' wings that swept from between her shoulder blades down to her waist. The only clue that she may have been a little older than I would have expected was the accentuated flare of her hips leading down to her beautifully rounded behind. Her head moved backwards and forwards, pleasuring him while he filmed.

Everyone, apart from the few people who were otherwise occupied, was looking towards me. They were smiling and looking at me with dewy-eyed pride like parents at a graduation.

I smiled back and gave them a nervous wave and a 'Hello', suddenly feeling self-conscious, my confidence having taken two steps back.

'Now then!' Linda announced to the room in general, taking charge again. 'It's almost time for the grand finale!' There was a cheer from the back and a smattering of laughter broke out around the room. Her expression darkened. 'But first, though, you'll have to meet 'The Beast'.'

What now? I'd come this far. There would be no backing down.

'Beast! Beast! Beast!' began the chant from some of the younger guys. A squat, balding man in his forties stepped forward. He was thick-set, dark and very hairy and reminded me of a gorilla; not the sort of man I would normally go for at all.

But then there was his cock. *Fucking hell!*

It wasn't all that long but it was as thick as my wrist with a fat, rounded end and it was heading straight for my mouth. I had a good idea what was expected of me and I was determined not to disappoint.

I opened my mouth wide to stretch my lips around that brute of a cock, and keeping a firm hold on my head he began to fuck my mouth deeply. I could smell the muskiness of his skin and I looked up at the twisted grimace of pleasure on his face while he continued to pump my throat. Thankfully I knew what I was doing and relaxed to allow him full access. I might have expected him to be really rough with me, especially after my earlier treatment, but he wasn't. He was firm but not aggressive, filling my mouth over and over again with surprising tenderness.

A slow handclap got underway and his muscular body began to tense. His strokes became shorter and sharper as his orgasm approached. I opened my mouth wide and with a groan, he ejaculated a thick coil of salty come which piled up on my outstretched tongue, stroking and squeezing himself like a half-empty tube of toothpaste. I pulled in my tongue and swallowed down his copious issue, only to have it replaced seconds later by another cock which soon pulled back to let fly a jet of semen which arced into the air, raining down on one side of my face and into my mouth. I made a big show of licking my lips for the assembled crowd.

From then on, men kept on stepping forward so there were several around me at any one time. I managed to get some of them in my mouth before they came and took others in hand, but most couldn't contain themselves any longer and stroked themselves until they came all over me. The procession continued until it seemed that every man in the room had emptied himself. It was in my hair, my eyes, all over my face, in my mouth and down my chin, running over my breasts and down my body in little rivers towards my crotch. It was everywhere.

Right at the end, I became aware of a groan from behind me. In the middle of everything else, I had completely forgotten about the young man in whose lap I was still perched. I rolled my hips and ground my arse onto him until he unleashed his orgasm deep inside me, slamming his head backwards against the upholstery as he came. His prick began to soften and his breathing slowed, the whole room erupting into tumultuous applause and wolf-whistles. I slipped off his lap and wiping my eyes, turned around to look at him for the first time. A familiar face with a mop of sandy-blonde hair looked back at me, grinning.

I clapped my hand over my mouth in shock.

'Ryan! What the f . . . ?'

'Hello, Rebecca. Fancy meeting you here!'

Linda, laughing, clapped her hands together in delight.

'Happy birthday, honey! I hope you liked your present.'

She took my face in her hands and slowly, lovingly, licked a long trail of semen from my cheek then kissed me passionately on the mouth. I could taste the saltiness when our tongues met. There was another round of cheers and applause as Linda broke off the kiss and took me by the hand.

'Come on, sweetie! Let's go and get you cleaned up, then you can meet everybody properly.'

I turned and waved weakly at Ryan as Linda steered me out of the room.

'Speak to you later!' he mouthed back at me.

CHAPTER ELEVEN

I was still in a daze when Linda led me through two sets of doors to a bathroom, turned on the shower and stripped off, ready to join me under the warm, invigorating spray. I undid my shoes, trying to process what had just happened. I couldn't take it in.

Neither of us spoke while she started soaping me down. I didn't know where to start; there were so many questions. From somewhere there rose a tide of anger which I did my best to quell. I wasn't even sure which of the things fighting for space in my brain I was angry about.

When we did try to speak, we both blurted out our words together.

'Go on. You first,' she said.

I marshalled my thoughts. *Start at the beginning. Take it from there.*

'How on earth did you organise this?

'Well, you know about my parent's leisure activities?'

'Yes, of course!'

'I've always known the people they swing with. They've become like old family friends over the years.'

'Didn't you find it a bit strange getting involved in this

with people you grew up knowing?' I asked.

Linda looked taken aback.

'Says the girl who lost her virginity to her step-dad's best mate!' she retorted.

I rolled my eyes in contrition.

'I guess you got me there.' A dreadful thought hit me like running headlong into a brick wall. 'Oh my God! Your parents aren't here tonight are they?' I asked in horror.

Linda squeezed some shampoo into her hand and began massaging it into my hair.

'No, no. They only do couples, but some swingers like to mix and match a bit more. You get to know people who know other people if you see what I mean. It's a lifestyle community. I had to wait till I was eighteen to go to one of these get-togethers but I couldn't wait to introduce you. I knew you'd have a ball.'

I began to chuckle.

'I think I had a few of them tonight.'

'I was worried I might have pushed things too far,' she said, relaxing visibly.

'No,' I replied, 'although I think I surprised myself.'

'Jesus! You surprised everyone, even me, and there's not much about you I don't know. You really are an animal when you're on a roll.'

Sadie, take a bow!

By now I was full of questions. The floodgates had opened.

'Is Ryan usually a part of all this?'

'Not usually. He came down from university especially. I invited him because the two of you used to fancy the pants off each other. Well, the pants definitely

114

came off tonight. It was about time the two of you got it on, even if it was in company.'

'He fancied me? Why didn't you say?'

Linda began rinsing the shampoo out of my hair.

'You'd not long turned fifteen the last time you spent any real time together. What could he have done?'

'You must have been planning this for ages.' It was her turn to nod. 'What would you have done if I hadn't gone ahead with it?'

She shrugged her shoulders.

'I guess I'd have stepped into the breach and gone for the rematch. After all, I couldn't very well leave them high and dry, all dressed up with no one to do, could I? I'm glad you said yes, though. Aren't you?'

I thought for a moment, still dealing with an array of conflicting thoughts and emotions. I wanted to kiss her and punch her at the same time.

'It was unforgettable; I'll give you that, although I don't think I'm going to be able to move tomorrow. You haven't got a wheelchair handy, have you?'

She grinned.

'No, but I might manage to find some crutches.'

Linda turned off the water, opened the shower door and took a pair of thick, fluffy towels from the vanity unit. She handed one of them to me. I still had so many unanswered questions going round in my head, but I needed time to process them. Besides, by now everybody would be waiting for us to make our grand entrance.

This time I might even have my clothes on. That'll be a novelty.

'Shit! My clothes are still in the other room.'

Linda shook her head.

'No, they're not. Look over there.'

Sure enough, my dress was waiting for me on a hanger behind the bathroom door and my clutch bag and underwear had been placed neatly on the vanity unit.

'When the . . . ?'

'All part of the service, my dear. It's a different world for people with real money. They might as well go through life walking on a carpet of rose petals.'

Once we were dry and dressed again, we redid our hair and makeup side by side in the oversized mirror and returned to the reception room. The chaise longue had been moved back against the wall and the room was dotted with little tables laid out with trays of canapés and other tasty morsels. At the far end was a well-stocked bar I hadn't even noticed before.

I presumed the room was filled with the same people as earlier, except now they were dressed and either sitting at tables relaxing or standing around chatting in small groups as if nothing untoward had happened. I hardly recognised them with their clothes on. None of them wore masks anymore either. It was the strangest thing, having almost no idea who had done what to me. If I was totally honest with myself, though, it was also part of the thrill.

A flute of champagne appeared in my hand, courtesy of an elegant, perfectly-manicured lady in her late forties wearing a lot of large, expensive jewellery. Linda introduced her as Melissa, our hostess for the evening.

'Rebecca! Congratulations!' she said graciously, kissing me on both cheeks.

'Thank you,' I replied as sweetly as I could, not absolutely sure if she was congratulating me on my birthday or my earlier performance.

'Welcome to the club,' she added.

Ah! There's my answer.

An image flashed through my mind. She hadn't looked quite so ladylike on all fours being attended to from both ends while her husband watched, issuing words of encouragement and slowly masturbating.

'Has Linda had the talk with you yet?'

My brow knitted.

'Don't worry dear; it's nothing to fret about. I'm sure she'll fill you in later.' She laid a hand gently on my wrist and winked. 'There are just a few house rules for those in the know. It's for everyone's benefit. In the meantime, please make yourself at home. You really were quite breathtaking tonight. Linda spoke very highly of you. Believe me when I say you are an absolute darling.'

I didn't have a clue how to reply to that.

'Thank you,' I said again, completely out of my depth.

I really must learn how to make small talk.

If there are such things as books on small talk, I felt quite sure they didn't include a chapter on the social politics of swinging amongst the wealthy. I was going to have to learn as I went.

Linda led me around, introducing me to everyone by name as we circulated the room. I don't know why I was surprised to find them all such a nice group of people, but I was.

We approached a lady in a long, backless dress who was facing the other way, chatting to a man in a dinner jacket who I didn't recognise. I knew her from her glorious hourglass shape and the tattoo of a pair of feathered wings down her back, which her outfit framed

117

perfectly.

'Janine, Alan, may I introduce Rebecca?' Linda seemed in her element, completely at ease.

Turning to face us, Janine was no less striking from the front. Beneath her neatly-cut, incendiary hair she had a rounded face and startlingly blue eyes. Her low-cut dress struggled to contain her generous bosom and her blood-red lips were outlined in a much darker colour that contrasted with her flawless, pale skin giving her a hard-edged, almost gothic beauty. I could imagine them as they must have been earlier, wrapped around a stiff cock and sucking with enthusiasm.

She took my hand gently in hers and kissed me on both cheeks. It was clearly the greeting of choice amongst this social group. I would have to remember that.

'It's so nice to meet you. Linda has been full of praise and you didn't disappoint. This is my husband, Alan. He was filming tonight for you as a little souvenir.'

He took my hand and kissed my cheeks just as his wife had done.

'Thank you. I wondered what all that was about,' I said, looking from one to the other.

'He's a professional cameraman so it should come out quite well. We'll edit it together and get a copy to you via Linda. Don't worry; it won't fall into enemy hands. You can be assured of our discretion. In fact, that's very important; there are a lot of people here with too much to lose if their private lives were ever made public. Not everyone appreciates or understands the lifestyle. Linda seemed to think you might enjoy having a record of your evening, though.'

I stared at Linda, open-mouthed.

'What are you looking at me like that for?' she said. 'It's just that you've rather enjoyed your spicy little home movies in the past and I thought it might be a nice touch.'

Not for the first time in my life, I shook my head at her in disbelief but found myself unable to avoid breaking out into a smile.

'You're unbelievable! Definitely a one-off!'

Linda gave me her enigmatic, self-satisfied smile. Janine regarded me carefully, weighing me up.

'So you're an Aries then?' she asked.

'Oh, here we go!' Linda muttered under her breath.

'Yes, I am. Why?'

'That figures. Let me guess: you're fiery; creative; determined and passionate about things that matter to you, in fact, just plain passionate.' She regarded me warmly. 'You're also fearless; adventurous; impatient; and a tad impulsive, I'm betting.'

'That's not a bad summary, to be honest.'

'Hmm!' She fixed me with those piercing blue eyes. 'Something tells me I ought to read your cards.'

'My cards?'

Linda's eyes rolled so far back in her head that only the whites were showing.

'Yes, tarot cards.' Janine explained.

'I don't know. It's not something I've ever had done.'

'There will come a time when you might want me to, and any friend of Linda is a friend of mine. Linda has my number and I'm sure she'll pass it on if you're interested, even though she doesn't set much store by that sort of thing.' She looked across at Linda with affectionate disdain.

'We've agreed to disagree,' Linda chipped in.

Alan looked on genially, amused at the interplay between Linda and Janine but keeping his opinions to himself. Perhaps Janine did enough talking for the both of them.

'Anyway, if you'll excuse us there's someone who is dying to talk to Rebecca. We'll catch up later,' Linda went on.

'It was lovely to meet you, Rebecca. I feel sure we'll meet again,' said Janine.

'Likewise!' I smiled at her and followed Linda across the room. 'What was all that about?' I asked, my voice lowered.

'Oh, she's into all that hocus-pocus stuff. Load of superstitious nonsense!'

'She seemed pretty spot-on with her character assessment.'

'Coincidence? Guesswork? Bunkum if you ask me! Don't get me wrong: I love her to bits and I've known her for years; I just don't hold with all that stuff.'

Finally, we reached Ryan, who was waiting patiently at a table with an empty chair by it. He stood up to greet us as we came over, polite as always.

Linda winked at me.

'I'll leave the two of you to catch up. There's somebody I need to speak to. I'm sure you both have plenty to talk about.'

We sat down to chat like the old friends that we were, although some part of me still reeled in astonishment at what we'd been doing to each other less than an hour ago. It was as if it happened to someone else.

'I can't believe how long it's been,' I said, taking a sip of my champagne.

'I know. Crazy, isn't it? Every time I've been around lately, you've been busy working and whenever you're around, I'm at university.'

I blushed. Suddenly I was my fifteen-year-old self again. Why did he always make me feel like that?

'I don't know where the time's gone,' he continued. 'My degree finals will be in a couple of months. You seem to be doing alright for yourself what with the album in the bag and everything. You must be really happy with that.'

I sighed.

'In a way, it's a dream come true. I'm making music which is what I've always wanted to do. I'm just not making much of a living yet. There's a long way to go still. I never seem to get much time off, though, so I have to make the most of it when I do.'

'Like tonight?'

'Like tonight,' I replied, looking self-consciously down at my glass.

Ryan looked momentarily awkward.

'I take it Linda's explained our connection to all this?' he enquired.

'Yes. I'm still in shock, though. I can't quite believe it. I knew Linda was up to something but I never expected this.'

Ryan nodded sagely.

'She's full of surprises alright.'

'And I still can't believe that we . . .'

'It's just sex, Rebecca. Nobody died tonight. Everyone will leave here with a smile on their face.'

'She says you fancied me ages ago.'

'And I still do. Linda knew how I felt about you a long

time ago, but the timing has always sucked. I would have liked to have had you all to myself but since that doesn't seem to be on the cards then I'll take what I can get of you; it's better than nothing. That's why I leapt at the chance to come along tonight when Linda mentioned it.'

'I never knew.'

It was true. I never thought he'd be interested in me when he could have anyone he wanted. To me, he'd always seemed to be something untouchably remote, despite the obvious warmth between us.

'You don't regret tonight do you?' he asked.

'No! It was fun.' I grinned. 'I'd do it again, except maybe not until I can walk straight again. I had no idea that was you. Are you shocked?'

'Shocked? No, I thoroughly enjoyed it, but I had no idea things would take the direction they did. Like I said, it's just sex. It's nothing to get hung up about.'

'So: friends with benefits then?'

Ryan's eyes were smiling and he appeared to be turning something over in his mind.

'Who's Sadie? Linda said I should ask you about Sadie.'

I was stunned. I'd never even told Steve about her, despite him been on the receiving end of her attentions enough times. How was I going to explain this one?

'What did she say?'

'Nothing, she just said I should ask you. It won't go any further; I promise. Our family is pretty good at keeping secrets in case you hadn't noticed.'

I had.

Here goes nothing I suppose.

'Sadie is a name we gave to my sexual side. She's a

tigress. It kind of sounds stupid, now I say it.'

Ryan shook his head.

'It doesn't sound stupid at all. It's very apt. You were a force of nature tonight. In fact, you *are* a force of nature. There's always been something wild and wonderful about you. Sadie's perfect and I hope you're very proud of her.'

He leant forwards across the table and took my hands in his, looking into my eyes. In that moment I knew that he understood.

'Maybe there's something of that in all of us except not everyone dares to let it out. Perhaps . . .' He seemed to be struggling with his own hidden depths. 'Perhaps in our own way we're all tigers.'

CHAPTER TWELVE

It was well after one in the morning before we finally made our way around wishing everyone good night and climbed into Linda's Mini. I spent ages chatting to Ryan. We hadn't talked like that in such a long time and it felt so good to catch up, despite the bizarre circumstances.

Eventually, though, Linda peeled me away to circulate around the room again and observe the social niceties. I still couldn't believe I'd just had sex with many of them and I was sure when I stopped to think about it that quite a few of the hands and lips I'd felt on my body had been female. Whoever they were, my skin still tingled when I thought about their touch.

'So,' Linda asked, putting the key in its slot, 'have you had a good time?'

'Yes, although I'm still not sure whether to kiss you or kill you. To be honest, I'm still in shock.'

'Okay, so what's bugging you? Talk to me.'

'There are so many things going round in my head I don't know where to start.'

'Then let me start by putting your mind at rest over a few things. None of the people there will ever identify you to anyone else. There's no threat to your career because everybody would have too much to lose by opening their mouths. Even within the wider swinging community people might talk about what they've done, but not who it was with; it's just not done.'

'What about the video?' I asked.

'The same applies. It was done for you. It won't be available to anyone else. If you want, all the rest of the footage will be destroyed and you'll have the only copy to do with as you wish. That said, I wouldn't mind having a copy myself, you know, for quiet moments. After all, I have got a nickname to live up to.'

I giggled.

'There is a Code of Conduct amongst this group,' she continued. 'It's all pretty straightforward really. I've put a copy of it in the glove compartment for you. Basically, all it does is put common-sense and consideration down in black and white. It's not rocket science.'

Linda eased the Mini up the driveway, and the gates slowly opened to let us out into the night.

'Do you think the lifestyle's for you?' she asked.

'Not permanently. Someday I'd like to find the one man I could happily spend the rest of my life with. You know, settle down and have a family; be a mum. I don't know when that's likely to happen, though. I mean, I've only just turned eighteen so I've got a lot of living to do yet and I need to make my way in the world first. It could be fun to dabble in it now and again.'

She pulled up at the end of the driveway and glanced across at me before checking the road and pulling out.

'As Woody Allen once said: 'I feel sex is a beautiful thing between two people. Between five, it's fantastic.' He kind of summed up what this is all about. I mean, don't get me wrong, there's nothing wrong with monogamy as long as it's not monotony.'

I couldn't contain my amusement, spluttering into my hand.

'I'd love to know where you get some of the things you say from. I wish I had your brain.'

Linda shook her head, looking serious for a moment.

'No, you don't,' she said, pursing her lips. 'Anyway, this lot liked you,' she added more brightly, 'so you're in if you want to be. You're not obliged to be there on every occasion. In fact, there's no obligation at all. They tend to keep people informed by text, although we're thinking of setting up a secure website which will make things easier to organise. Melissa and Don are pretty much the hub of this group, the movers and shakers if you will. They do a lot of the hosting for things like this. After all, they've got the space and it isn't as if they can't afford it. There are plenty of other groups out there too. It's a case of networking, getting to know people.'

'Speaking of which, there are a few things that happened tonight I need to talk to you about.'

Linda shifted a little in her seat as she drove, looking awkward.

'Go on.'

'Starting with a few of the individuals there.'

She visibly relaxed.

I'd decided to work my way up to the biggest thing.

'The man you called The Beast, where have I seen him before? There's something familiar about him.'

'Ian? It's not surprising he looks familiar. He's an ex-rugby player. You've probably seen him on the telly. Isn't he a blast?'

'That's one word for it.'

'He's a sweetie, really. Bet you can't guess what his other nickname is.' Now she looked smug.

'No idea.'

'They call him Mister Whippy.'

'You mean, like the soft ice cream that squirts . . . ?'

'That's the one. Get it now?'

An image passed momentarily through my mind and I realised I was pressing my tongue against the roof of my mouth. I got it alright. Linda started to look a bit uncomfortable again.

'I suppose there's another individual and his tastes that you'll be wanting to know about, isn't there?'

'Yes. That was going to be my next question.'

'I know you like to get kind of rough sometimes, but I didn't know he was going to unleash on you quite like that. He was . . . enthusiastic enough when he did it to me. It's definitely his thing. You remember Kevin?'

'Kevin?'

'Yes, you know; the softly spoken guy in his early thirties you were talking to at the bar when you went back for more champagne. That was him.'

My jaw dropped.

'You're kidding. He seemed so sweet and unassuming: so polite.'

'He is. That's the thing; it's always the quiet ones you've got to watch out for. The surprise is what lies beneath the surface when the veneer of civilised life is stripped away. There's an animal lurking inside all of us. You of all people ought to know that.'

I was still reeling with astonishment.

'He didn't strike me as the kind of person who would

say boo to a goose. Does he have a partner?'

'No. Not one that's lasted! He's a lovely man, but do you think you could deal with that kind of treatment on a regular basis?'

It was my turn to shift uneasily in my seat. I wondered if we had any cream for bruises in the medicine cabinet at home.

'No. It was an interesting experience for a one-off, but I think I'd end up crippled if I had to deal with that too often. I can see your point.' I paused, looking directly at her. 'And then there's us.'

Linda hesitated for a moment, then launched in.

'I'm so sorry. I just got carried away. It won't happen again and I . . .' she burbled.

'It's alright.'

'What?'

'It's alright. I don't mind. In fact, I quite enjoyed it. When did you start to feel that way about girls?'

Linda's relief was palpable.

'I suppose deep down I've always been attracted to you. I can't remember exactly when I started seeing things differently, but I didn't want to do anything to jeopardise our friendship; you mean too much to me for that. There's no one else in the whole world I trust as much as you, except maybe Ryan. He's like a rock to me.'

My mind went off on another tangent and my mouth opened to let the words out before my brain was fully in gear.

'If I'd chickened out tonight and you'd stepped in instead of me, you wouldn't have . . . ?'

'Eughh! No!' In her horror, she swerved the car as we rounded a bend in the road, regained her composure, and slowed down a bit. 'He's my brother. What do you think I am? Even I've got my limits.' She shuddered. 'Anyway, I suppose it was coming to things like tonight that opened my eyes and made me even more curious to know what it would be like with another woman.'

'Have you tried it yet?' I asked.

'No more than you have. I guess you realise that some of the attention you were getting tonight was from women, don't you?'

'I'd worked it out. Why do you want me, though?'

'You seriously need to ask? It's because you're just so sensual and vibrant and because I can't think of anybody I'd rather share that experience with. Don't worry; I haven't suddenly changed. I'm not looking for hearts and flowers or commitment. I just think it might be nice. I'll understand if you don't want to. The most important thing is that nothing spoils our friendship. I hope you know how much that means to me.'

I thought for a moment.

'I don't see why it should do any harm and it would be nice to try it. Like you said, I can't think of anybody I'd rather explore that with other than you. Just, not tonight eh?'

Linda's face cracked into a smile.

'If I was in your shoes right now, I don't think I'd be considering anything for the next week, but bloody hell, you don't half give as good as you get! I mean, you can take it, but you can dish it out too. Ryan's face was a picture. I know you didn't know who it was, but the look on his face when you turned the tables on him was priceless. I don't think he expected that at all, not after the Kevin episode. If we'd been charging people to be there, it would have been worth the cost of admission just for that. I've got enough ammunition to tease him with for months.'

It was around two in the morning before we arrived home. I was starting to feel incredibly tired by the time Linda pulled the car up at the front of the house.

'Thank you,' I said. 'Thank you for an amazing evening. You'll be pleased to know I feel less like killing you and more like kissing you now.'

Linda's eyes locked wantonly with mine.

'Then why don't you?'

I undid my seatbelt and leant towards her. Laying her hands either side of my face, she brought her lips to mine and kissed me deeply, gently at first then more eagerly, open-mouthed. Our tongues connected, snaking around each other, each savouring the other until eventually, we separated, regaining our breath.

'Till next time,' I assured her. 'But right now I need sleep and recuperation.'

Linda smiled.

'I don't blame you. I'll hold you to it, though. We're on a promise now.'

'I think you know I'm pretty good at following through on my word' I said, giving her my most smouldering look.

'You'd better stop that right now or neither of us will get any sleep. I'll speak to you later on tomorrow. I think Ryan might be popping over to see you in the morning. He said he was going to fetch something for you but he wouldn't say what.'

'Oh, okay.' *What's he up to?* 'It'll be nice to see him again. It seems to be famine or feast with him.'

'Tell me about it. That's how it's been ever since he went away to uni. Go on. You'd better go in before I change my mind and take you home with me now.'

I reached out to touch her face and she nuzzled her cheek against it.

'Good night, sweetie.'

'Good night.'

I stepped out of the car door and stretched as I stood up.

'Ooh, don't forget your copy of the Code of Conduct.' She reached across to open the glove compartment and handed me two sheets of paper stapled together. 'Peruse it at your leisure.'

'Thank you.'

I closed the car door and waved her off, folded the code of conduct in half and placed it in my clutch bag, then made my way inside. Mum was still up and sitting in the kitchen with a cup of coffee, playing a game on her tablet.

'Did you have a good evening?' she asked.

'It was really interesting: something different. It was nice to just let my hair down for a change. You didn't stay up just for me, did you?'

'I'm still your mum, aren't I? I'm allowed to worry.'

'You needn't have. I'm fine, but it's late and I'm really tired,' I said, yawning. 'I'm going to head straight up to bed.' Drowsily, I put my hand on her shoulder. The evening's activities and the champagne were really starting to catch up with me. 'Good night, Mum.'

'Goodnight, sweetheart.'

I barely remembered climbing the stairs, undressing and clambering into bed. The last thing I was conscious of was my head hitting the pillow.

CHAPTER THIRTEEN

'Wake up, sweetheart. You've got a visitor.'

Surely it wasn't morning already.

'What time is it?' I asked, opening my eyes.

'It's just after ten,' said Mum. 'Ryan's downstairs in the kitchen. I told him you'll be down when you're ready. There's a cup of tea on the bedside table.'

'Thanks, Mum,' I mumbled. 'I'd better make myself presentable first.'

Mum left the room and I sat up, now aware that I was naked under the covers. I never usually slept naked when I was at home. If I was with somebody then it was a different story.

How out of it was I when I came to bed?

I put the flat of my hand in front of my face. Not good; morning breath! At least I'd showered the previous evening; that was something to be grateful for. Despite still aching like I'd boxed ten rounds, I quickly dressed in a tee-shirt and jeans, scrubbed my face and cleaned my teeth then ran a brush through my hair. No fuss, no makeup. I probably looked a sight, but I didn't want to keep Ryan waiting too long. As a last thought, I poured a capful of mouthwash and gargled with it. That was it; I would have to do.

When I entered the room with the remainder of my mug of tea in hand, he was sitting at the breakfast bar sipping a coffee, looking effortless as always.

'Sorry to keep you waiting. I was still asleep. If Mum hadn't woken me up, I think I'd have slept till lunch.' I joined him at the breakfast bar and sat cautiously on one of the stools, relieved to be able to sit down without too much discomfort. 'This is an unexpected pleasure, although I think Linda mentioned something about you coming over last night. It's quite rare to see you over here.'

'True. It's been a while. I got you something as a late birthday present.' He handed me a small, velvet-covered box. 'Go on. Open it up.'

I lifted the lid. Inside was a necklace with a small but heavy gold pendant on it in the shape of a letter S.

'Where did you get this at such short notice on a Sunday morning?'

'Oh, it's amazing what you can do when you call in a few favours. I thought Sadie needed official recognition, seeing as she's such an important part of you.'

'Thank you. It's beautiful, but I still don't understand how you managed it.'

'I made a call last night while we were still at the house. A friend who works for one of the top London jewellers owes me a favour, so they opened up specially and I went in and picked it up this morning.'

'Blimey! What time did you get up?'

He gave me an amused look.

'Early, that's all I'm saying. It's part birthday present and part apology for springing things on you yesterday.'

'I've made my peace with it already. Besides which, there's nothing you need to apologise for. I enjoyed myself.'

He gave me that magic smile, obviously relieved that I was still okay about everything.

'Are you able to stay for lunch?' I asked him.

'If you're sure, that would be really nice. I'll have to go back later on this afternoon, though. There's stuff I've got to finish in preparation for my finals.'

'What happens after that?'

'Providing I pass.'

'Which you should,' I assured him.

He held up his hands in supplication.

'Which I should, then there's a job lined up in the city with Goldberg, Lehmann and Strauss. I had some dealings with them during the degree course and they liked me, so they offered me a permanent position.'

'That's brilliant. So you'll be a high flier in the world of finance then?'

'Hardly! It's a long way to the top, but it's a foot in the door.'

I had a feeling he was just being modest.

'Come on then,' he said. 'Let's try it on you.'

I looked at him for a moment, bemused.

'Oh, the necklace! Of course.'

I lifted it from its box and Ryan stepped around behind me, taking it gently from my fingers and securing the clip while I lifted my hair. I closed my eyes when his fingers brushed the skin at the back of my neck, lost for a moment in the sensation of his touch, so different from the contact of our bodies the previous evening. This time it was sensuous, personal.

I was wandering in my tropical paradise again with the warm sea breezes fanning my hair and the kiss of the sun on my back, my bare feet leaving a trail of impressions in the damp sand at the water's edge. I squished the pale golden grains between my toes, waves lapping at my ankles.

My eyes snapped open. All of a sudden I was back in the kitchen. I looked down at the gold 'S' around my neck and placed my hand over it. Ryan's fingertips parted company with my skin, which yearned for them to return.

'Thank you so much. It's very special and I can't believe you went to all that trouble just to get it.'

'I'm glad you like it,' he said, sitting back down.

'It's on and it's staying on, although I don't know how I'm going to explain the 'S' to people. Sadie is kind of a private thing and I wouldn't use Linda's other nickname for me in public.'

He raised one questioning eyebrow at me.

'I won't ask.'

'Don't!' I retorted, trying to conceal my sudden awkwardness.

He thought for a moment.

'What's your middle name?'

I screwed my face up and looked at him sideways.

'It doesn't begin with an 'S' if that's what you're wondering.'

'What is it then, or aren't you going to tell me?'

'No, I'm not. I hate it. I won't even tell Linda what that is!'

'So just keep the 'S' a mystery. Let people wonder. They wouldn't guess it in a million years anyway.'

I sniggered.

'You're making me sound like Rumpelstiltskin.'

Now he was sniggering too.

'Why? Your middle name's not Rumpelstiltskin, is it?'

'No, but it's almost as bad.'

Mum came into the kitchen on her way to the utility room with a basket of washing and gave us both a peculiar look. Ryan and I looked at each other and burst out laughing. Mum smiled to herself and carried on through the other door, shaking her head.

It had been so long since we'd spent time together like this. Now it was as if we'd never been apart; two kids laughing at the wrestling again. I missed his easy-going humour.

'I tell you what, though,' I added.

'What?'

'Mum calls me sweetheart and Linda sometimes calls me sweetie, so I can always say that's what the S stands for if I'm asked.'

'There you go then. I know where Linda gets that from too. Our Mum calls Linda sweetie from time to time.'

Now there was a suitable explanation in place, I could wear the necklace without feeling self-conscious. I looked at it again and kissed him affectionately on the cheek.

'Thank you,' I said.

He gave me an unusually shy smile. Some part of me wanted to kiss him again, this time on the lips, and if we both could have got past our hesitancy we probably would have, but the words went unsaid and the kiss never happened.

When it was time for him to go I wished he didn't have to leave. I could feel him slipping through my fingers again as he drove away. We had separate lives and much work to do. I put it from my mind. Besides, there was something nagging at me, something I needed to do.

Ah, yes! That's it. There was reading that required my attention.

I made my way upstairs and checked on the rocking chair for my clutch bag. Sure enough, the folded sheets of paper were inside. I settled down on the bed to read them through carefully.

Code of Conduct

These rules exist for the benefit and well-being of everyone. Failure to remain within these rules may result in individuals being refused entry or being asked to leave an event. This is at the discretion of the host(s) and/or organiser(s). Any serious infraction of these rules will result in the individual or individuals concerned being barred from entry to future events.

Conduct With Each Other
- *Every person present deserves respect as an individual. The wishes and preferences of everyone involved must always be taken into account.*
- *Consideration for others is paramount.*
- *No one should feel obliged to do anything they don't want to.*
- *All activities are to be safe, sane and consensual.*
- *No means no.*
- *There will be no intimidation.*
- *There will be no arguments.*
- *Couples or individuals should leave any personal differences or issues at home. If they can't, they should not attend.*

- *If you are engaged in sexual activity in a couple or in a group, then be clear but polite with others about who may or may not join in.*
- *More experienced guests should be patient and understanding of the inexperience of others. Everybody starts somewhere and attending an event for the first time can be overwhelming to newcomers.*

Personal Conduct
- *What happens at events is not to be discussed outside the circle of those involved.*
- *No one present is to be identified to anyone outside the circle of those involved.*
- *The right to privacy of everyone present is to be maintained at all times.*
- *No cameras or mobile phones, or other similar electronic devices are to be used in any areas designated for entertainment or play without the express permission of the event organiser who will first consult with anyone likely to be present in advance of the event.*
- *Mobile phones etc. are to be left outside of entertainment and play areas including those for general use (see below for definition). They may be used outside of these areas to make calls if necessary.*
- *There will be no use of illicit or prohibited drugs.*
- *While the consumption of alcohol is allowed and may help people to relax and enjoy themselves, drinking to excess is not.*

Venue
- *The venue for each event is usually the host and/or hostesses home. Please treat it with respect.*
- *There are four classes of area in any venue:*
1. *'General' areas are for the use of all including those used for socialising. Some may be specified for socialising only*

and not for sexual activity, others may be for both.

2. 'Open' areas are those which are made available for the use of guests for particular activities. They may allow access to a limited number of people, however, individuals are free to come and go from these areas to participate or to watch.

3. 'Private' areas may be assigned for the use of specific groups of individuals by agreement with the host(s) to afford greater privacy if desired. These will usually be bedrooms.

4. 'No go' areas are not for the use of guests and will either be locked or marked as 'no entry'.

- Food and drink should only be taken into areas specified (usually general areas) and not into the bedrooms. If wet play or food sex is intended, there may be an area set aside for this. If in doubt, ask.

- Please leave all rooms in the condition in which you would like to find them. There is usually a supply of fresh sheets and/or towels in play areas to help ensure this.

- No smoking is allowed in the play area or areas. There will usually be other places designated for smoking. If in doubt, please consult the host(s).

Dress

- Guests should wear smart casual clothing as a minimum standard.
- Jeans are not permitted.
- Sports/training shoes are not permitted.
- If there are specific dress requirements for an event, this will be made clear at the time of invitation.

Health and Hygiene

- Safe sex is to be practised at all times.
- Anyone with an STI or other communicable illness should not attend until it is deemed medically safe.

- *Condoms must be used with anyone other than a regular partner. They are often provided but this is not to be relied upon. Individuals should make their own arrangements for this, including using hypoallergenic condoms if necessary.*
- *All guests are expected to maintain a high standard of personal hygiene and presentation, including but not limited to: bathing or showering before attending an event, good oral hygiene, good hand and nail care (especially ensuring that nails are not rough or snagged) and not wearing an excess of cologne or perfume (as some people may be allergic to these).*

After reading both sheets again I came to a simple conclusion. What it all boiled down to was anything goes as long as you're not a dick to people and respect your surroundings. That seemed fair enough. One question remained. What was 'wet play'? Surely hot tubs and swimming pools would be classed as 'general' or 'open' areas.

Oh! No! Hang on. Now I understood what they meant, not that that appealed particularly. Then again, never say never, eh?

CHAPTER FOURTEEN

The next few weeks were spent mixing and making final tweaks to the album.

When we met with Pristeen to play them the rush mixes, their reaction was predictable. My song was an obvious single, but they didn't want to release it first in case it limited our audience. Exactly as Doug and Mitchell had foreseen, the lyrics made them nervous, although they were relieved to have a less full-on version to exploit for radio airplay. The irony of it was that if we'd been a rap band, we could have got away with far worse and no one would have batted an eyelid. Their reservations were entirely driven by concerns about marketing strategy, not moral indignation on their part.

When I arrived home from the meeting with Pristeen at half past five, Linda was already in the kitchen, talking to Mum. They turned to face me as I came in and put my bag down on the floor before flopping onto a stool. Linda gave me a look that told me she wanted to talk but couldn't say anything. I had a good idea what it was about.

'Hi, sweetheart!' said Mum. 'Good meeting?'

'Yup! Everything's a go for the release of the first

single, even though they won't release the one we really want them to. We've got a photo shoot on Friday, followed by a mad dash to a gig on Friday night and another one on Saturday. Then we need to start gearing up for all the promotional stuff.'

'Bloody hell!' said Linda. 'Pardon my French, Mrs Taylor,' she said, turning to Mum, 'but that's a pretty full-on schedule.'

'Well, I'm proud of you Rebecca. You deserve to have some success after all the hard work you've put in.' Mum was radiant.

'Deserving success and achieving it are two different things, though,' I said.

Mum decided to change the subject before my good mood dissipated.

'Dinner's going to be a bit late tonight. Jeff and Steve are still working in the studio and Rob's round at a friend's at the moment. Will you stay to dinner too, Linda?'

'Thanks. If it's not too much trouble, that would be great.'

'Of course not,' Mum beamed. 'You're always welcome.'

'We'll go upstairs until dinner if that's alright,' I said.

'That's fine. I'll call you when it's ready.'

By the time we got up to my room I couldn't contain my excitement any longer.

'Well? Have you got it?'

Linda nodded, eyes shining with the same enthusiasm as me. She produced a DVD from her bag and waved it under my nose.

'Have you seen it yet?' I asked.

'No. I was waiting for you. I've been fit to explode all day today. School was insufferable. I can't wait till the A-levels are over.'

'Come on then. I expect we've got time to watch some of it before dinner. No one is going to disturb us at the moment.'

I put the disk into the player and settled down alongside Linda with the remote controls in my hand. The television screen flickered to life.

Well, here goes nothing.

The first surprise was that it had a proper title screen that read: 'Rebecca's Eighteenth Birthday Celebration' in fancy letters. It had music too. The elegant strains of a chamber orchestra accompanied opening shots of the house from the driveway by daylight, then the front door opening into the hallway with its grand staircase and a view looking down from the top of the steps, which tilted up to show the enormous chandelier.

I turned to Linda.

'This isn't what I was expecting.'

'Well, don't forget Alan is a professional cameraman.'

'What does he work in? Porn? I can imagine Janine being an ex-porn star.'

Linda shook her head.

'No. Telly actually! Janine's something to do with television too. I'm sure she'll be quite amused you think she looks like a porn star.'

The scene changed to a shot taken from inside a ground floor window, looking along the driveway towards the gates. Linda's Mini made its twilit way slowly towards the house. Alan must have been ready and waiting with the camera, tucked out of sight behind a curtain to get the shot. We stepped out of the car and walked towards the front door. I looked so nervous. Linda looked stunning in her long silver dress and matching heels, oozing sensuality and confidence.

It cut to a view of a large, oak-panelled door from behind which came three loud knocks. A man in an elaborate, white and gold mask moved into view, turned the key in the lock and stepped back, opening the door to reveal me framed in the doorway; naked and blindfold. Linda steered me through into the room, let go of my hands and stood beside me looking triumphant while the camera lingered on my naked form, inspecting me down to my shoes and back up to my face again. I had to admit I didn't look too bad in high heels and a blindfold, even if I did have the air of a lamb being brought to the slaughter. My body was really quite toned; our sessions in the gym hadn't done either of us any harm.

Two masked women lifted my arms out to my sides and two more stepped towards me with brightly coloured feathers from a peacock's tail in their hands.

So that's what they were!

'In case you were wondering where they came from,' said Linda, leaning in towards me, 'Melissa keeps several peacocks at the house. By the time we arrived, they'd probably gone in to roost for the night or whatever it is that peacocks do to avoid ending up as dinner for foxes.'

I squinted at the screen.

'Is that Melissa there with the ornate silver mask and the feathers in her hand?'

'Yes, I think it is. She does like her bling, doesn't she?'

We watched the feathers gliding over my body. I could see my breathing changing; my mouth falling open and my head tipping back as I submitted to the caress of the iridescent fronds against my skin. A man holding a doubled-over leather belt stepped up behind me from the edge of the shot and struck me hard across the buttocks with it. My whole body quivered with the shock.

'Ooh, that looks worse on camera than I thought it did at the time,' said Linda, screwing up her face. 'I thought you might appreciate the whole juxtaposition of pleasure and pain thing but perhaps it was a tad harsh. You're not mad at me, are you?'

'I'm still here aren't I? It's not as if it's the worst punishment my derriere had to endure that night is it?'

There was another loud slap of leather against my buttocks.

'I guess not.' Linda winced, now looking doubly sheepish. I was quite enjoying twisting the knife, at least a little.

Hands began to appear from everywhere, stroking against my skin, helping themselves to every part of me; men's hands, women's hands, it no longer mattered. The mouths that closed over my nipples belonged to the two women who had been tantalising me all over with the feathers.

I knew it.

We watched as more hands guided me over to the chaise longue and manoeuvred me into position, legs straight, with my pussy exposed to the view of the lens and everyone else for that matter. The camera moved around to linger on me and an agile man in his twenties, who I now recognised from my later introductions, sat between my legs reaching up with his tongue while another probed and teased me from above.

'The bloke underneath me must have had a crick in his neck afterwards,' I joked.

'I think he did,' chuckled Linda. 'Although I don't think it was anything a dose of Ibuprofen wouldn't cure and I'm sure he would have said it was worth it.'

'I can't say I minded it either. He knew what he was doing. They both did.'

Now a queue of men had formed, each waiting in line as the first of them slid smoothly into me.

I was getting so turned on again, despite feeling like I was watching it all happen to someone else. I looked across at Linda who shifted position slightly, moving her thighs against each other and I knew it was having the same effect on her too. We watched the men take their turn with me, one by one. Alan had been careful not to film most people's faces and had pixelated others out so I still had no idea who was who for the most part.

'Oh, there we go!' Linda sighed, still staring intently at the screen while the first of them took me the other way. Her hand strayed down her body and began caressing the valley between her thighs through her jeans.

The camera moved in for a close-up shot accompanied by a torrent of dirty talk from off camera. The strangest thing of all wasn't what we were watching; it was the sound of my voice issuing a string of obscenities from the television. I couldn't even remember saying half of that stuff.

Linda moaned next to me, pressing harder between her thighs.

'You're fucking enjoying this, aren't you?' I poked her arm with my finger.

'Hmm,' she murmured, already carried away on a

sensual tide that threatened to take her out to sea.

Now the queue was becoming shorter and the sex more vigorous. Some of them, emboldened by my obvious enjoyment, were getting quite carried away until a gesture from Linda told them their number was up.

I looked across at her, incredulous.

'You were running the whole show, weren't you? You planned it all down to the last detail.'

'Pretty much, yeah.' Now her breathing was becoming more stilted. I wasn't sure which I wanted to watch more, Linda or the screen. On the television in front of us another man took over, pounding into me hard; my body moving to and fro in time with him.

Leaning across, I lifted Linda's top, sliding it up and over her breasts and unclipping her bra. She didn't try to stop me. I moved around to stroke her breasts and closed my mouth around one nipple, sucking it into my mouth then letting go with a smack of my lips.

'Oh, don't stop.' Linda was breathless now, digging her fingers into the crotch of her jeans. I opened my mouth wider, pressing my lips around the whole areola, swirling with my tongue, caressing and squeezing her other breast with my free hand.

'Fuck!' The word exploded from Linda's mouth as she tensed beneath me then came apart at the seams like a rag doll, flopping back against the pillows with a sigh. More gently now, I rolled my tongue around her nipple while her orgasm subsided then lifted my head, watching her face.

'Oh, my God!' she sighed, still regaining her breath.

'I didn't think you believed in God.'

'I don't, but let's not split hairs, eh?' Her sea-green

eyes looked up at me. For the moment at least, the DVD was forgotten. 'It's funny, isn't it?'

'What's funny?'

'People say that when they come whether they're religious or not.

'I suppose it's a kind of spiritual experience; that moment of just being.'

Linda nodded.

'Hence the point of tantric sex, perhaps. They say that tantric masters can hold themselves at the point of climax for hours or even days. That's got to be exhausting.'

'But fun, or interesting, or deep and meaningful, or whatever you want it to be.' I hesitated to ask the question. 'Do you still want more?' I asked her.

The look on her face told me she was anything but ready to stop.

'Much more! We haven't even taken our clothes off yet.'

I had a thought.

'Why don't you stay the night? Nobody will bat an eyelid. You're always staying over anyway and nobody ever bothers us. The only thing is, we might need to keep the volume down if Rob's in his room.'

'If you're sure.'

'Of course I'm sure. I want this too.'

She thought for a moment, but in all honesty not for very long.

'You're on. This is so happening.'

'Dinner's ready!' called Mum's voice up the stairs.

I paused the DVD, putting the television on standby just for good measure while Linda straightened her top again.

'Let's eat.' I said.

'Don't tempt me!' Linda's expression became lascivious.

'Later! Food first!'

Downstairs, Rob seemed in a buoyant mood, humming to himself while he laid the table, something Jeff noticed as soon as he came in from the studio. Steve didn't join us of course; he'd gone straight home to Valentina and their baby boy. I wondered if he looked anything like Steve and just for a moment, my mind strayed to what our own children might have looked like.

Mum had prepared a lovely meal. The conversation flowed easily while the five of us sat around the big breakfast bar eating our pasta Carbonara and garlic bread. She'd even made Italian meatballs in a tomato and basil sauce so we could have a bit of both. Jeff took down some glasses and opened up a bottle of Chianti.

'So Rob,' said Mum, 'are you going to tell everyone your news?'

He put down his knife and fork and finished his mouthful.

'Well . . .' He paused, possibly for effect, a hint of smugness playing around the corners of his mouth. 'The letter came through this morning. I've been accepted into Fulton United's youth academy. I'm going to be training to become a professional footballer.'

We all chorused our congratulations.

'Well done!' said Jeff, clapping him on the back. 'We always knew you had it in you. It had to be one or the other of the cricket, the tennis or the football eventually.'

Linda appraised him with her eyes.

'Congratulations. You and Rebecca are both on the

cusp of great things.'

'I've still got to earn my place on the first team.' Rob remained modest. 'Nothing's done and dusted, but it's definitely a milestone.' He looked towards me, still addressing Linda. 'Rebecca's day's about to come, though; I can feel it.'

'Shh! Don't jinx it,' I half-teased, reaching for more garlic bread.

At least Linda and I have both been eating it. It would be a bit unfair otherwise.

I blushed as an image of the two of us locked in a passionate kiss flitted across my mind. If the others noticed, at least they would assume it was my modesty over the music.

After ice cream and strawberries, Linda and I helped to clear everything away and fill the dishwasher, but our minds were elsewhere. As soon as we could do so without arousing any suspicion, we dashed back upstairs.

'What do you want to do first?' I asked, closing the door. 'Watch the rest of the DVD, or . . . ?'

'As much as I'm tempted by the 'or', if we don't watch the rest of the film now, we won't get around to it at all, and I so want to see your face for some of it.'

'Well, we shouldn't be disturbed. There's a match on TV, so that'll be Rob out of the way for a couple of hours and we do have the whole night ahead of us. He never comes in here anyway.'

We propped ourselves up against the headboard and I pressed the standby button on the remote. A deliciously obscene image of me leaning forwards against the chaise longue with a naked man behind me, mid-thrust, popped up on the screen.

'Oh yes!' I said. 'That's where we were.'

I hit 'play' and he continued his thrusting motion, rocking my whole body against the furniture. Linda, resplendent in her silver gown, looked on in delight with a familiar glint in her eyes until eventually she waved him away and leant in towards me. As she made her announcements to the assembly of guests, a woman stepped up with a leather belt in her hand. It looked like the same one that had been used on me earlier. I recognised the woman instantly by her dark-lined lips and her red hair.

'Oh, she's tattooed there as well!' I exclaimed in surprise when she turned to face the camera. 'That's gotta hurt; right over the pubic bone!'

'Pierced too, or so she tells me. I haven't got close enough yet to find out for myself yet, though.'

'I tell you what,' I said, 'you talk about me being a natural performer but you sure know how to work a room full of people. You were totally playing to the crowd.'

Linda glanced back at the screen.

'Oh, here we go! I apologise in advance for what Kevin did. I told him you weren't exactly shy and retiring in that department but I never . . .'

Her words faded then halted and she sat transfixed by the unfolding events on the screen. Sure enough, the mild-mannered young man I'd been talking to at the bar stepped up, smearing lube over his engorged manhood and stroking himself while Janine placed the belt between my teeth. Without warning he drove into me, forcing my body forwards and fucking me with savage ferocity.

Linda grabbed a pillow from behind her and covered

her eyes but it couldn't block out the stifled sobs coming from the television.

'I'm so sorry. It was worse than I thought. It didn't look as bad from where I was at the time.'

I sat and watched, unable to tear my eyes away, like watching a car crash happen in slow motion. It was as if it were happening to someone else. On the screen, Linda cradled my head, nuzzling into my hair and whispering something inaudible into my ear.

'Has he finished yet?' she asked, still cowering behind the pillow.

'No. Not yet.'

The bombardment continued.

'Now?'

'No.'

'Holy Fuck! Doesn't that guy ever come?'

'Oh, wait, wait! Yes, you can look now.'

Linda peered round the edge of the pillow in time to see him sandwich his cock between the cheeks of my arse and unleash a stream of come up my back.

'Fucking Nora!' It was my turn to be astonished. 'It felt like quite a lot at the time, but bloody hell!'

Linda and Janine both leant over me while I lay collapsed over the chaise longue.

'Oh!' I said, to yet another moment of on-screen revelation. Linda's hair brushed the area between my shoulders while she held Janine's head and guided her outstretched tongue down my spine towards where Kevin's ejaculate had pooled.

I turned to Linda who, by now, had lowered the pillow away from her face and down into her lap.

'You do enjoy being in charge, don't you?' I said. It

was more of a statement than a question.

'Maybe I do. There's nothing wrong with that.'

A gowned and commanding Linda pointed to the end of the chaise longue. Ryan stepped forward from the assembly of people and lay down on it, nursing his condom-covered erection.

Wow! He's got a fit body.

The thought ran through my head that it must be a result of all his outdoor pursuits, or maybe some of his indoor ones. I didn't remember him being that buff when he went away to university, but then again I never got to see him without his clothes.

Several men lifted me clean off my feet and carried me bodily round to the end of the chaise longue. The camera followed them and zoomed in for another close-up, then tilted up towards my face while they lowered me slowly onto him. Now knowing who was on the other end of the erection that slid into my welcoming body made me even more turned on than I already was.

Still blindfolded and with Ryan's hands cupping my breasts, my high-heeled feet planted firmly on the floor, I could see myself, thigh muscles tensing and relaxing, riding up and down on him, then holding still when another man positioned himself between my open legs, entering me alongside Ryan.

My hand strayed down to undo the top button of my jeans, eased down the zip and slid inside my briefs, my fingertip slipping easily into the hot dampness.

On the screen, I threw my head back in orgasm and fell back into Ryan's arms before another slightly older man took his turn with me.

When I closed my eyes I could still remember how the

two of them felt inside me, together. My fingertip caressed the front wall of my vagina, circling. I opened my eyes again, fixing them on the screen in front of me.

Now he was gone and I was lifting myself up, reaching beneath me to reposition the tip of Ryan's erection. I plunged myself down onto him. Linda had been right; his face was an absolute picture of surprise, so were the faces of most of the people in the room. I was in charge again now, working him hard. Yet another man took up position between my open legs, followed shortly by the other two taking turns in my mouth.

My fingers found their way up to my clitoris, circling then pressing then circling again.

My screen-self slipped the man from her mouth, gasping as she came.

I followed, dissolving into the bed with a deep sigh, freefalling.

I opened my eyes to see Linda propped up on one elbow, staring at me with the DVD remote in her hand.

'Welcome back. You were away with the fairies there. I must admit I do like watching you come. I would have helped out, but by the time I realised how far gone you were, you didn't need any assistance from me. I think we'll call that 'one all' as Rob might say.' She sniggered and began imitating a football commentator's inane chatter. 'Who knows what the final score's going to be? After all, it's a game of two halves. It's never over till it's over.'

We both broke into a chortle.

I looked across at the image on the screen, frozen in time.

'Why did you pause it?'

'Because I don't want you to miss any of what happens next.'

I blew air up my face in an attempt to dislodge the hair that had fallen across my forehead and over my eyes.

'Fuck me! It was a bit of a marathon, wasn't it?'

'Are you ready for the final instalment?' asked Linda.

'Go for it!'

She pressed the 'play' button.

There was a bit of camera wobble at this point and it didn't take me long to realise why. The on-screen Linda slowly removed the blindfold and tossed it aside with a dramatic flourish. I must have been in total darkness for well over an hour because at first, I looked disorientated and confused. My expression turned more to one of shock as I scanned the room and the scene around me sunk in. I looked directly towards the camera, finally breaking out into a wry smile. The camera was beginning to wobble backwards and forwards even more now and the cameraman's ragged breathing could be heard, close behind the onboard microphone. Linda addressed the room again, conducting them like an orchestra, and 'The Beast' stepped towards me.

'I've got to admit I'm proud of you. You didn't flinch with him at all,' Linda said.

'I seem to remember someone once encouraging me to train myself for just such occasions. Besides, he was surprisingly gentle. I was kind of expecting the worst, but it wasn't like that.'

We sat and stared at the screen, waiting for the moment.

'Come on . . . come on . . . oh, oh, there he goes!' cried Linda, leaning forwards in excitement and pointing at the screen.

The camera zoomed in again, trying to keep steady and failing. There was a deep groan from behind the camera closely followed by the climax on screen.

'Mister Whippy strikes again!' Linda rocked with unalloyed delight.

'And Alan got what he came for too, by the sound of things.'

I laughed, as much at Linda as anything else, although the scene did have a strange comedy about it. In my mind, I could picture the smiling, cruelly beautiful Janine licking those wicked lips and patting her husband's waning erection.

Now the camera had come in quite close and from a high angle as the men crowded round, one by one and sometimes several at once reaching their peak and emptying themselves all over me.

'I'd hate to think what Melissa's upholstery cleaning bill must be like,' I quipped.

Linda snorted with laughter.

'I wouldn't worry. She and her husband are minted; it won't make too much of a dent.'

Eventually, the queue subsided and the camera moved back to capture a shot of me sitting in Ryan's lap, dazed and dripping.

'Fuck! You look like you've been caught up in an explosion at a glue factory. Mind you, I'm sure I looked much the same at my welcoming party.'

'Thank you for that delicate assessment of my situation,' I replied.

'Ooh, hark at you! Who's talking like a dictionary now?' She waved her hands around excitedly. 'Right, here we go; the moment to end them all.'

We turned back towards the television.

Ryan's face screwed up tight at the moment he couldn't contain himself any longer and gave in to his orgasm, bucking and heaving beneath me. In the midst of a round of tumultuous applause, there was a look of triumphant achievement on my face which was replaced by a look of utter disbelief when I turned to face him and realisation dawned.

Next to me, Linda's delight almost matched that of her on-screen self.

'Wonderful! I don't think I'm ever going to tire of that moment. DVDs don't wear out, do they?'

'I don't think so. You know, I'm still a bit in shock over it all.'

'What's to worry about? You had the night of your life, plus you and Ryan had a major reboot and you just massively increased your social circle. You've got to admit, you do tend to shut yourself away and that's such a waste.'

Out of the corner of my eye, I could see Linda leading me out of the door, and the picture slowly faded to black then went back to the menu screen.

'It's the curse of the creative; the need to lock ourselves away from the world and dig deep for inspiration. I guess that's the price artists pay for seeking their muse and the antidote to being public property the rest of the time, not that many members of the public know who I am yet. I've been asked for my autograph all of three times so far.'

'And what was that like?'

'Weird! Very weird! The first time, I had to keep checking behind where I was standing to make sure it was me they were actually talking to.'

My gaze met Linda's and we looked at each other nervously.

'So what are we going to do with the rest of our evening?' she asked.

'I think we both know, but there's no rush is there? If Mum and Jeff haven't drunk it all we could have a glass of wine to put us in the right mood. In fact, even if they have, I know we keep plenty of bottles of that one. Jeff buys it by the case.'

She smiled.

'That sounds like a good idea.'

I could see a thought pass through her mind. I knew that expression well by now, but sometimes it was better not to ask.

'I'll go and get us a bottle and a couple of glasses. Back in a jiffy,' I said.

When I returned two minutes later with a newly opened bottle of Chianti and two large glasses, the main light in my bedroom had been switched off and only the bedside light lent a cosy glow to the room.

'Honestly Linda, there's no need to se . . .'

Linda lay snuggled in bed with the covers up to her shoulders and her hands over the top, grinning.

'I just thought I'd warm it up. After all, it is a chilly evening.'

I smiled to myself. Holding the two glasses in one hand, I poured a generous amount into each, placed the bottle on the bedside table and handed one to Linda. She sat up to take it and the covers fell away, revealing her small but perfect breasts.

I sat on the edge of the bed and our glasses rang as we

touched them together, the wine inside them rocking against the sides.

'To us,' I said simply.

'To friends and lovers.'

Linda looked breathtaking with her long, straight hair cascading over her shoulders, eyes shining in the warm glow of the lamp. Her moist lips parted in expectation and she lifted the glass to them, taking a sip. I still couldn't believe we were doing this. We'd shared this bed so many times but only to sleep; it had always been platonic. This time was different; it would be a whole new kind of sleepover. Linda could see my hesitation.

'You can change your mind if you want to. I understand if you don't want to go there.'

I shook my head.

'I want this. I want you. You're the most beautiful girl in the world to me and you always have been.'

'I don't think I can wait any longer, can you?' she asked, looking relieved.

I gently took the wine from her hand and placed both glasses on the bedside table next to the bottle.

'No.'

I leant towards Linda and she drew me into her arms, kissing me tentatively. At first, our lips barely touched, neither of us wanting to overpower the other, but within seconds the kiss had escalated and we pulled in tight, fingers in each other's hair, heads tilted to the side and tongues wrapped around each other. We broke away from the kiss, panting, eyes locked.

Her trembling hands reached for the hem of my top and I raised my arms so she could lift it over my head, freeing my breasts. Linda tossed it aside and leant my head back, raining kisses down my throat and over my collarbone while my hands traversed the smooth skin of her shoulders and arms. Her lips closed around one nipple, tongue flicking, teeth rasping, torturing it with her sweet mouth, only stopping when the tension became too much for either of us to bear.

'Let's get you out of these jeans,' she said breathlessly, her fingers struggling with the button on the waistband. I stood up to make things a little easier.

'Ah, that's better,' Linda said, more confidently this time, sliding the zip down and peeling the denim over the rounded cheeks of my behind; edging it down my thighs. Taking my hand, she pulled me over onto the bed and stood up. I rolled onto my back, giggling while she pulled off my shoes and slid the legs of my jeans over my feet.

'You know,' she said, still wrestling with the second leg, 'I've come to the conclusion that dresses are much easier to get a woman out of. Maybe that's why men resisted women wearing trousers for so long.'

She handed me my wine glass and sipped deeply from her own then put it down again with a look of resolve.

'Rebecca Taylor, I'm so going to absolutely devour you.'

'What with? Some fava beans and a nice Chianti?' I smirked.

She sucked air through her teeth, making a stuttering sound.

'I think I'll skip the fava beans and I've just had some Chianti, so I'll focus my attention on you, but don't worry; unlike Hannibal Lecter, I would prefer you very much alive.'

'I'm relieved to hear it,' I said.

I lifted my behind off the bed and eased the lacy material of my briefs over it, then stretched out my legs so Linda could take them off. She took her time, though, sliding them smoothly over my feet before letting my underwear fall to the floor. For a few seconds, her hands remained poised between my knees, pressed together in a moment of quiet supplication, then slid slowly down the inside of my thighs, pushing outwards and opening my legs wide as she descended. She stopped, her face coming to rest so close to me that I could feel the heat of her breath on the bare skin at the apex of my thighs, her fingers tracing softly upwards, teasing me open. I ached to feel her mouth against me.

'Are you ready for this?' she asked, licking her lips.

I looked down at her flushed and eager face.

'God yes! Aren't you?'

She reminded me of a cat about to enjoy a saucer of milk.

'Just you try and stop me.'

Linda lowered her head and flicked me lightly with the tip of her tongue, dancing against me, then as she gained in confidence her tongue lingered, pressing harder and working its way into the moist grove, making me tingle with electricity. I moaned softly and hooked one leg across her back, stroking the hair that hung over her shoulders with the sole of my foot which only made her redouble her efforts when she realised how much she was affecting me. Again there was a surge of power: stronger this time, arcing through me until it reached the tips of my fingers.

Linda glanced up my body, her eyes meeting mine. She placed her hands on my thighs and pushed my bent knees back, opening me up to her. The tip of her tongue brushed against my perineum then worked slowly upwards, teasing my labia apart again and she sucked them into her mouth before releasing them and circling my clitoris lightly, teasingly.

'Oh yes, Linda. Yes,' I encouraged breathlessly, power crackling at my fingertips which raked the bedcover, seeking purchase. I was a Tesla coil, radiating sparks in every direction.

She held me open with her thumbs, circling harder with her tongue, ramping up the voltage and now the power thrummed through my body, looking for its escape. Linda made a low humming noise that began in the back of her throat and vibrated right through me, her tongue pressing hard, throbbing with the sound.

'Oh yes. Don't stop. I'm . . . I'm . . .'

The circuits blew and I exploded in a shower of sparks then plunged into darkness.

One by one, the lights in my head slowly blinked back on and I opened my eyes.

Linda was looking at me in wonder and smiling, her eyes radiant. The area around her mouth glistened with moisture in the lamplight.

'You taste even better than I thought you would,' she said, licking her lips, 'like liquid sunshine!'

Visions of me encircled by twittering bluebirds and followed by a trail of butterflies and woodland creatures filled my head. I lifted myself up onto my elbows, breaking out into laughter.

'You make me sound like some kind of Disney princess.'

'I was thinking more like an English rose,' she said,

'somehow more Kate Winslet than Ariel the mermaid. I can't say I've ever seen Disney princesses getting it on with each other, but then again, who knows what cartoon characters get up to when the cameras stop rolling and they're back in their trailers? I've heard Sleeping Beauty spent a lot of time on her back off screen too, and as for Snow White, well, we've all heard the stories about how *she* paid the rent. That's Hollywood for you. It's been said that if all the actresses in Hollywood were laid end to end, nobody would be the least bit surprised.'

When I stopped laughing for long enough to pull myself back into the moment, I looked at her incredulously, probably sounding even more surprised than I felt.

'You're telling me you've never done that before!

'No, I haven't. I just tried to copy the things I like done to me. It works then?' she asked, taking another sip of wine.

I flopped back against the bedcovers.

'You could say that.'

Standing up, Linda took my wine from the bedside cabinet and held it out to me. I sat up to accept it but instead of taking it from her I put my hands on her waist and pulled her in close.

'Ooh, careful! You'll spill the . . .'

I began stroking her behind through the thin material that covered her and kissed my way across the flat of her stomach.

'Hmm.' She sighed long and low from somewhere deep down. I didn't so much hear it as feel her skin vibrating against my lips. 'Never mind, it wasn't important.'

I hooked my fingers over the sides of her lace-trimmed knickers and slid them smoothly down her legs, looking up at her.

'I reckon kindness deserves kindness, don't you think?'

Linda placed the glasses back on the bedside table.

'Well, alright then; since you put it like that.'

I glanced down and caught my breath.

'Not what you were expecting?' she asked.

When I thought about it, it hadn't even occurred to me to look when we were in the shower at Melissa's house.

'I thought you'd be all shaved.'

'I was until recently. I thought I'd let it grow back a bit so I could style it. Do you like the topiary?'

A neatly shaped triangle of hair pointed down towards her otherwise shaven pussy.

'Topiary?' I asked.

'Yes. You know, trimming a bush into interesting shapes.'

Sniggering, I ran my fingers through her pubic hair then trapped it between my fingers, pulling sharply. She gasped.

'I guess it gives me more purchase: something to hang on to,' I said, looking up into her surprised face, 'so you can't escape me.'

'What makes you think I'd want to?'

'You don't know what I'm planning to do to you yet.'

Chewing one side of her lower lip, Linda brushed my hair away from my face.

'Right now I don't care. You could do anything you wanted.'

'Don't worry,' I said. 'I think you'll like it.'

I spread my hands across the cheeks of Linda's behind, pulling her towards me and kissing just above the triangle of hair. Her skin smelled like peaches. My fingers strayed between the tops of her thighs, tracing the folds of her labia until they found the opening between and I slipped two of them inside her, massaging with my fingertips. She moaned and her legs began to buckle. I gently withdrew my fingers and sampled the honey pot, revelling in the sweet, hot taste of her, watching her eyes widen.

Maybe it's not something everybody does. Watch and learn, baby!

'Let's lie you down so we can do this properly,' I said. My suggestion met with no resistance. I guided her onto the bed and she laid back against the pillows, looking at me with her arms up in surrender, her long, dark hair framing her face. I'd never seen her look more beautiful.

'I'm all yours,' she said softly.

Starting just below the line of her jaw, I ran my hands slowly down over the contours of her long, supple frame: a whole new world yet to be explored. Linda's inquisitive and expecting eyes didn't leave me as inch by sweet inch I kissed my way across her breasts then carried on downwards.

Go on, do a Steve; make her wait. You know she'll thank you for it eventually.

Smirking at the thought I began again at Linda's feet, working gradually upwards, building her up to a fever pitch of anticipation until I was positioned on my front between her legs with my arms wrapped around her slender thighs. She was almost silent now; hardly breathing. I adjusted my weight slightly.

'There! That's better.' I took one last look up at Linda's expectant face. 'Now, where was I? Oh yes . . . Here!'

I buried my tongue inside her, scooping the moisture up towards her clitoris and stabbing at it with the tip. Linda groaned and spread her hands out flat on the bed, hissing air through her teeth. Rolling slightly to one side, I laid one hand against her inner thigh and with the other, slid my first two fingers inside her, stroking them in and out rhythmically while my tongue went to work, pressing harder. Linda's hands clamped over her breasts, squeezing them tight and pinching roughly at her hardened nipples.

'Oh, Rebecca! Fuck!' She threw her head back, gasping, but I wasn't finished yet; I had yet another trick up my sleeve. Remembering how it felt when Steve did it to me, I couldn't wait to make her feel the same. I moistened my other two fingers with saliva and straightened them so the fingertips were poised at her anus and inched them slowly forward. After a moment, I could feel her opening up to me and I slid them all the way in.

She was whimpering now as my fingers moved in and out, fucking her in tandem. I circled hard with my tongue and closed my lips around her clitoris, rocking my head from side to side. Her whole body began to tense, her back arching as she fought for breath.

'Oh fuck, yes.'

I was already gaining the impression that this was unusually vocal for her, at least when she wasn't being screwed senseless by a pair of oversexed roofers. She must have been dangerously close to being swept away by the wave that was about to break.

Linda went rigid. *Breathe, damn it. Breathe!* I could swear she was turning blue.

'Gaaah!' She exhaled forcefully, releasing all the pent up tension in her muscles and dissolving to my touch, carried away by the riptide. A trickle of wetness escaped around my deeply embedded fingers. I withdrew them and licked it slowly away while she eventually stopped convulsing and came round again.

I slid up her body and we cradled with our arms wrapped around each other, looking wordlessly into each other's eyes. Linda stroked my face and ran her finger across my lips.

'I've wanted you for such a long time,' she confessed. 'Is that wrong of me?'

'How can anything so nice be wrong? We both wanted it. I think it's wonderful that we can find comfort in each other like this.'

She looked at me, tracing the curve of my waist and hips with her fingertips while I scissored my leg between hers, rocking my thigh slowly against her crotch.

'I don't suppose you're ready to give up the opposite sex, though. I know I'm not, but why limit ourselves?' she said.

I rolled over and topped up the wine glasses, then handed one to Linda.

'I think that one's yours, although it hardly seems to matter now. Another toast then: to sharing!'

We clinked our glasses together and took a sip.

'To sharing!' she reiterated.

When I looked into Linda's eyes they were aquamarine pools of boundless mystery. Now we shared something even more than we already had before, something else: a beautiful, tender secret. I took another mouthful of Chianti, savouring it.

The lustful glint in Linda's eyes had returned.

'So!' she said, 'What would you like to do next?'

'Well,' I turned the possibilities over in my mind, 'there are a few things I've heard about.' A couple in particular presented themselves at the forefront of my imagination. I lowered my eyes, shyly stroking the fingers of my left hand over her skin, following the line of her collarbone.

'Yes?' she prompted.

'I've been thinking. Why don't we try . . . ?' I breathed the words into her ear.

'Hmm,' she sighed appreciatively, 'and you call me kinky!'

A self-satisfied smirk spread from both corners of my mouth, dimpling my cheeks.

'I guess I'm just lucky to have learned from some of the best.'

CHAPTER FIFTEEN

We returned to our gigging schedule while Mitchell fought our corner with the people in suits and they argued back and forth over how to market us. Stylists and photographers came and went, as did the first two proposed release dates for the debut single, which at least gave us time to make a modest video to accompany it. It wasn't my choice of single, or Mitchell's, but the record company insisted on testing the water with a low-key release first, before ploughing their resources into marketing on a larger scale.

Pristeen Records finally released our debut single, 'Cross My Heart', in the second week of July. We backed it up with a number of radio interviews, even recording a live session for national radio, and it sold in a steady trickle but we didn't set the world on fire. There was no great fanfare, no adoring crowds. It charted low down for a few weeks then faded again.

Pristeen were no less disappointed than we were. Mitchell pushed for them to release our favourite song, but still they resisted. They chose another track again. It was good, no doubt about it, but it didn't have the same magic as that one, special song. We all knew it. We could sense Mitchell's frustration but we soldiered on regardless. What else could we do? Our second single was released to even less publicity than the first and barely charted at all.

In the meantime, Linda left for university to study for a degree in Psychology after breezing her A-levels. We spoke as often as we could but there was very little opportunity to see each other. I missed her. When we did get to catch up it was as if we'd never been apart; we just picked up exactly where we left off.

I found the time for the odd brief fling with one or two of the musicians that came and went from the studio at The Gables. Having a car certainly came in handy, although it did prove a little bit cramped for some of the uses I put it to. Linda's Mini was somewhat newer than my old, red Fiesta, but I'd insisted on paying for my car with my own money and I still didn't have very much of that. The royalties from the first single had helped, what there were of them, but they weren't exactly life-changing.

No relationship lasted, though. I didn't really expect it to. The only one I thought might have become something more than just a fling turned out to be a big disappointment. He was the drummer with one of the bands that came to record, and there was an air of wildness, something of the bad boy about him that I found exciting. It ended the day I went over to his place and found him in the bathroom with a needle in his arm. I still remember the conflicted look in his eyes when he realised his little secret had been discovered at the same moment the heroin rushed into his bloodstream and they began to glaze over.

I closed the door and walked away.

Linda was typically circumspect about it when I spoke to her on the phone.

'You're better off out of there. There's no point getting dragged down by anyone else's self-destructive tendencies. I don't care how good a fuck he is when he's not off his face. Good bloody riddance!'

As a precaution, I decided to get myself tested. Thankfully everything came back clear. I breathed a sigh of relief and moved on.

Finally, Pristeen relented and agreed to release my song, but their patience wasn't going to last forever. Mitchell didn't want them to lose faith and start concentrating their efforts elsewhere. If they did, we were dead in the water. It was all or nothing; everything hung in the balance. Our song and its video would probably be the last chance we had to make our mark with anything off this album, and Pristeen would be reluctant to put their resources behind another if there was no singles success to boost this one on its release.

Mitchell called me to a meeting in his office. He and the video director were already deep in discussion when Penny showed me in.

'Oh, good afternoon, Rebecca.' Mitchell extended a hand. 'This is Damien Price. He'll be directing the shoot next week.'

He was quite young for a director, probably in his late twenties, but he had youthful enthusiasm on his side and exuded a sense of purpose despite his air of art school chic. We shook hands and exchanged the usual pleasantries.

Mitchell continued, still on a roll.

'I was just explaining how long it's taken us to persuade Pristeen to go with this particular song as a single and how they've finally agreed to go all out to promote it on the proviso that we use the version with the less edgy lyrics for single release.'

I must have pulled a face about it because Damien chipped right in.

'If it's any consolation, I've listened to both versions of the song and I love the uncensored one, although I can understand their caution. What I'd like to do is a sexier version of the video to go with the uncut song.'

'Oh? What have you got in mind?' My head teemed with possibilities.

'Well, don't feel like you have to say yes to this but I'd like to cut in additional material that includes more of a sex scene instead of just suggesting it; all simulated of course.'

'Of course,' I said, although thoughts of the footage from my birthday celebrations did bring to mind that maybe simulation wouldn't be necessary. 'How far do you want to push it?'

'It's more a question of how far you're prepared to go for your art,' he said, looking straight at me.

How about all the way?

'As far as we dare,' I said. 'I'm all in on this one.'

He nodded, pressing his lips together.

'Okay, we'll go for it then. It will involve you and a couple of the dancers. I just wanted to make sure you were okay with that. It's going to be a fairly raunchy video anyway but with the extra footage cut in it should certainly get people talking.'

'That's what we're looking for, though,' said Mitchell,

looking at Damien. 'At this stage, the record company don't need to know about the other version of the video. We'll negotiate making it available on the internet alongside the single release. Playing it safe hasn't had the impact we'd hoped for so far, so they should be more open to suggestion. After all, what they really want is a return on their investment and what we need is a big breakthrough for Rebecca.'

'Well, if anything's going to do it, this will, but you know how fickle sales are. There's no knowing what will happen. The set and props people have gone all out, in fact, the sets are nearly ready. Oh, that reminds me,' he turned to face me, 'wardrobe wants to do a fitting session for the whole band the day after tomorrow. It's at Rivermead, the warehouse studio where we'll be filming, so I'm intending to be there to run through more of the details on the shoot afterwards. I can show you around the sets as well. Sound good?'

'Yup!' I nodded while Damien continued.

'We're rehearsing the choreography on Monday, which shouldn't take too long for you guys. Shooting starts on Tuesday and should go on for three to four days because of the number of sets involved. They'll be long days, so Mitchell's booked you all into a hotel in London, not too far from where we're filming.'

'I can't wait.' I wasn't lying. Inside I was practically jumping up and down with excitement despite my relatively calm exterior.

'Great! Let's go for it. I'm looking forward to pulling out all the stops on this one.'

CHAPTER SIXTEEN

It was well before six in the morning when the limousine arrived to pick me up. I had already showered and dressed and was just finishing my tea and toast when it pulled up outside the house. Mitchell told me not to worry about my hair or makeup since all that would be taken care of at the studio, but he wanted everybody on set at seven.

'Good morning, Miss Taylor,' said the smartly dressed chauffeur, opening the door.

I thanked him as I leant forwards and stepped into the cavernous, cream leather upholstered interior. Such five-star treatment was a bit of a novelty, but the rest of the band were being picked up in the limo too and Mitchell had insisted that it was worth it to ensure we all got to the shoot on time.

'Besides,' he said when I spoke to him on the phone, 'it's the day we've all been waiting for. If you go in there feeling like a million dollars then it'll come across in your performance and that's what we all want, isn't it?'

The chauffeur put my small suitcase in the boot before easing himself into the driver's seat and pulling smoothly away.

If it's a limo should it be a boot or a trunk? I wasn't sure.

Since the driver hadn't volunteered his name, I asked him.

'It's Derek, Miss Taylor. I'll be with you for the next few days.'

He took me to the rented house down the road to pick up the rest of the band, who were in good spirits when they clambered in. Rafael looked around himself, open-mouthed. It was a bit of a novelty for all of us.

'Wow! It's got a fully stocked bar and everything.'

'Shame we can't do much with it unless they've got orange juice in the fridge,' chipped in Helena, sensible as always.

'Well it still beats going everywhere in the van with a stack of amps and Mick's farts for company,' Daniel added.

Alex just smiled and looked at me.

'You ready?'

'Ready as I'll ever be. I guess this is another of those crunch moments when we've just got to take the bull by the horns and go for it. We've done alright whenever the chips have been down so far.'

The journey into the East End of London seemed to take no time at all and we arrived raring to go, but before we could film anything we would have to spend the next hour and a half being prepared in hair, makeup and wardrobe.

Inside the inauspicious-looking converted warehouse, several sets were ready and waiting: an area with a big, blank backdrop where we could be filmed performing; the front of a house complete with street lamps outside; a bedroom; and a more abstract set, with clouds suspended on wires and a variety of sexual implements. A lot of them had been my idea, although they had required a little research. Linda, as always, had been a fount of information on the obscure and the bizarre. Most of it was stuff I'd never used but I'd bet money she would.

By eight thirty we were fitted out and ready to film the band's performance. The director busily checked his notes while everything around him was a hive of activity. Several cameras were being wheeled into position on tracks, the sound people were checking the playback that we had to mime to, and still others stood behind monitor screens with headsets and clipboards. The last video we made was nothing like this big. It had been very low-key and low-budget.

Most of our equipment stood to one side of the set, ready to be brought into position later. It had all been brought down previously when we rehearsed and went through the choreography, which to be fair mostly involved the dancers around us although I was going to have to bust some moves of one kind or another at various points. I was no dancer but Damien and the choreographer had been very encouraging.

'If you can capture the graceful seductiveness we're after, then you've got it. Be slinky,' she said at the rehearsal. I could manage that. After all, I had assistance; Sadie would be sure to lend a helping paw.

Damien looked up from his notes as we walked onto the set.

'Good morning!'

We greeted him cheerfully.

'Good to see you all bright and early and ready to go. Just like we discussed the other day, I want to start with just Rebecca and Alex and then as the other instruments come in, we'll bring the rest of you on. When it cuts back to the band from other shots, you'll just magically appear one by one. We'll film each segment a number of times from different angles and then cut it together from the best bits. It's all in the editing. A lot of the visual effects and other touches can be added in post-production.'

We all nodded our agreement.

'So if the rest of you want to grab a coffee, I'll send someone to give you a call when we're ready. As you probably realise by now, there's a lot of waiting around followed by periods of intense activity, so you'll just have to be patient I'm afraid. It's going to be a long day, so settle in.'

While Rafael, Daniel and Helena traipsed off in the direction of the refreshments stand which was away from the studio floor and down the corridor, Alex and I were guided towards the two stools which had been positioned in the large area in front of the backdrop, surrounded by banks of bright lights. It took a moment to adjust to the glare. A shapely young female assistant with a headset on handed Alex his acoustic guitar, giving him a shy smile before scurrying off again.

She fancies you.

Perhaps they were both too unassuming to do anything about it. Besides, in his nervousness, Alex seemed not to have noticed. By now I knew that focussed look well.

I sat demurely on the stool, adjusting my fifties-style tea dress so as not to show too much leg . . . yet. My hair was piled up and sculpted on my head without a strand out of place and my lips and nails had been painted a fire-engine red, all in keeping with the era. In front of the stool was a stand with an old-fashioned, chrome-caged microphone perched on top.

'Okay! Remember,' said Damien, 'keep your eyes down at first. Alex, you're concentrating on the guitar. Rebecca, you're looking down and to your left, away from Alex. We're going for shyly seductive and alluring, to begin with. We don't want to peak too early do we?'

He caught my eye and raised his eyebrows, smirking, then retreated to a position behind the cameras.

'We're going to do the intro and the first two verses, then we'll go back and bring on the drums and redo from the start of the vocals. Don't worry about staying silent. Play and sing as tight to the playback as you can, but don't worry about how it sounds. Rebecca, save your voice; it's going to be a long day. How it looks is more important because the actual sound on the video will be the record anyway. You both okay?'

We nodded and took our positions.

'Head a little bit more to the left, Rebecca. That's it. Remember, we're going for moody and atmospheric to start with and don't worry; we will be doing lots of takes so just go with it.'

He checked around him, making sure everyone was ready. Someone stepped in front of the main camera with a clapper board. Two words, the name of the song, were chalked on its surface.

'Come Inside' it invited.

'And . . . action! Roll playback.'

I held my position while Alex played along to the opening chords, lifting my head slowly to look straight into the camera in front of me before opening my mouth to sing in time with my own voice. The opening verse was crooning, soft and seductive, a prelude to what lay ahead.

It's been a wonderful evening
And I don't want it to end
If you come with me
Then you will see
How we could be more than just friends

I want the touch of your lips on my body
I need the feel of your hands in my hair
We can take all night
Till the morning light
I can't let you go home, it just wouldn't be right

Something long-forgotten had resurfaced in my head about how Marilyn Monroe made love to the camera. Sadie rubbed herself against my legs with her tail in the air, a low, contented purr resonating in her throat.

Damien signalled to keep everything rolling and I dissolved into the lens in front of me. The song lifted, shifting up into the next gear as it entered the first chorus and I opened up a little more to the power in my voice, singing through the higher notes. My words had become a sultry invitation, husky like a lounge singer yet gliding from note to note on a bed of silk.

Do what you want to with my body
I need that rush to find my release
Give me your touch
It could never be too much for me

'Okay, cut!'

The music stopped.

Damien was all business, yet I could see he was pleased.

'Guys, that was amazing. We need more of the same. Let's do another take. Camera one I want you to really zoom in on Rebecca's eyes for the second half of the verse.' He turned towards me, lowering his voice. 'I don't know where that look came from Rebecca, but I think the polar ice caps just melted. The camera loves you.' He spoke up again, addressing everybody. 'Okay, let's reset from the top and go again.'

A handful of takes later, we were ready to move on and bring the drum kit into shot.

'Okay, take a five-minute break.' He turned to the assistant who had handed Alex his guitar. 'Sarah, can you fetch the drummer, Daniel? He's up next.'

Clutching her clipboard, she disappeared through the double doors and down the corridor in search of Daniel and reappeared with him in tow, coffee cup in one hand and sticks in the other. Having clearly got the message that things were going well so far, he was in an ebullient mood.

'No jokes about rim shots, please. I think I must have heard them all about a dozen times. In fact, I think I probably made most of them up.'

Despite looking relaxed, Damien remained businesslike.

'Okay Daniel, we're going from the top again with you in place. Don't be put off by the cameras. We'll come in close on your hands for some of it; when you're doing the, um . . . rim shots through the verse.'

Forty minutes and several takes later it was time for the bass and keyboards to join in. Once they had taken their turns, bodies appeared from nowhere, moving the banks of Marshalls into place behind where we would be playing. We would be on our feet from now on.

'Twenty-minute break, people! I want everybody back in their places by eleven thirty. Let's get as far as we can with the whole band stuff by the time we stop for lunch.'

We joined the queue for the refreshments along with everybody else and I smiled to myself to see Alex relaxed and chatting with the assistant who had handed him the guitar earlier. Maybe he had noticed her after all. She was all eyes, hanging on every word while they talked about the shoot and our upcoming support slots on the British leg of another artist's tour.

It just happened to be one of Mitchell's more successful acts we were supporting. There were definite advantages to being part of a stable working under one management company; it helped open doors. At least the gigs were going to pay decent money too, even if we were going to be on the road for a while. Both Rafael and Daniel had become increasingly restless about the poor state of their finances. Daniel had threatened more than once to pack it all in and get a regular job. Alex and I persuaded him to stick with it.

We were still halfway through our polystyrene cups of coffee when the call came through for everybody to be back on set in five minutes.

Here we go! No rest for the wicked.

I drained my cup and threw it in the bin before heading back onto set. We took our places and the makeup artist scurried around, checking the others and touching up my lipstick before filming could recommence. Sarah the assistant handed me my gleaming Les Paul. Someone had been busy polishing.

Damien seemed ready to attack things again.

'Okay, places everybody. We're just going to go straight through in one take to start with. What we're looking for now is energy. Most of this footage is for later on in the song, so step things up between the second and third verses and really lay into the choruses and the solo, but without being overly showy for the moment. Slightly exaggerated movements will work best on camera. Got it?'

We all nodded.

'Rebecca?'

'Yup!'

'You can smoulder all you like; the more the merrier.'

'I think I can manage that.'

In fact, the more I thought about the other verses, the more turned on I got. Smouldering wasn't going to be a problem, putting out the ensuing fire might.

'Everybody good?' asked Damien, looking around him. 'Good! Okay, and . . . action! Cue playback.'

The song started over and we eased ourselves into it, running through the now familiar beginning section before burning into the second verse. I caressed the old-fashioned microphone on the stand in front of me, wrapping my scarlet nails around it, and leant in towards the camera.

Come inside if you want to
Come inside if you dare

You can do what you do
Till we're black and blue
I don't think I'd ever get enough of you

You can come inside if you want to
Come inside if you dare
You can pull my hair
Touch me everywhere
We can do it how you like it baby, don't fight fair

With fluid ease, Alex launched into his solo before the chorus repeated. Sadie paced back and forth, eager for the final verse, waiting for the reaction.

Now that I've got your attention
There's something you ought to know
I've got a friend here with me
Who is wild and free
Come on baby; tell me, honey, what'll it be?

You can come inside if you want to
Come inside if you dare
You can do what you do
Till we're all black and blue
I don't think we'll ever get enough of you

Do what you want to with my body
I need that rush to find my release, yeah
Give me your touch
It could never be too much . . . for me

I poured myself into the last blistering, sustained note

and the music played out to its final percussive chord.

Sadie sat down, licking her lips.

When I looked around the room it was a silent sea of open mouths. The young assistant's pencil rolled off her clipboard and fell to the floor with a clatter.

Damien grinned. I had a feeling it was the first time he'd let most of the crew hear the whole song because it was obvious he'd been expecting this reaction. He was the first to break the silence.

'Well everybody, you might be surprised to hear that was the clean version. Oh, and 'cut' by the way,' he announced. He was enjoying the song's impact as much as I was.

As one, the room began to breathe again and a lone pair of hands began to clap, followed by another and then another. Soon the studio floor had erupted into applause. Damien held up his hands and quiet eventually returned.

'Now I hope everyone here understands what a unique piece of music we're working with. This is not your average pop song. Over the next few days, we're making a video which I'd like to think does it justice. So far we've been doing the conventional stuff, but some of this video will be a little less so. This is a song which some might think is a bit controversial, but I want you all to be proud of what we're doing here. I already am.'

He looked at me and winked, then picked the pencil up off the floor and handed it to Sarah.

'Right everybody, let's get back to work and go for another take. After that, we can alter the track for an arc shot. Cameras two and three, can you move a little further round for more of a side-on view . . . ? Okay, that's far enough. Places please and reset.'

A few takes later and we were ready for lunch. I was famished, but we only had a short break for food before I needed to be back in wardrobe for a change of mood and outfit. Most of the dancers had already arrived during the second half of the morning and were now dressed for the occasion, if dressed was the right word for it. Acres of skin were broken up by the odd scrap of black leather. Now they were milling around in the hospitality area, chatting and warming up.

On my way to be changed into my next outfit and have my hair restyled, I bumped into one of the dancers on his way out of wardrobe. I barely came up past his shoulders, but it afforded me a perfect view of his muscles moving beneath his burnished, chestnut skin when he held the door open for me. Thankfully, wardrobe hadn't covered very much of him; there was plenty of his athletic frame on show.

'Thank you,' I said as he let me through.

'My pleasure!' He flashed me a pearly smile, all the more dazzling against the darkness of his skin. I turned to take in the rear view as he disappeared out into the corridor.

Damn!

'Are you ready, Rebecca?'

'Hmm? Oh, yes!' I turned back to face the wardrobe lady, suddenly remembering what I was supposed to be there for. She glanced towards the door then back to me with the tight-lipped beginnings of a smile and took my next costume down off the rail. This time it was a black leather one piece suit that had been made especially to fit me. It took a bit of getting into but it fitted like a glove: hugging my curves, accentuating my waist, and making the most of my cleavage.

Once my makeup had been updated and my hair restyled into something a bit more rock-chick, I looked myself up and down in the big mirror. It didn't look bad, even if I do say so myself.

When I strode onto the set wearing the black stilettos that completed the ensemble, heads turned. Those that hadn't noticed straight away soon had their elbows nudged.

Rafael was standing by the door as I came in.

'Wow, Rebecca! Te ves increíble.'

I wasn't totally sure what it meant, but it sounded good.

Damien waved me into position behind a stand which now had a more modern, wireless microphone on it and the rest of the band took their places behind their instruments.

'Alright, listen up everybody. There are three phases to this afternoon's shooting. Firstly, we're going to film all the way through with just the band until we're comfortable with that, then we're going to film again with the dancers as well. Finally, Rebecca's going to join in with the dancers for the section during the guitar solo.' He turned towards us. 'Right guys, I really want you to rock out this time, big showy movements. Rebecca, you don't need me to tell you what to do, just go for it. Let's take it all the way through from the top.'

By the third take, Damien was happy to bring on the dancers. They writhed and gyrated around us while we played, sometimes forming into pairs or threes before spinning off in opposite directions again. The choreographer had gone as all out as everyone else. Their movements perfectly captured the song's unbridled sexuality.

I was no dancer, and certainly not while wearing stiletto heels, but I did my best to keep up with them during the middle section. Mostly it involved me with my arms up over my head, looking as seductive as I could without falling over and the dancers writhing up against me in time to the music. Damien was happy that it looked good on camera anyway.

By the time we had been on set for almost twelve hours we were exhausted, but Damien seemed pleased with the day's work.

'Okay, that's a wrap for today, people. The dancers who are doing the fantasy sequence, I need you back on set by eight am tomorrow. Rebecca and band, I believe your bags have already been taken to your hotel. Once you've paid wardrobe a visit, your car should be waiting outside, ready to take you there. Get a good night's sleep; we've got another busy day ahead.'

Sure enough, by the time we emerged from the studio the limo was ready and waiting. When Derek our driver opened up the door, it was lit up inside like a Christmas tree by blue and lilac concealed lights. By now it was dark outside and we were all hungry and tired, but exhilarated. As we climbed in, we noticed the chilled bottle of champagne already on ice in a silver bucket.

'Alright, now we're talking!' enthused Daniel, reaching for the champagne glasses.

Derek slid into the driver's seat and turned to speak over his shoulder.

'Compliments of Mr Sacker. He thought you would appreciate it after today.'

'Too right!' Rafael chimed in.

'Then tell him thank you, if you speak to him before we do,' I said.

'I'd settle in and enjoy the journey if I were you. Your hotel's a little way across town. Mr Sacker has arranged a slight upgrade to your accommodation.'

What's Mitchell up to?

'Where are we staying?'

'Oh, you'll see! He asked me to keep it a surprise. Just sit back and enjoy the journey.' Derek seemed to be quietly enjoying the mystery of it all.

Alex opened the bottle of champagne with a satisfying 'pop' and poured it into five glasses before we pulled smoothly away. It tasted like heaven after drinking instant coffee out of polystyrene cups all day.

We chattered excitedly and sipped at the crisp, straw-coloured effervescence, heading west through Central London and the City of Westminster. Moving slowly through the evening traffic we could see people peering at the tinted windows, trying and failing to see who was inside. Helena laughed at Daniel and Rafael pulling faces at them through the glass.

We turned down the Edgware Road then onto Park Lane. Hyde Park was away to our right and lit up in blue, the facade of a tall building stretched skywards to our left. Almost imperceptibly, we pulled to a halt.

'Here we are. I think you'll find one of Mr Sacker's people should be here to meet you in reception. Have a good evening and I'll see you back here at seven thirty.'

Thanking him, we stowed our empty glasses in the ice bucket, stepped out onto the pavement in the chill evening air and looked up at the modern edifice in front of us.

'Wow!' said Alex, 'I never thought we'd be staying at the Walton-Astor. This is definitely a step up from the usual B and Bs.'

Waiting for us in reception was a familiar face. Penny's ever-changing hair had now been dyed light green.

'Hi, guys! How did today's filming go?'

She was met with an enthusiastic babble of voices.

'We'll just check you in and get your keys. I've taken the liberty of reserving a table for you in Explorers. The food has an eastern twist and I can recommend the cocktails. It's all on Mitchell's tab: his treat. Just don't indulge too much on the booze; it sounds like tomorrow's going to be another busy one.'

'How come you're working so late?' I asked. 'I've never seen you outside the office.'

'I don't live very far from here and we . . . Mitchell thought it would be a good idea to make sure everything went smoothly.'

Is there something you ought to tell me?

She blushed as if she could read my thoughts and hastily moved on.

'Let's get your room keys. Your bags have already been taken up, and the restaurant's booked for eight thirty so you'd better go straight in there. You're all probably starving.'

There was a murmur of general agreement.

She watched us collect our key cards from reception and waved us off to our exotic feast.

'Good luck for tomorrow!' she called after us.

CHAPTER SEVENTEEN

The phone rang. It sounded clinical and unfamiliar.

I picked it up to the sound of an automated voice informing me it was my morning alarm call. Fumbling around blindly, I eventually manoeuvred the handset back to its resting place then prised my eyes open and looked at the clock.

Six am.

My head felt surprisingly clear. It was certainly nothing a good cup of tea wouldn't cure. A couple of the guys might not fare quite so well but on the whole, we'd been fairly restrained. We were all too tired to drink much and had turned in quite early.

Onwards and upwards.

I showered, dried and dressed before meeting the band for a quick breakfast and heading out through hotel reception to meet the car. Derek pulled up in the limo exactly on time. How he managed that in London traffic I would never know.

The crew were nearly ready to start when we arrived. Since Central London was even more congested than usual, the trip across town had been slow.

'Morning, guys!' said Damien. 'I've been reviewing

yesterday's footage, so what I want to do first is get some close-up shots of the band including the guitar solo while Rebecca gets kitted out and then we can move on. By then the dancers should be ready. The rest of you won't be needed for that so you can either stick around and watch, or be driven back to your hotel when you're ready. I've spoken to Mitchell to give him an update so he knows we're making good progress. You're all still booked in for tonight but only Rebecca will be needed for tomorrow's filming, so you'll be free to enjoy yourselves.'

Daniel and Rafael looked quietly pleased. They could get on with the serious business of propping up the bar, playing at being celebrity rock stars, and skirt-watching. Helena would probably want to make the most of the spa. I had a feeling Alex might stick around for a while; he had an ulterior motive.

By ten thirty all the close-ups were done and the crew moved the equipment across to the fantasy set. Several large model clouds hung against a sky blue backdrop and the rest of the set was laid out with an assortment of wild and wonderful things: a swing with a suspended harness which could rotate through three hundred and sixty degrees, sex chairs (for those awkward positions - according to Linda), suspension cuffs for wrists and ankles, spreader bars, restraints, gags, whips, floggers and a selection of toys that ranged from the sublime to the ridiculous to 'you must be kidding'.

Out of everything, it was the swing that most caught my eye. It looked fun.

Maybe someday.

I left wardrobe feeling self-conscious. I'd never dressed in the sort of get-up I was now wearing, but it was strangely exhilarating. I could feel the eyes of everyone I passed in the corridor boring into me. Maybe it was exciting precisely because they were. If the leather suit had been eye-catching, this was sure to turn heads.

What the hell. Here goes.

Somewhere inside me, a switch flipped. Rebecca Taylor the performer had come out to play again.

The band were enjoying the comings and goings on set from the back of the studio, standing around with cups of coffee in their hands when I entered the room wearing the same black stilettos as the day before. This time, though, they were partnered with a black lace-up corset that just about contained my bust, along with black briefs, stockings and suspenders.

'¡Mierda!' Rafael nearly dropped his cup.

Helena clapped her hands together in delight and made a whooping sound.

'Whoa, Rebecca! Go, sister!'

Daniel was typically laddish, whistling through his fingers while even Alex went wide-eyed.

Damien, however, was typically focussed.

'Looking good, Rebecca! Okay, here's what I want to do. We're going to film you singing the song from various places, first just you, then with the dancers doing their thing. We'll start with you lying draped across the central cloud, then do you on the swing and see where we go from there.

It was tempting to say I wouldn't mind being done on the swing but I thought better of it; after all, there was work to do, but I was pleased to see that one of the dancers was the same rather delicious young man I had seen leaving wardrobe the day before. At least he was still around. In my mind's eye, I could picture myself suspended in the harness, swinging to and fro while he attended to me. Maybe I could persuade Damien to include that in the raunchier version of the video. It was worth a try.

The male dancers were dressed in silver thongs and the women in matching silver bikinis. They all had white, feathered wings attached to their backs and their skin was dusted with silvery powder giving them an ethereal glow. They were exactly as I'd imagined when I sent my ideas to Damien. My 'angels of ecstasy' would be cavorting and frolicking around me while I draped myself around the set: the mistress of all I surveyed.

By lunch break, we had several takes under our belt (or corset in my case) but Damien still wanted to do more in the afternoon. Alex and Sarah were cosseted in their own little world together, chatting animatedly over their pasta.

I brought my tray over to an empty table and sat down, hoping I didn't drop any lamb hotpot down my front; that would rather spoil the sex siren effect. I was just tucking in when a dark voice spoke.

'Mind if I join you?'

Looking up into the face of my own personal angel of ecstasy I gestured for him to sit. Thankfully I made sure to finish my mouthful before speaking.

'Go ahead! Nice moves by the way; it's looking great.'

'Thank you. You don't look so bad yourself. I'm Lee, by the way.'

There it was; that pearly smile. I held out my hand in greeting.

'Rebecca.'

'It's one hell of a song you're making the video for. I don't think I've worked on anything as daring. Who wrote it?'

'I did!'

He put his knife and fork back on his tray and looked at me with a mixture of respect and amazement. His vegetarian cannelloni could wait.

'So you're not just a pretty face with an amazing voice, you write great songs too. I'm in awe. Is there anything you can't do?'

'Yes. I'm no good at sports and I can't dance like you can.'

'I wouldn't worry. I think you're holding your own out there.'

I wouldn't mind holding yours.

'You're very kind, but I feel like a total amateur at times. It's all very new.'

'Nobody would know. Besides, your outfit is quite a distraction.'

So you're straight then. That was a start.

Lunch seemed over all too quickly. We were just as much in our own world as Alex and Sarah. The five-minute call came through for everyone to be back on set.

'Here we go again,' he said, picking up his tray.

'I'll see you later.' *I can hope.*

He flashed a smile back in my direction before disappearing through the double doors, taking care not to trap his wings as they closed.

The rest of the band stayed until after lunch but the hotel and its temptations were calling and they bailed out, leaving me to it. They waved goodbye while I settled onto the sex chair for the next take. At first, I hadn't seen the point of that particular piece of furniture. Now I was actually sitting in it the possibilities were becoming apparent, although Melissa's chaise longue had fulfilled many of the same functions in its own way. It seems the French had it all worked out centuries ago.

Alex, as I had suspected, stayed behind when the others left.

Two hours later, Damien announced that we had finished with the dancers and they were free to leave. He wanted to go straight into doing some more close-ups with just me. I had to watch as my angel followed the others out of the door, although he did turn around and smile in my direction before he left. My opportunity had evaporated.

It was six before Alex and I left the building. Derek was ready and waiting with the limo.

'So, Alex, what are you going to do with your evening?' I asked as we clambered into the VIP padded cell on wheels.

He looked suddenly coy.

'Um . . . I don't think I'll be joining the rest of you for dinner. I've made other plans.'

'They wouldn't happen to involve the lovely Sarah by any chance, would they?'

He grinned.

'I guess you got me there. You seemed well away with that dancer you were talking to. What are you going to be doing?'

I screwed my face up.

'Nothing that exciting, unfortunately; we never got each other's numbers. It looks like I'll be working off my frustration in the gym before getting an early night. I'm going to be busy filming tomorrow anyway.'

'Oh, yeah! Those scenes! You'll be up early again then?'

'Yes. It's alright for you guys. You can take your time over breakfast before the limo comes back to take you home. Meanwhile, I'm going to be suffering for my art.'

Alex sat back in his seat as we pulled away.

'You mean with two hot strangers' hands all over you?'

'Basically, yes. I suppose it could be worse.'

CHAPTER EIGHTEEN

I had finished my breakfast and was heading out to meet the limo when Alex sauntered into reception, whistling.

'Where have you been? As if I didn't know, you dirty stop-out.'

He looked self-conscious but he wasn't denying it.

'It seems a bit of a waste of an expensive hotel room.'

'Never mind, I'm sure you had a very comfortable night, and even this hotel doesn't come with that kind of room service, not officially anyway. I don't think the others are up yet; they spent last night in the bar. If you move quickly you can make it back up to your room before they realise you never made it back. You know Helena will only give you the third degree, and Daniel and Rafael will be merciless.'

Even though his shyness had partly returned, there was a different bounce in his step. He turned back to face me, on his way to the lift.

'Thanks for the heads up. Good luck for today.'

At the studio, things seemed quieter. The dancers had gone and even the crew was slightly reduced. Wardrobe had put me in much more everyday clothes this time and my make-up looked much more subdued.

Damien had a serious look about him as he stood talking to a slight, elfin-featured brunette and a well-built, finely chiselled young man in his early twenties. I recognised them from among the dancers who had been present the day before. They certainly looked the part as my screen lovers. It was just a shame my angel wasn't there.

'Ah Rebecca, I'd like you to meet the two people you'll be filming with today. This is Hannah,' he gestured towards the girl, who gave me a sweet but mischievous smile, 'and this is Bruce.'

I shook his hand, but nice as he was, I felt no spark of attraction between us. Perhaps acting a sex scene with him would be easier that way; we were here to work after all. Hannah, on the other hand, I could have eaten alive. My night with Linda had definitely made its mark on me.

'The first thing we're going to do is the scene outside the door,' said Damien. 'Bruce and Rebecca, you've both seen the script for that, not that there's much to say. It all needs to be in the body language and the eyes. Got it?'

We both nodded.

'It's only a short sequence, but it will be right at the start before the music comes in. What we're filming today, including the bedroom scene, will have the sound we record with it mixed into the video. I suggest the three of you grab refreshments and run through everything while we finish getting the lighting right, then we're ready to go.'

We sat down with our cups of tea and discussed how we were going to make the bedroom scene look realistic. Bruce seemed very matter of fact about it although I couldn't completely account for his professional distance.

Hannah seemed to know him quite well, so when he went for a toilet break I seized my chance to ask her about him.

She giggled.

'He's probably a bit out of his comfort zone faking sex with one woman, let alone two.'

I still didn't get it. Hannah looked at me as if I'd just landed from outer space.

'He's gay!' she said.

The light bulb came on over my head.

'So that's it. I couldn't quite put my finger on it.'

'I wouldn't worry. He's been pretty convincing so far, hasn't he? He acts as well as dances. Maybe the director didn't want to involve a man who was going to get too carried away with the scene, if you get what I mean. I think he wanted to make sure we couldn't be accused of anything improper, no matter how real the scenes look.'

I sighed, still a little disappointed.

'I suppose he's just covering himself but between you and me I'd have considered shooting them for real, even if all that's shown is just clever camera angles and lots of skin. It needs to have passion.'

'Oh, I think we'll manage that.' There was a sparkle in Hannah's eyes when they briefly met mine before she averted her gaze, blushing. That made me feel a whole lot better about things; maybe the day wasn't going to be such a loss after all.

Sarah breezed in to fetch us just as Bruce came back from the restroom. The previous evening must have agreed with her as much as it had with Alex; she seemed very chipper.

'Five minutes,' she said, holding up one hand, 'then we're ready to go.'

There was a different sway to her denim-clad hips as she made her way back out of the door. I knew that feeling.

Minutes later, Bruce and I found ourselves standing in the lamplight on a fake street corner, looking down towards one camera while another ran alongside us on tracks. Two more handheld cameras were ready to follow us. We looked at each other, both feeling like fish out of water for our different reasons. I'd never really acted much unless you counted being a star in the nativity play, and the bits I'd done as part of my Performing Arts studies.

Capture the feeling . . . capture the feeling!

'And . . . action!'

We strolled hand in hand from the street corner down to the front of the house looking into each other's eyes and stopped at the front door. I was about to open my mouth to speak my line when Damien interjected.

'Cut! Let's go for another take. We're looking for the same smouldering magic here that we've had all the rest of the shoot, Rebecca. Bruce, I need you to come in a little closer.'

We tried again. Damien interrupted before we had finished the take.

'I'm just not feeling it guys. There's no spark. Let's reset and roll again.'

Bruce and I shrugged our shoulders, went back to the street corner and tried again with the same result. Damien looked agitated.

'Do you mind if I try something?' I asked Bruce.

He looked pensive.

'What have you got in mind?'

I pulled him aside and quietly told him.

'Ooh! That'll put the cat among the pigeons.'

'Promise you won't be offended?

'No. Go for it!'

I turned to Damien.

'Can I make a suggestion?'

'I'm listening.' By now he was getting curious about what I was up to.

'I've got an idea. Give me a minute to run it past somebody. I'm just going on instinct here but it's got to be worth a try and if you don't like it, don't keep the footage.'

Damien gave me a quizzical look then resigned himself with a sigh.

'What have we got to lose? Okay everybody, take five.'

I was back in four, dashing up to Damien and holding an excited Hannah by the hand. She hadn't been to wardrobe yet, so she was still dressed in the clothes she arrived in. She looked hot regardless.

'Let's try switching this around. The song's ambiguous anyway, so why don't we make it that I bring a girl home, not a boy?'

It took a moment to sink in.

'You certainly know how to stir up a hornets' nest. The record company's going to hate this. It's one thing using sex to sell everything from music to perfume to toothpaste, but another thing turning people's attitudes and preconceptions on their heads.'

'I thought we were aiming to challenge. You said so yourself.'

He puffed out his cheeks.

'We're up against a whole raft of double standards but

if we're aiming to ruffle feathers then what the hell; let's go the whole hog.'

My hunch about Hannah had been right. She took Bruce's hand, trying to keep her enthusiasm in check.

'Thank you.' she said softly.

'Don't sweat it. If this works I'll still get my spotlight moment as the meat in the sandwich.' His tongue remained firmly planted in his cheek.

A quick trip to makeup and Hannah was ready to go. We'd opted for a natural look to contrast with the other scenes and she was so pretty anyway, she didn't need much more than what was necessary under the lights.

'Alright! Places, please! We'll try this Rebecca's way.'

Hannah and I moved to the street corner. Damien took up position behind the monitor screen that allowed him to see all the camera feeds simultaneously.

'Okay, quiet please on set and . . . action!'

Hannah looked both nervous and excited at the same time as we made our way slowly to the front of the house. Our fingertips touched, unwilling to part. We turned to each other at the front door, our breathing falling in step. My heart skipped a beat.

Just go with it.

I touched Hannah's face and drew her gently towards me into a kiss. Our lips met, softly at first then with increasing fervour. We broke away, lips moist and parted.

The script! Oh yes, the script.

'Why don't you come in for . . . coffee?' I asked. We were lost in the moment, eyes locked.

'Cut!' Damien looked suddenly excited. 'Holy shit you two; I think I just had an unprofessional response.'

When I looked around me, he wasn't the only one.

Several members of the crew were shifting uncomfortably from foot to foot, trying to hide their awkwardness. Bruce applauded.

'I don't know where that came from. The kiss wasn't in the script but we'll keep it,' Damien continued. 'I think there was a bit of camera shake on the handhelds so we're going to have to do it again if you don't mind.'

We didn't.

Two more takes and Damien was satisfied that we had what we needed. Hannah and I were anything but satisfied; we were ready to tear each other's clothes off.

'Okay, let's break to set up for the bedroom scene. Rebecca, Bruce and Hannah, you'd better get yourselves down to wardrobe.'

We emerged from the changing room wearing flesh-coloured underwear, although when I examined myself in the mirror I wasn't totally happy with what the top did to the curve of my breasts; it didn't look natural. Hannah seemed to be of the same opinion by the look on her face.

'What do you think?' I asked her. 'I'd be happy not to bother with the top.'

She looked at me for a moment, turning it over in her mind.

'What the hell! I'm game if you are.'

We re-emerged topless, although the make-up artist had insisted on powdering around our nipples to cover them, and strode onto the bedroom set presenting a united front.

Damien remained surprisingly circumspect.

'I suppose I shouldn't be surprised by anything you do anymore, Rebecca. Some shots are definitely not going to be for the general release version, but have it your way.

This is either going to make my career or kill it stone dead unless I go into directing adult movies. Come on then. Let's do this.'

The three of us clambered onto the big bed with Bruce in the middle, and Hannah and me on either side of him with our arms draped across his chest. Sarah covered us up to the waist with a silk sheet, adjusting it here and there until she appeared satisfied that it was decorously arranged.

'Lucky bastard!' muttered one of the cameramen under his breath, little knowing that Bruce would probably be more interested in him than either of us.

I mimed the third verse to camera a couple of times, then again with me in the middle looking up towards an overhead camera. Bruce and Hannah were carefully positioned over my breasts looking into each other's eyes for stylistic effect. After that, Damien cleared the set of all but essential crew which included two cameramen, the sound guy and Sarah. Everyone else had been instructed to take an extended tea break and we were back to our original places with Bruce in the middle.

'Right!' Damien looked more nervous than the three of us on the bed. 'I think the best thing we can do is let you guys freestyle this. Please, no actual sex acts and nothing too . . . specific. What we're looking for is lots of writhing, lots of hands on skin, plenty of noise, moments that we can intercut with the other footage to spice things up. Steamy as it is, don't forget we're still making a music video.'

I must have pouted because Bruce grinned, Hannah laughed and Damien just shook his head.

'Rebecca, you're a one-off and no mistake. Just take

your time with it.' He checked everyone was ready. 'Roll cameras.'

For a moment the three of us looked at each other wondering what to do then a look of inspiration crossed Hannah's face. She lowered her mouth over Bruce's left nipple, running one hand slowly up and down his chiselled torso. I followed suit on the other side before we leant across his chest and kissed each other deeply. Soon the bed was a writhing, groaning mass of arms and legs and skin.

Before long I found myself in the middle again with two pairs of lips and hands worshipping my body, gripping hold of the bedstead behind me. There was nobody else left but the three of us, except for Sadie curled up at the bottom of the bed making contented purring noises; all others had faded into the distance. Despite the fact that we weren't actually doing anything in particular, it was still affecting me; I could feel myself getting wet.

Somewhere in the distance, I heard Damien's voice.

'What we need to capture is one good loud moan, Rebecca. Think you can fake an orgasm? I've got an idea for the final part of the video.'

I wasn't sure. I'd never really needed to.

'I'll try.'

After a few moments, I felt Bruce tense when Hannah's left hand snaked, unseen, beneath the covers, but he soon relaxed again when she bypassed him and reached downwards, brushing her fingers up the inside of my leg. In the midst of everything else, Damien was unaware what was happening, but Bruce had worked it out.

Hannah's fingers found their way up to the valley between my thighs, teasing and caressing me through my invisible underwear. I propped myself up slightly and allowed my head to fall back against the pillow. Now her hand had made its way up to the waistband and crept underneath the material, finding the smooth curve of my pubic mound and heading south again. Bruce's lips brushed my skin, his strong hand lay across my right breast, stroking gently but although he played his part well, it was all for the cameras. When it came down to it, he was set decoration.

I threw my head back, struggling for breath, not daring to let myself go but Hannah was determined to push me over the edge. Her fingers slipped inside me, circling and pressing, urging me on with their insistence. This was all about Hannah and me now; an express locomotive that was gathering a momentum of its own. Her fingertips went deeper, stroking the walls of my vagina. Her palm pressed flat against my crotch, grinding against me. I closed my eyes, not daring to look at the camera. My orgasm was now a runaway train; there would be no stopping it until it reached the end of the tracks and came off the rails. I couldn't hold it back any longer.

With a final explosive exhalation, I sank back against the pillows, no longer caring where I was or who else was there. Eventually, I opened my eyes to see Bruce give Hannah a surreptitious look of disbelief while her eyes danced in triumph and she quietly slipped her hand away from me underneath the covers.

All of a sudden I became aware of the eyes that were watching us and looked around me. Damien and the sound man holding the boom microphone were staring, slack-jawed.

'Oh! Um . . . cut!' Damien composed himself. 'That was very well . . . acted. I think we got our loud sigh too.'

The sound man tapped his headphones and nodded. Sarah looked flushed, her chest heaving. She swallowed hard. Damien breathed a sigh of relief.

'Okay everybody, that's a wrap for today and a wrap for the video. Well done! Good work, people. We've captured something very special here and just in time for lunch too.'

Sarah appeared with three robes and laid them on the bed, unable to take her eyes off us.

'We'll let you get dressed in peace. See you in a few minutes.'

Now, after everything, we were alone together on the studio floor. The double doors swung noisily shut behind the retreating crew and we stared at each other. Bruce broke into a grin.

'I don't fucking believe you two, and on film as well!'

'Do you think they noticed we weren't entirely pretending?' I asked.

'I don't know. If they did, nobody's saying anything so let's just act like nothing happened.' He picked up his robe and slipped it over his muscular shoulders. 'I'll leave you two lovebirds to it.'

Hannah looked at me, bright-eyed.

'I'm sorry, I couldn't help it. I just got carried away and when he said he wanted you to moan loudly, well, I . . .'

'Shh!'

I gently took her hand and slipped her fingers into my

mouth. She still tasted of me.

Hannah caught her breath.

'So what now?' she asked.

'I think we need to finish what we started, don't you?'

She nodded, her delicate features alive with vitality, her eyes sparkling.

'I'd like that.'

'Then when we get out of here, you're coming with me.'

'In the limo?'

'Yes. We'll have it all to ourselves.'

Her eyes lit up even more.

'Where are we going? My place is in a bit of a rough neighbourhood.'

'Well, just in case we needed to film tomorrow, I'm still booked in at the hotel for another night and I haven't got around to cancelling it. How do you fancy spending the night together at the Walton-Astor?'

'Oh, fuck yes! You had me at 'finish what we started'.'

'Good! But first, let's eat. I'm frigging hungry.' A thought occurred to me. 'I don't suppose you've ever got it on in the back of a limo, have you?'

'No. I've never even been in one. Why? Have you? Got it on in the back of a limo, I mean!'

I shook my head and broke out into a grin.

'No, but I guess there's a first time for everything.'

CHAPTER NINETEEN

Life on tour was certainly hectic.

We had become part of a circus that moved from city to city, never in the same place for more than two nights in a row, living together on a tour bus en route from one gig to the next while another truck followed behind with all our gear in flight cases. I kept my favourite Les Paul with me, though. I didn't like leaving her in the truck with the half-dozen other guitars I'd taken on tour. Apart from my anklet and the gold letter S that always hung around my neck, she was my prize possession.

We soon found out who the messy ones were. I was quite tidy, much more so than I had been when I was younger, but nowhere near as finicky as Helena. That brought her into direct opposition with Daniel who seemed to be followed everywhere by a wake of clutter. There's nothing like living in a cramped space with four other people and a driver to test your relationships. On the whole, though, we got along well.

Although the gigs were fun, they were too short. We were just getting warmed up by the time we'd completed our forty minute slot and it was time to leave the stage again. At least the audiences received us with something better than indifference which was as much as a support band could hope for. We didn't get hassled for autographs much. I wasn't sure if that was a good thing or a bad thing.

We'd hardly been home in a month, living out of suitcases and staying in hotels whenever we could for a better night's sleep, when 'Come Inside' was released. Pristeen insisted on bringing out the radio edit along with its video first before they would let the full version out of the bag. They would have run a mile from the video if they could; the spineless suits were too terrified of adverse public opinion.

It wasn't even a question of taking the moral high ground, in fact far from it. They would have sold their grandmothers if they thought there was profit to be made, because when push came to shove they existed to make money rather than music. To them, it was just a vehicle, a product to be sold to consumers like breakfast cereal or ballpoint pens.

Whenever we found ourselves in meetings at the record company, I was reminded of something Linda had once said. Most of them were Linda's sharks personified. They used shallow, persuasive, well-chosen words and had intelligence to spare, but hadn't a soul to share between them. They didn't lack the courage of their convictions; they had no convictions beyond those of self-preservation, and no fucking imagination either.

The song caused a bit of a stir on its release in mid-November, but television channels didn't want to play the video and most radio stations wouldn't playlist the record, all quoting the same excuses as the record company. It would be the public who decided our future.

Everything changed when Pristeen finally released the uncut version of the song and the video over the internet, albeit under duress. We couldn't be at the office to preview the video when Damien took it to show Mitchell, but we were itching to see it nonetheless. As soon as we got the phone call to let us know it was out, I downloaded it via the Wi-Fi on the bus and we crowded round my tablet to watch.

The video opened with our shy, lamplit progress from the street corner to the front door, the first excitement-charged kiss with Hannah, and my hesitant invitation. You could feel the attraction between us; it leapt out of the screen.

'Okay, I got wood already,' admitted Rafael.

'We all know what your fantasy is, then. Keep watching to the end; you're going to love it,' I promised. 'You missed all the juicy stuff on the last day.'

It faded into the atmospherically stylish two-shot of me and Alex sitting on the stools. I purred softly into the microphone accompanied by the acoustic guitar's jazzy, clipped chords. The muted colours and occasional crackles made it look like old film except for the fact that my nails and lips stood out even redder than they had in real life. Line by line as the verse continued, the crackling diminished and the other band members appeared in shot, one by one.

The song lifted into the chorus and we were standing now. Still wearing the tea dress and guitar in hand, I opened up into the microphone before the music reined in momentarily. Through the second verse, it cut back and forth between the cloud fantasy scene and shots of us performing.

It was nice to have been able to keep the leather one-piece since it was made to fit, although I couldn't wear it on stage for more than one or two numbers; it would be too hot under the lights. As sexy as it felt when it was on, the outfit was only for show. Wearing it in the bedroom had crossed my mind, but I couldn't zip myself into it without help, and trying to peel myself out again in the heat of the moment promised to be a bit of a challenge. Although I was more patient than I used to be, taking it off involved so much grunting and heaving, the mood of the moment would be ruined. It was like trying to skin a rabbit without removing the feet.

Alex transitioned smoothly into his solo, the video cutting between Alex's hands hard at work on the neck of the guitar and me on my cloud surrounded by the writhing dancers. By the time the chorus arrived I was suspended on the swing with my head tipped back, hair almost brushing the floor, with my legs wrapped around my angel. His hands roamed my skin while I sang, his body undulating in time with the music. It was a shame we never got any closer than that. How I wished I could have got him alone or, come to think of it, with Hannah too if she liked boys that way. Now there was a thought! It never occurred to me to ask.

I began the third verse singing directly to the viewer from the bed. The camera pulled back to show Hannah and Bruce looking into each other's eyes across my body and there was an increasingly complex series of cuts from one section of footage to another, but it was the missing fourth verse we were all waiting for.

Now the band were throwing themselves into their performance, and the occupants of the bed were doing the same. Damien had been masterful with his camera angles and editing. Just as I suspected, it showed nothing but suggested everything. Our hands pressed tightly to each other's skin and clutched at the covers as the three of us writhed and moaned. It was beautifully done: erotic and passionate, perfectly counterpointing my lyrics which suggested everything without actually saying anything. It was all in the mind.

'Damn! That last verse still gets me every time.' Rafael shook his head. 'I think I've only ever heard that referred to in one other song.'

He was right; I could only think of a couple of veiled references off the top of my head; once by Led Zeppelin and once by The Doors. 'Back Door Man' was one of the songs on the compilation that Steve had put together for me. I still listened to them sometimes when I was in the mood for a little 'inspiration'. Even though it was an old blues song, supposedly about serial adultery not 'that', The Doors probably knew exactly how audiences would interpret it. Jim Morrison would have been an interesting person to meet: magnetically good looking with a filthy mind. He would have been my kind of man if he hadn't been yet another casualty of the music business, living his whole life with one finger hovering over the self-destruct button.

The closing bars saw us playing together as a band again. I unleashed the last notes into the microphone and we laid into the punchy final chords. Damien had saved his 'pièce de resistance' for last. There was a rising chorus of cries in darkness before the image of us in bed faded back in. I threw my head back against the pillows with a gasp and let out a long sigh before opening my eyes and looking directly into the camera in close-up. The image faded out.

Daniel was the first to speak.

'Oh yeah! Fuck me, that's hot!'

'I'm kind of sorry we missed the last day of filming now,' agreed Helena. 'That must have been so much fun and the last bit . . . well, it's hard to believe it was just acting.'

'It was, wasn't it?' asked Rafael.

'Of course!' I assured him. 'Besides, the bloke was gay so nothing happened there.'

I conveniently omitted to mention Hannah. Derek had been the soul of discretion when we clambered into the back of the limo and closed the connecting screen between us and the cab. He must have known what was going on because we practically attacked each other in our fervour as the car drove away, but he never said anything. All sorts of things probably happened in the back of the Lincoln. I just hope they cleaned the seats regularly and vacuumed up the cocaine from the carpets after other people had been in there. What we got up to was probably mild by comparison.

She was so sweet and wild and uninhibited with me that night. We couldn't get enough of each other. In fact, we called room service for food because neither of us could be bothered to dress and go out; we were having too much fun right where we were.

I snapped myself out of my daydream.

'What do you think, Alex?' I asked.

'I think it's great. It really does the song justice and it looks amazing. You absolutely shine all the way through and as for that last bit, well . . .' He gave me a knowing look but I said nothing. Only three people really knew the truth and a handful of others might have thought they did. Everyone else would just have to wonder.

For the first day or so, we were so busy with the tour that we were ignorant of the effect it had, then everything went mad. Within days it had gone viral all over social media and download sales went through the roof. Word spread like wildfire. The radio stations could no longer ignore the public clamour and agreed to playlist the song. The music channels finally screened the cut down version of the video after nine in the evening which only fuelled further demand for the download.

It was while we were on our way to another show that Mitchell rang.

'Rebecca, I've got some news. You might want to put this on speaker.'

I fiddled with the screen for a moment and put the phone down on the table in front of us.

'Okay, done. What is it, Mitchell?'

'Are you all sitting down?'

'Yes!' we chorused.

There was a pause.

'Congratulations, the record is now number four in the UK, with France and Germany not far behind and sales are still rising.'

We looked at each other in disbelief and would have erupted but Mitchell was still talking.

'Not only that, but sales in the States are going up exponentially. You should be top ten in the US and at least five other major markets by next week. Japan is lapping it up. Ladies and gentlemen, you've got what is rapidly becoming a worldwide hit on your hands.'

We couldn't contain ourselves anymore, whooping and yelling, jumping up and down and hugging each other. Our driver probably wondered what had happened to the suspension on the bus.

Mitchell waited patiently for quiet to return before continuing.

'You'd better get ready for the ride of your lives because this is where it all changes. You've all worked so hard for this and I'm really proud of you, but if you thought your schedule was full before, just you wait.'

We were also relieved; there would be no more struggling to make ends meet. Even then, we had no idea just how much our world was about to change.

-0-

It wasn't long before the backlash started. Self-appointed moral guardians began popping out of the woodwork, bemoaning the song's lax morality, while others applauded its honesty. LGBT groups waded into the fight in its defence, which further fuelled the righteous indignation of the more conservative elements, including some religious groups.

All I'd done was write a song. There wasn't even any swearing in it and there was none of the misogyny that seemed to be so common in rap videos. There was no violence either. What was so wrong about three people taking pleasure in each other? Mitchell remained placid. He advised me to rise above the arguments and say nothing in public until things died down.

'There's no such thing as bad publicity,' he said when we spoke on the phone. 'Just stay out of the fray for now.

Meanwhile, you can watch the sales figures go up and your career take off. Even the record company are starting to see the value in controversy now they're shifting units. Sit back and watch them fawn all over you and tell you how they've always had faith in you, how they were just waiting for the right time and all the other stuff they're bound to come out with. Take it all with a big pinch of salt. As long as you're making them money you'll be able to do no wrong.'

He was right of course. The top brass at Pristeen fell over themselves to show their support now that I had become their bestselling artist overnight. Sales of the previous singles started to go up again too. By the time the album came out, presales and online orders pushed it straight to the number one slot in the UK, and other countries followed in quick succession.

It was the strangest thing, to finally hold in my hand the tangible result of everything I'd spent my life working for, with my name and a beckoning picture of me on the cover. Of course, we had to call the album 'Come Inside' too; it was the perfect invitation to the voyage of discovery it was meant to be.

The support slots were reaching the end of their run. The plan had been to continue with the European leg of the tour as a support act but there was now such a clamour for tickets that Mitchell hastily arranged a series of headlining gigs instead. We began playing to bigger and bigger venues and it was such a buzz to hear the audiences shouting for us and not someone else. Now we could really throw ourselves into the live performances, expand the stage show and give them a full hour and three-quarter set. Between gigs, we even flew to the US to make some appearances too.

The band and I worked and worked, and yet when everything was one mad, dizzying rush of adrenaline and excitement, it didn't feel like a chore despite the exhausting schedule of gigs, interviews and television appearances. We burned the candle at both ends and got away with it, riding high on the wave of our success.

It didn't take the press long to latch on to me. To them, I was the latest sex symbol, another excuse to sell copy. Photographers began following me everywhere in the hope of catching a 'wardrobe malfunction' or an episode of drunken behaviour they could splash across the papers but I was mostly too busy for indiscretions, sexual or otherwise. It was quite amusing to watch the paparazzi out of the window of hotel bedrooms, camped out waiting for me in the vain hope that I was going to do something newsworthy.

When I did emerge into the street, I was usually met by a crowd of outstretched hands eager for autographs. I would sign as many of them as I could reach before impatient security people steered me towards a waiting car and whisked me away to whatever appointment was next on the schedule.

In the meantime, 'Come Inside' had been nominated for a UK Music Award in the category for 'Best British Video' and I had been put forward for 'Best British Breakthrough Act'. Even though we didn't actually come top in either of them, there were worthy winners and the whole thing did our profile no harm at all.

Every so often I would receive a message inviting me to one of Linda's friends 'events'. As much as the idea appealed, I had to turn them down; I was always too busy. It would have been nice to be able to let my hair down. The thought of the sexual adventure still out there for the taking was still such a secret thrill but my private life had been on hold for months. I didn't even know how many events Linda made it to, seeing as she was away at university and probably didn't have the money to travel back very often. It was a safe bet she didn't run short of other entertainment, though.

Pristeen released another single which continued our success, but they were pressing for a new album, keen for more high profile singles. It was a good job I had plenty of songs up my sleeve. Whenever we had some quiet time on the tour bus or sat around in hotels I would write. Alex and I started writing together too. It was an interesting combination; we both had such different approaches and yet somehow it worked. Doug flew back over to the UK to make the new album with us. It was good to see him again.

'Listen, honey,' he said when we met at Mitchell's office, 'I had so much fun with you guys the last time I wasn't going to miss this for the world and besides which, the roll you're on, we'd have to really screw it up not to have another success on our hands.'

'Well it's good to have you back with us,' added Mitchell. 'I know there were things you wanted to do last time but couldn't. We should have a much bigger production budget this time around, so your hands won't be as tied when it comes to drafting in things like horns or strings. Don't let Pristeen rush things either. Rebecca and the band have worked really hard this last year or so since everything kicked off and it will do everyone good to catch their breath.'

Doug nodded.

'Nobody wants burnout. We've all been there.'

'Exactly! We're in this for the long haul.' Mitchell turned to me. 'So Rebecca, relax and take a few days off. Recharge your batteries and we'll take the time to get this record right before you go back into the arena to face the lions again.'

'I think I'll try to catch up with a few old friends. It's going to be strange being back at home for more than a day here and there. Even my birthday was spent on the road. Jeff's planning to have a barbeque, supposedly to celebrate his birthday, but I think it's just a good excuse for a knees-up and a get-together if you ask me.'

Mitchell smiled.

'Yes, I've been invited too. I think just about everyone your folks know is going, plus a few more besides.'

'Why don't you come as well?' I asked Doug.

He looked perplexed.

'Your step-dad doesn't know me, though.'

'That doesn't matter; I'm inviting you. Besides, I think you'd have a lot in common, not least record production. It's the first Saturday in July if you can make it. Hopefully, the weather will hold, but we'll put up a marquee in case it rains. After all, you never know for sure what the British weather is going to do.'

'Well, I haven't made any other plans for my stay yet, so that would be really nice, as long as I'm not intruding.'

It was so like Doug to be unassuming. Although he looked the part, he never played the star outside of the public gaze. I liked that about him.

'Of course not, it would be good to have you there,' I said. 'If your wife and children have come over with you this time, you could bring them too.'

'Thank you. They're here for the first couple of months. After that, they'll have to go back before the kids start school again in the fall and I don't suppose we'll finish making the album until the end of October at least.'

CHAPTER TWENTY

'Sweetie!' Linda flung her arms around me as soon as I stepped through the front door. 'I can't believe you're here at last. It's been so long.'

'I know, but what a whirlwind it's been! My feet haven't touched the ground.'

'So who's been sweeping you off your feet lately then?' Linda looked at me quizzically.

'No one, more's the pity. At least my bank balance looks a bit healthier than it did this time last year but my love life is close to non-existent at the moment. Speaking of which, how's Scott?'

'Oh, he's got a girlfriend at university who doesn't let him out of her sight. A bit over-possessive if you ask me! She'd turn into a right bunny-boiler if she thought he so much as looked at anyone else, never mind someone he had history with, so I wouldn't hold out much hope of getting reacquainted there.'

'And he puts up with that?'

She looked at me and pulled a face.

'For now, but I don't think it'll last. I mean, how can it, not when he's tasted the kind of freedom he had with us? Maybe she'll learn the hard way that you don't hold onto someone by suffocating them, but by then it'll be too late.'

'What about Dean? Don't you ever see him anymore?'

'Nah! That went quiet a long time ago.' For a moment I wasn't sure if she was being overly dismissive, but then her expression darkened. 'Things got too complicated for their own good.'

Loretta Maloney appeared at the top of the stairs and came down to greet me, removing her reading glasses.

'Rebecca, it's so good to see you.' She placed her hands either side of my face and took a good look at me. 'You look well. Fame is obviously agreeing with you. How's life as a rock star?'

'It might sound strange to say it but I wouldn't know.'

She gave me a questioning look.

'I still think of myself as a musician, not as a celebrity,' I explained. 'It's like I'm someone else when the spotlight of publicity is on me. In fact, I'm quite looking forward to a few days of just being me instead of public property. It's nice to get back home for some sanity. In fairness, my manager always warned me it would be like that and so did Jeff.'

'Well, sweetie, to us you'll always be part of the furniture here, as well as Linda's closest friend, so if you're looking to get your feet back on the ground then you've come to the right place.'

'Thank you. I mean, I can't complain. I'm where I always hoped to be, successfully making music. We're starting work on a new album and there's none of the uncertainty we had before, just the pressure to keep delivering, but mostly it's good.'

'Well I'm sure the two of you have a lot of catching up to do, so I'll let you get on with it. I'm making tea. Would you like one, Rebecca?'

'Yes please, Mrs M.'

'What about you, Linda?'

'I'll have a coffee if that's alright, Mum.'

'Yes, okay.' Her tone was grudging but good natured, a hint of a smile playing around the corners of her mouth. 'You've always got to be the odd one out.'

'That's me to a T.'

Loretta shook her head.

'You always were a contrary child. Go on up, you two. I'll bring them in when they're ready.'

It was almost like nothing had changed and the events of the last year were a bizarre dream as we bounded excitedly up the stairs. Now, though, when I followed Linda's long, jeans-covered legs up to her room, I could imagine sinking my teeth into that slender behind and making her squeal. I could console myself that it was all Linda's fault in the first place; she'd started it.

'So,' I asked as we sat down on the bed, 'how's university?'

She nodded sagely.

'Good, I suppose: confirming most of my theories about humanity and its foibles.'

'And Ryan?'

'Oh, I was wondering how long it would take you to get round to him. He's fine, working his way up the ladder and doing his Masters Degree as well. He's in with all the big shots. You know what he's like; he can charm the birds out of the trees.'

And out of their knickers too, I've no doubt.

I touched the gold letter hanging around my neck and smiled.

'I'll bet he's making good money too.'

'Alright I suppose, but not in your league.'

I shrugged my shoulders.

'Yes, but he'll still be earning good money long after the public have forgotten me. Besides, I've got no time to spend it.'

'Not yet,' Linda laid back on the bed and put her legs across my lap, 'but you will one day.'

'So come on then, what are these theories of yours?' I said, patting her knee. This had the potential to be one of those golden moments when Linda let her guard down.

'Well, I wouldn't exactly call them my theories, it's just that the more I learn about psychology, the more it confirms what I already thought about what drives people.'

'Which is?'

She propped herself up on her elbows.

'Sex, mostly! Freud might have had a bit of an Oedipus complex and projected his own peculiarities onto his assessment of others but he was definitely onto something. Beyond our own instinct for survival and our basic needs, what motivates people is sex. Oh sure, we might dress it up in fancy terms or try to deny it, even to ourselves, but we're all the same underneath.'

'Is that why you keep the company you keep? They're subjects for study?' I realised I had been absent-mindedly stroking her leg.

'More than that, they're friends, but it is a doorway to my prospective career.'

There always seemed to be an angle with Linda; nothing happened without purpose.

Loretta knocked on the door and dropped off a tray

with the drinks and a plate of cake bars on it. We put the tray on the bedside table and thanked her before she disappeared back to her office.

'Go on,' I said, turning to face Linda again, propping a pillow behind me then leaning back against the headboard with my mug of tea. We dovetailed our legs together.

'It's all about Maslow's Hierarchy of Needs, even though I don't think he ever placed sexuality at the top of the triangle himself. He was too preoccupied with western values and aspirations. I think Freud might have.'

'You've lost me.'

Linda took up position on her mental soap box and I settled in. This was beginning to sound like it had become another hobbyhorse of hers.

'Abraham Maslow ranked people's wants and needs in terms of importance. It's often shown as a triangle or pyramid to make it easier to get to grips with. We tend to focus on the lowest level of the triangle that is missing from our lives. To cut a long story short, once our needs are met we turn our attention to what we want and ultimately to what fulfils us as human beings. He called it self-actualisation. He placed sex itself right at the bottom of the triangle among basic needs, but I think it comes full circle to find itself at the top as well because Maslow was more concerned with altruism than hedonism. I think he underestimated people's capacity for selfishness and their inability to see beyond material wealth. You only have to look at the behaviour patterns of the new class of super-rich to see that in action.'

Linda sat upright and paused for a moment. I just

listened, waiting for her to pull the threads together.

'So what expresses the fulfilment and gratification of an individual's desires more than sex?' she continued. 'It explains why it can become a major preoccupation to the wealthy and privileged. They're free to indulge themselves because they have opportunity as well as motive. They don't spend their lives chained to the yoke of necessity. Looking at it the other way, there's nothing less sexy than poverty and deprivation is there? Nobody fantasises about hardship and hunger. Opulence is more alluring than degradation.'

'That's true enough.'

Linda sipped her coffee and took a bite out of her cake bar.

'What really bothers me,' she said through a mouthful of cake crumbs before swallowing, 'is that we live in a more unequal society than at any time in the last hundred years. We've gone backwards. An ever increasing proportion of the wealth is being concentrated into the hands of an ever decreasing proportion of the population.'

'So where does that leave you? You sound like a socialist but you mix with the top one percent.'

She waved the remainder of her cake bar while she spoke, like she was conducting an imaginary orchestra.

'It's simple. I intend to make my living extracting money from the top of the pile by making wealthy hedonists wishes come true. Everybody wins.'

'And you're going to do that how?'

'I'm still working on the fine print, but watch this space. I don't want to say too much until things are finalised but the plan is to be ready to launch the business by the time I finish my degree.'

I'd never seen her looking so determined. She understood what she meant, even if I was still trying to work it out.

'How long have you been working on this? You sound pretty certain about it all.'

'Just like you, I think I've spent my whole life working up to this in one way or another. You were born to make music and I was born to be in the high-end leisure industry.'

'Well, that's one way of putting it.' I chortled. 'It sounds a lot like high-class prostitution to me.'

Linda shook her head.

'Think of it more as specialist events organising and you'll be closer, but the real perk of the job,' she said with a self-satisfied glance in my direction, 'is I get to join in if I feel like it.'

CHAPTER TWENTY-ONE

A small team of people arrived in a van shortly after breakfast and set about putting up the marquee. By mid-morning, they had finished, including laying the floor and setting up lights. If it hadn't been for the size of the back lawn the marquee would have dominated the garden, but there was plenty of room to spare, whatever the weather did. We were in luck, though; it looked like it was going to be a beautiful day.

Rolo would have loved all the hustle and bustle of the preparations. He'd been my friend and companion since I was a little girl, joining in with me as I danced and sang in front of the sofa, getting under our feet, sharing in all our highs and lows, and now he just wasn't around anymore. I could hardly remember a time when he hadn't been there.

When we lost him in the February at the ripe old age of fifteen, Mum phoned and told me he was gone, but it didn't seem real in amongst all the madness of life in the public eye. Now I was home I keenly felt the empty space left behind, but the rest of the family had already moved on. Even though Rob attended the football academy, he was home more often than I was and he'd never been as close to Rolo as me, so he didn't seem as affected. What really brought it home was discovering a bag of doggy treats in the pocket of my jacket which I found still hanging up in the utility room.

Today, though, it was all hands to the pumps; there was no time to brood.

Rob and I set out the tables and chairs. Mum decorated the inside of the marquee with a little help from Nanna while Jeff and Pappy moved the big grill onto the patio. Even though a catering company was preparing a lot of the food, Jeff had insisted on setting up the barbeque to grill steaks and sausages. Maybe it fulfilled a primal male need because there had been no shortage of volunteers to do a stint on the grill as long as the drinks kept flowing.

It was already getting hotter, so thankfully I had enough time to shower and change. We were just about ready by the time it reached two in the afternoon and people began to arrive. I was still helping to put the drinks out when Linda and her parents appeared. She emerged through the patio doors from the lounge in a beautiful, figure-hugging dress and high-heeled shoes that showed off her legs to maximum effect, not that she needed the extra height. She looked amazing. I wondered who she was hoping to impress.

Moving with deliberate, giraffe-like grace, she made her way over.

'Hey, sweetie!'

'You look dressed to make a killing. Who's the target?'

'Oh, no one,' she said with airy nonchalance. 'It's just nice to dress for the occasion. Anyway, you look lovely too.'

'It's only a summer dress I had in the wardrobe. I think I've got a bit curvier since I wore it last. What do you think?' I ran my hands over my hips through the thin cotton.

Linda gave me a heated look and lowered her voice.

'Stop that you saucy minx or I'll take you upstairs myself before the party's even started, and we'll end up missing the whole thing.'

'So you're in one of those moods too then; it must be the weather. Anyway, is Ryan coming?'

Linda smiled mischievously. Maybe she'd followed my train of thought.

'Yes, actually he is. He's coming down from London.' Her face dropped. 'And I think he's bringing his new girlfriend.'

'Oh!' I tried not to let the disappointment register in my voice. 'You don't sound too enamoured.'

'I've only met her once. I'm sure he'd be up for a rematch but I don't think Samantha's the sharing kind. You'll have to make up your own mind about her. I'd be interested to know what you think.'

'It'll be nice to meet her.' *Oh well, there goes that idea.* 'Punch?'

'I think that's a bit extreme. You haven't even met her yet.'

'No!' I said, picking up a glass, pointing to the bowl on the table and grinning. 'Punch!'

'Oh, go on then. I might as well start as I mean to carry on.'

I ladled us out a couple of glasses of the fruity concoction, handed Linda one and took a sip of mine, running it thoughtfully round my mouth.

'Hmm. I'm getting peaches, white wine, mangoes, ginger ale and a hint of elderflower.'

Linda raised her glass.

'And I'm getting plastered. Here's to a monster party. Cheers!'

The garden was already starting to fill up as more people arrived. A steady trickle of them came round the corner between the house and the studio. Still more emerged from the house onto the patio. Jeff had put Rob on front door duties for the time being while he and Mum greeted people when they came through into the garden.

The rest of the band had arrived and I waved to them as the guys predictably made straight for the beer. Helena looked over in my direction and rolled her eyes, laughing. Mitchell stood on the patio, shaking hands with Jeff, and standing by his side, beaming, was Penny.

I knew it.

'Excuse me a minute,' I said to Linda. 'I need to catch my manager or rather, his PA.'

Penny saw me walking towards her. Her hair was growing longer now and had turned a more natural auburn colour. She said something briefly to Mitchell who was already involved in a conversation with Jeff and placed her hand on his arm before coming down the steps to meet me halfway.

'So,' I said, 'fess up! I thought there was something between you two ages ago but you've kept a tight lid on it.'

She smiled coyly.

'We've always had a close working relationship, but I didn't think anything was going to happen for a long time because Mitchell's so dedicated to the job. In fact, when I first started working for him I thought he might be gay. It turns out I was completely wrong on that one! One day we were working late on some press releases and 'boom'; that was it! We've been together a while now. We didn't say anything about it for a long time until we knew how it would pan out and now we're going public, you're among the first to know.'

'So what prompted the coming out?'

Penny held out her hand.

'This!'

It took me a moment to register the diamond engagement ring on her finger.

'Oh my God! Congratulations!' I flung my arms around her, nearly spilling my punch. 'So do they know at the agency yet?'

'Mitchell told them yesterday. We'd kept it quiet because we didn't want it to affect our work. I'm so glad it's all out in the open now.'

'I had a feeling you fancied Mitchell but I didn't know how he felt about you until the first time we had a meeting with Doug. Mitchell got all jealous when he could see how attracted you were to him.'

'You don't miss much, do you? I confess I did that on purpose to try and provoke a response. Mitchell can be so reserved but underneath the surface, he's not what people expect at all.'

Mitchell called her over from the patio, where Mum had now joined in the conversation.

'I'll catch you later,' she said. 'Mitchell obviously wants to do some introductions.'

As I watched her go back up the steps, I noticed a petite woman with a mass of blonde, curly hair whose eyes were fixed on me. She looked about six months pregnant. Holding her hand was a little boy maybe a bit over a year old with hair so blonde it was almost white. She looked away when she noticed that I had seen her, and turned her attention back to the boy who looked up at her and said something.

I had no idea who she might be until Steve came and stood by her side. He smiled, kissed her briefly and picked up the boy, who laughed when Steve placed him on his shoulders. Valentina looked nothing like the image of her I'd always had in my head. In reality, she looked a bit like I would with curls.

Maybe Steve has a type.

She glanced furtively across at me then looked away again. I hoped she wasn't going to make a scene. Even though Steve had always tried to put me at ease about her, I had a feeling she harboured unspoken words and Latin passions might run high.

Doug arrived with his wife and their two young sons, saving me from dwelling on my thoughts. I filled some more glasses with punch and went over to greet them.

It was while we were talking that Ryan and Samantha turned up and went over to his parents. Good looking as she was in a brittle sort of way, there was something in her plastic smile that didn't fill me with confidence, and when she happened to glance over in my direction her face dropped momentarily when she recognised me. After a short round of introductions, Ryan brought her over towards me and I excused myself with Doug and his family.

'Hi, Rebecca! This is Samantha.'

When I greeted her, she gave a wide smile but the

message never reached her eyes. They remained appraising, with all the warmth of an iceberg.

'It's so nice to meet you. I love your music. It's so . . . liberated.'

'Thank you.' *I think.* 'We're just about to start work on the next album.'

'How nice.' Her smile remained pinned to her cheeks, presenting a wall of perfectly white teeth. 'Will it be the same sort of thing as the last one?'

Ryan looked at Samantha then back at me, sensing the tension I was doing my best to diffuse.

'To be honest,' I replied, 'there were only a few songs in a 'liberated' vein on the last album. The record company are pushing us to do more like that this time around now that they have a handle on how to market my music, so 1 guess it will probably be even more so, yes.'

'I see. Well, best of luck with it.'

'Thank you. So how did you two meet?'

Ryan opened his mouth to speak, but Samantha spoke for him.

'Work: Ryan works in the City, you know.'

'Yes, I did know.' She was really starting to grate on me and we'd only met two minutes ago.

Samantha hooked her arm through Ryan's, fixing her eyes on him.

'How long have you known each other?' she asked.

Ryan looked questioningly at me, puffing out his cheeks.

'Since you moved into the area, wasn't it? That must have been in the spring before I went off to university. Doesn't time fly?'

'It certainly does,' I said. 'So much has happened since then.' I resisted the temptation to touch the gold letter S hanging around my neck for fear of blushing.

Samantha slid her hand down to take hold of Ryan's, cementing her territorial claim.

'Well, we'd better circulate. There are so many people Ryan says he wants to introduce me to.'

Like who? He doesn't know many of the people here that well.

I nodded graciously. At least the uncomfortable conversation was over.

'I'll catch you later,' Ryan said, with a brief glance in my direction that Samantha didn't fully register as she led him away.

'Well, what do you think?' said a voice behind me.

'I didn't realise you were there, Linda,' I said, still watching Ryan and Samantha walking away. Samantha seemed to think that they were now out of earshot, or maybe she didn't. She turned to Ryan with a look of spite and I could just make out her words.

'I know you said we were going to a party at your friend Rebecca's, but you never told me it was that slapper.'

Ryan looked as shocked and injured as I felt.

'That's my sister's best friend and practically a member of the family you're talking about. I suggest you mind your words if you want to remain welcome here.' I don't think I'd ever seen him so furious, despite trying to keep his voice down.

If she'd been within range I'd have punched Samantha's lights out. Linda's hand took hold of my arm, holding me back, and I turned to face her.

'Don't rise to it,' she said. 'It's exactly what that two-faced bitch wants. I had a feeling about her but that just confirmed it. What a piece of work!'

'She's a reptile. Where the fuck did he find her? Underneath a rock?'

'She's probably a colleague at Goldbergs: legal department if I'm not mistaken.'

'A lawyer: that figures! I don't suppose he's told her about your family's leisure activities, has he? If she's as judgemental as that about a song, fuck knows what she'd be like if she knew the truth about that.'

'If he's got any sense he'll ditch the bitch pronto. I don't care how good she is in the sack.'

I drained my glass.

'I need another drink; a proper one, not some pussy-assed punch this time. Where's the wine?'

'That's my girl. Just don't be tempted to hit her with the bottle. It'll be all over the papers by Monday and she'll have some gilt-edged legal eagle suing the arse off you before you know what's happening.'

'Don't worry,' I assured Linda. 'I wouldn't give her the satisfaction.'

Even though Ryan and Samantha had disappeared out of view round the corner of the house, we could hear the raised voices from where we stood and so could half the party. Ryan re-appeared a couple of minutes later, just as I was pouring myself a glass of Pinotage. He looked red-faced and fuming as he came up to me.

'I'm so sorry. I had no idea she would be like that or I wouldn't have brought her. I was so looking forward to seeing everybody again, you especially, but I don't see how we can stay. I think half the people here heard at least some of the stuff she said.' He looked at me, gauging my mood. 'Are you alright? If I was you I'd have decked her.'

'I'm not going to lie and say I wasn't tempted. I'll be alright, though.' I took a good swig of the wine before I realised I had bypassed the glass and was drinking straight from the bottle. 'Where is she now?'

'In the car. I'm going to take her home. It's funny how you find out what someone's really like, isn't it? I don't think we'll be seeing each other again outside of work and that's going to be awkward enough.'

'I'm sorry. I didn't mean to cause any trouble.'

Ryan's jaw dropped. He took the wine gently from my hand, placed it on the table and wrapped his arms around me.

'You've done nothing wrong. I'm just glad I've seen Samantha for what she is before anything got too serious.'

He kissed me briefly on the lips, then stepped back to look at me, still holding onto my fingertips, a whole melting pot of emotions playing across his face.

'I'd better go and get Samantha out of here before she's lynched. Enjoy the rest of the party.'

Then he was gone again. For how long this time I didn't know. It never occurred to me to ask him if he was coming back again later; I was still reeling from that simple, honest kiss. I put my fingers to my lips as he walked away, stopping momentarily to make his apologies to Brian, Loretta and Linda.

Mum hurried over to see what was going on, now that Ryan had gone.

'Are you okay? I overheard some of the vile stuff that was coming out of that young woman's mouth.'

'I'm fine. If I see her again, though, I'm not sure I can be held responsible for my actions.'

'Well she won't be welcome here again, I can tell you that.'

The caterers brought the food out and laid it all out on a long table in the marquee. I was hungry. I hadn't eaten since breakfast; none of us had. The wine was beginning to go to my head a little and I needed to soak it up. Jeff and his crew had been busy on the grill. A stockpile of food was already keeping warm on the top rack and there was more on the way.

I made my way over to the marquee, picked up a plate and was so busy helping myself to rolls, coleslaw and kebabs on sticks that I barely noticed the woman who came up to the buffet behind me.

'It's so nice to finally get the chance to meet you, Rebecca.'

Even though her English was good, she spoke with the slow deliberation of someone who still translates their words in their head. I knew who it was before I even turned around.

'Valentina, it's nice to meet you too.'

Her eyes measured me carefully.

'It seems we share something important in our lives.'

Here we go again. What is it about people spoiling for fights today?

'What's that?' I knew what the answer was already.

'My husband.'

The set of her jaw told me she meant business. I put down my plate and looked her in the eyes, trying to keep my voice level.

'Not anymore. That was over a long time ago. He

made his choice and he chose you.'

'Yes, he did, and I suppose there are things I should be thanking you for.'

I waited for the punch line and she didn't disappoint.

'I don't know what you did to him but he came back to me a changed man and a completely different lover.'

I wasn't sure how she meant it to come across, but her words cut me more deeply than any knife ever could and far more than any of Samantha's meaningless vitriol. It must have shown on my face how much it hurt because Valentina's attitude softened and now she seemed to be fighting back tears.

More people were starting to file into the marquee now. I picked up my plate and gestured her to move to the end of the table so we could carry on our conversation. I owed her that much.

'I tried so hard to hate you,' she said, 'or at least the idea of you, you know. I love Steve; I always have. I loved him enough to leave my own family and country behind and start a new life here and I should never have let things get so bad between us that he moved out. It was hard for me, thinking about him being with someone else, although none of what happened between us was your fault. I believe him when he says it only happened after we split up.'

Valentina eyed me closely before continuing but I didn't flinch. After all, I had nothing to hide.

'It all started because we wanted children and it just wasn't happening for us.' She rested one hand on her rounded belly. 'It's funny how things turn out.'

'I'm happy for you both' I said. 'He was never mine to keep and yes, I did love him, but my career was about to take up all my time and it will for the foreseeable future. I won't lie; it was hard letting him go but he made the right choice.' Now I was close to tears as well, still finding the words difficult after all this time.

'I would like it if we could be friends,' she said.

'I'd like that too. It's always bothered me that there might be bad feeling left over.'

We put our arms around each other and hugged as closely as we could with her bump between us.

'And there is one more thing I should thank you for.'

'Oh, what's that?'

'Your honesty.'

I'd been about to take a bite of my tandoori kebab, but put it down again.

'What do you mean?'

'Your honesty right now: the way that you are speaking to me and also about the song. Nobody would have known if you had said you wrote it on your own and you would be richer too, no? Instead, it has changed our lives. If we are sensible we will never have to worry about money now and Steve wants to do more songwriting and production too. He's loyal to Jeff but he is capable of so much more than just being his engineer.' She broke out into a broad smile full of warmth and humour, nudging me heartily with her elbow. 'And we both know what a talented man he is, don't we?'

I couldn't help joining in with a big grin.

'Yes, I think we probably do. Shall we go and get something from the grill before it all goes?'

'Good idea. I'm ready to eat.'

Now there's a woman after my own heart.

We emerged into the sunlight, still chatting away.

Steve looked nervously across at us but visibly relaxed when he saw us talking. Valentina smiled at him and Steve waved his son's hand in reply.

'What's your little boy's name?' I asked.

'Aidan. We named him after Steve's grandfather from Ireland.'

'They both look happy,' I said.

'Yes, they are. We all are,' she reflected. 'Steve is a good father and we've put the past behind us. I'm glad you and I are talking too. I always wondered what you were like.'

'I know what you mean. I wondered about you too.'

'I couldn't believe the way that girl was with you earlier. She was so horrible and you'd done nothing to her. It made me think, you know?'

'I hope for Ryan's sake that's the last we see of her.'

'Ryan?'

'Her boyfriend, my best friend's brother,' I explained.

'Perhaps she felt, what's the word . . . scared? No . . . threatened! I saw the way he looks at you. You like him too, I think.'

We each collected one of everything from the barbeque.

'I'm eating for two,' she said. 'That's my excuse.'

'And I'm just hungry.' We laughed. 'Seriously, though, Ryan and I have very different lives and the timing's never been right. Life keeps getting in the way.'

'Maybe one day, no?'

'Maybe. I won't hold my breath.'

If being in Ryan's life meant keeping the company of people like Samantha, then maybe we really were worlds apart.

While we ate our food, I looked around me. Just about everybody we knew was there. Mum's friend Sandra and her husband Craig were sitting at a table eating with Jeff's Mum and Dad. Nanna and Pappy had bizarrely struck up a conversation with Doug and his wife while their boys played in and out of the bushes with other children of friends and family. It was a scene of harmony a million miles away from Samantha's earlier outburst.

I hadn't seen Rob in ages. The band members were busily mixing and chatting but he wasn't with them. Daniel's voice could be heard loud and clear above the music playing in the background. I wasn't sure how many beers he'd had but it would be a miracle if he lasted the evening. I would have thought he would be trying to chat Linda up. She'd be just his type although intellectually she could run rings around him, but there was no sign of her either.

I was just finishing my food when she appeared around the corner of the house, straightening her dress. Maybe she had been to the downstairs loo except she appeared a little flustered. It was a few moments before an overheated Rob emerged from the other end of the house through the back door of the gym, running his fingers through his untidy hair. I knew he was obsessive about using the equipment but this was a bit much even for him and . . .

I looked at Linda, calmly strolling across the lawn then back at Rob.

No! Surely not!

I had to admit it looked like they were studiously avoiding being seen together. This was a turn up for the books. I would have to press Linda for a confession. Rob was never particularly communicative at the best of times, so, secretive as she was, she was still my best chance of getting at the truth.

'Excuse me, Valentina,' I said. 'I'd better go and check something out.'

I caught up with Linda while she poured herself a drink and hauled her away into a quiet corner of the garden.

'Linda, is there something you ought to tell me?'

'What do you mean?'

'I think you know very well. Rob?'

She sighed heavily, knowing the game was up.

'Promise you won't tell anybody,' she pleaded.

'Of course not! Come on, you can tell me for Pete's sake.'

'Alright, alright!' She took a sip of her white wine and finally looked me in the eye. 'Yes.'

'Yes, what?'

'Yes, I shagged him, or rather he shagged me. Your brother's a very physical young man. You're not annoyed with me, are you?'

'Why should I be? You arranged for me to have sex with your brother while you watched if my memory serves me correctly.'

'I never thought of it like that.' Suddenly her face lit up. 'It was a right turn on too if I'm not mistaken.'

'Even though I . . .'

'Especially because you did what you did, you hot little slut.'

It was going to be one of those conversations.

'So, what did you do to Rob?' To be honest I was rather enjoying this interrogation.

'Oh, nothing too way out: Rob's very straightforward.' She winked. 'I wouldn't mind leading him further astray if I get the chance.'

'Is that the first time you've . . . ?'

She shook her head.

'It happened once before, while you were away. I was looking forward to the opportunity of getting reacquainted. Mission accomplished, I'm pleased to say.'

'Well, as long as you're both happy, who am I to stand in the way? I wish you'd told me, though; it would have been nice to know you were banging my brother.'

'Until today I thought it might have been a one-off.'

'Just don't go hurting his feelings, okay? As you've probably worked out, he's quite 'traditional' so make sure he understands where you're coming from on this. You can toy with his body all you like, but don't toy with his affections. Tread carefully.'

'Don't worry. I will. We're just having fun, but I'll make sure he understands that. The last thing I want is to hurt him or you.'

'Now that's sorted out, how about some dessert?'

Linda paused for a moment.

'Now I think about it, I haven't had any of the main course yet. I missed all that. Is there any left?'

'I expect so, but I reckon you've probably had enough meat for one afternoon.'

She stuck her tongue out.

'Ha, bloody ha! Strawberry gateau it is, then.'

On our way to the buffet, we passed Valentina and Rafael gabbling away nineteen to the dozen in Spanish. I'd wondered how long it would take them to find each other. Then we bumped into Mitchell.

'Ah Rebecca, I'm glad I caught up with you. I guess you've heard the good news.' He took off his little round glasses and began cleaning them on the hem of his shirt.

'Yes. I spoke to Penny earlier on. Congratulations! This is my friend, Linda, by the way. Linda, this is Mitchell.'

He replaced his glasses and Linda shook his hand.

'Rebecca talks about you a lot,' she said. 'If it weren't for you, she probably wouldn't be where she is now.'

'Or working with someone else, she's a pretty determined young lady. I'm just doing my job.'

'So,' I said, 'what made you take the plunge with Penny? I thought you had your private life on ice, waiting to ride off into the sunset on your Harley one day.'

'That's the problem, isn't it? Happiness is always just around the corner. Meanwhile, life passes you by. I realised I had to stop living for tomorrow and take the chance that was staring me in the face. I'm glad I did.'

On the face of it, Mitchell and Penny seemed a most unlikely couple. Until today I'd never seen him wearing jeans, it was always trousers and a shirt but no tie. On the other hand, she was twenty years younger than him and until recently at least, had always displayed a rather quirky dress sense. It seemed like they were somehow meeting each other in the middle.

'Besides,' he said, 'I've got to learn to let go of the reins a bit more with the business. I've got a good team of people now. I need to trust them to get on with it and allow myself to have a life. Penny taught me that. She's remarkably wise.'

'You certainly make quite a team,' I said.

Mitchell nodded.

'We always have. It just took me a while to see it. She's

less like a personal assistant at work and more like my right hand these days.'

Of all the people I knew, Mitchell was probably the only person who would be Linda's intellectual equal and yet, behind the bookish exterior what struck me most about him was his gentle humility. I was beginning to better understand what Penny had said earlier when she talked about what lay beneath the surface. The masks in his office were as apt a reminder to himself as anyone else about who we are behind our public facade.

By the evening, many of the younger children were beginning to flag. Steve came over to see me while Valentina led a tired Aidan to the car.

'It's been a long time. It was good to see you again,' I said.

'And you. I'm so relieved you and Valentina seem to be getting along.'

'She's nice. She was telling me about your hopes for the future.'

'Yeah, Jeff's very supportive. He understands my need to do more with myself. It's not about money; it's about being creatively fulfilled. I'm sure you'd understand that.'

I did.

'So what's next for you?' he asked.

'A new album and a new car. My old Fiesta hasn't moved much in the last year and it didn't want to start when I got home. We got it going but it's about time I replaced it, so I'm going to treat myself to something new.'

Grinning, Steve flashed me the keys to his brand new Audi.

'And why not? Great minds think alike. You've earned

it,' he said. 'I always knew you were destined for great things and I could never have allowed myself to stand in the way of that.' His smile remained but his eyes couldn't hide his emotions. 'It still hurts you know, the way things happened. I never meant for you to get caught up in my mess.'

I kissed him on the cheek.

'I still look up at my star and think of you sometimes, and I'll treasure what we shared forever. You'll always be very special to me. You know that don't you?'

'Yes.' He nodded thoughtfully and waved his hand back in the direction of the house. 'I'd better go. Valentina will be wondering what's happened to me.'

'Goodnight, Mr Bowes.'

He smiled wryly.

'Goodnight, Miss Taylor.'

I watched him walk away across the twilit lawn and turned back towards the marquee. Its sides lit up different colours as the disco got into full swing. The buffet tables had been cleared away to make a dance floor in the centre and Daniel was sleeping the alcohol off in one corner. Jeff was discussing the finer points of lawn care over a beer with Brian Maloney. Alex, Doug and Rafael were talking shop at a table away from the speakers while, as usual, it was the ladies who took possession of the dance floor.

Helena and Linda beckoned me over to the circle of dancing women which included Mum, Sandra, Doug's wife Serena, Loretta Maloney and a few others. I emptied my wine glass, kicked off my shoes and joined them.

I didn't even bother asking where Linda got to when she disappeared again after Rob had come over to join in.

One minute they were dancing together and the next they were nowhere to be seen. To my disappointment, Ryan hadn't come back. Maybe Samantha had won him over again. I hoped not. Maybe he felt awkward about returning after missing so much of the party. That was preferable.

It was well past midnight by the time we wound everything up and said goodbye to the last of the guests. Daniel had to be helped into the back of a waiting taxi by Alex and Rafael. Helena sat in the front, laughing at them. I told Loretta and Brian that Linda had crashed out up in my room and they weaved their way home, content that Linda was in safe hands.

Jeff, Mum and I waved them all off and traipsed wearily back into the house.

'Where's Rob, anyway?' asked Mum, pouring us all a glass of water.

'I think he went to bed early. Perhaps he had one beer too many?'

Mum gave me a look that told me maybe she didn't entirely believe my explanation.

Jeff wrapped his arm around Mum and kissed her.

'Time for bed,' he said, slurring slightly and swaying on his feet.

She looked at me.

'I'd better get this one upstairs as well or he won't make it. Can I leave you to lock up?'

'Sure.'

After securing the front door, I padded up the main staircase. On my way past Rob's room I could hear Linda's rhythmic, sighing breaths mingling with his and stood there for a moment, listening to the steady to and fro of their lovemaking. I checked the time on my phone. They must have disappeared from the party at about eleven and it was now nearly one. The boy had staying power, I'd give him that.

Little dramas aside, it had been a revealing and entertaining day. Things hadn't worked out quite how I'd imagined or hoped, and I was heading off to bed alone. Even so, it looked like we would still be setting an extra place at breakfast anyway.

CHAPTER TWENTY-TWO

The young man who showed me through to the office managed to be both fawning and officious at the same time: a remarkable feat in anybody's book. When we entered, Ms Ashton was still busy on the phone with her high-backed swivel chair facing away from us. Her assistant hovered nervously, waiting for her to turn around.

I'd been intrigued when Mitchell called to arrange the meeting.

'Hi, Rebecca! I know it's a bit short notice but I had an interesting conversation with a Ms Ashton at Circe Productions. They're quite a prominent independent program maker. She wants to meet with you at their offices this week. I explained that you're busy but she was quite determined. She says there's something she wants to discuss, that she knows you and that you've met before.'

Ashton . . . Ashton? It wasn't ringing any bells.

'I don't remember the name, but maybe we've met; so many people come and go in this job that it's entirely possible. Did she say what it was about?'

'I think she wants to discuss the possibility of more

regular TV appearances, but she wants to speak to you personally. To be honest it was all a bit cryptic. I must say it's not exactly a typical approach but the company checks out. What do you want to do?'

Something about it was telling me to go. I had no idea why.

'Make an appointment for later in the week. I'm already committed Monday and Tuesday, but I should be able to break away from things after that.'

'Good. I'll phone Circe Productions back and let you know,' Mitchell said.

The week after that there would have been no chance because we'd be away on promotional work for another month or so, although I was determined to be back in time for Linda's twenty-first birthday celebrations.

The last few months had been another whirlwind of activity. Even before Doug had finished mixing the whole album, Pristeen had chosen the first single and had been keen to release it as soon as possible. The title track 'Devil on my Shoulder' which had just been released, already looked set to continue our success. At least we'd all agreed on the choice of track this time and I was really proud of the video we'd made for it. Now it was full steam ahead again.

In the meantime, here I was in Ms Ashton's office and still none the wiser . . . yet.

Behind the glass-topped desk, she shifted in her chair, still with her back to me.

'Look, I'm going to have to call you back later; I've got an important meeting to attend to. I need to see the viewing figures before we make a final decision, okay . . . ? Uh huh . . . ! Alright. Bye!'

There was something about that voice, but I still couldn't place it. She heaved a sigh before turning the chair around to place the receiver back on the hook. I found myself looking into a pale, rounded face with wide, piercingly blue eyes behind large glasses and a dark line around her full lips.

Janine!

Linda never mentioned her surname, but she had said Janine worked in television. I just never expected someone as uniquely individual as Janine to be the boss. Since I saw her last she had grown her hair a bit longer, but it was no less fiery red and she was just as strikingly beautiful as ever in her own gothic fairy tale way. Despite that, she looked extraordinarily efficient and every inch in charge in a grey pencil skirt and white blouse. None of her tattoos were showing.

She looked up from her desk, surprised to see us standing there.

'Oh, Rebecca! Hi!' Her face lit up.

Janine made her way around the desk, extending a hand in greeting, and kissed me on both cheeks. There was no air-kissing, no 'mwah' noises, nothing false; her honesty and directness hadn't altered.

'So glad you could come. I didn't realise you were here already.' She looked towards the young man who had shown me in. 'I didn't hear you enter.'

He cringed, realising he hadn't knocked.

'Before I rattle on about why I wanted to see you,' she said, 'would you like some tea or coffee?'

It often seemed to be coffee these days. I fancied a change.

'Tea please, that would be nice.'

'Two teas please, Thomas. In fact, better make it a

pot.'

He turned towards the door.

'And Thomas?'

'Yes, Ms Ashton.'

'Be a darling and knock before you come back in.'

'Yes, Ms Ashton.' He reddened before hastily disappearing.

Janine rolled her eyes and smiled.

'Ball of nerves, that one! If he just relaxed a little more without losing focus, he'd be fine. Please, take a seat.'

We arranged ourselves facing each other on a small sofa with a coffee table next to it.

'I suppose you're wondering what this is all about. I know your time must be precious.'

'I've got to admit I was curious,' I said, 'but I guess you're going to enlighten me. I didn't realise it was you when my manager told me about the call.'

She nodded, crossing her legs and leaning forwards, her generous bosom straining at the buttons on her blouse.

'I'm sure Linda's told you I've followed your career with interest. Ever since your unforgettable performance at your eighteenth birthday do, it's been quite clear the camera loves you, whatever you happen to be doing!' She raised one carefully plucked eyebrow. 'Besides, I love the music too. Your new album is on in my car all the time.'

'So you're the one who bought it! I always wondered if I'd get to meet them someday.'

Janine chuckled and waggled one finger in front of her.

'Now there it is, that spark! That's part of the reason

I asked to see you. I've been looking for a good excuse to remake your acquaintance for a long time. In the wake of your recent successes, it seemed like the perfect opportunity. I wanted to see if you were interested in doing some presenting. I think you'd be absolutely magnetic at hosting your own show.'

For a moment I was gobsmacked. Was she serious? My own TV show?

'I'm very flattered, but at this stage in my career, I don't think it's likely. I've never thought of myself as a TV personality; I'm a songwriter and performer. Life in the public eye is a vehicle for the music, not the other way around.'

She remained philosophical.

'I had a feeling you'd say that, but I had to ask. Your upfront nature would make for some brilliant viewing. The rest would come with practice. You're certainly an Aries through and through; you know your own mind.'

Her faith in astrology might have seemed strangely at odds with the power-dressed businesswoman sitting in front of me, but I'd seen the tattoos I was quite sure her colleagues hadn't, including the Gemini symbol with two interlinked hearts over her pubic region. There was far more to Janine than met the eye and she was intriguing enough at first glance.

Now she was gabbling away to me like a long-lost friend, patting me on the knee while she spoke. Even though we'd only met once in what now seemed like another lifetime, her familiarity was quite disarming. An image from my eighteenth birthday video of her tongue running the length of my back projected itself onto the silver screen in my mind. Maybe that familiarity wasn't so misplaced after all. We both knew things about each other which had no place in the public arena.

It was hard to believe all that happened over two years ago. Apart from the time spent in the studio when we could work in relative peace away from the limelight, it had continued to be one mad rush. After travelling to the US to mix the album with Doug, we'd been straight back into it. Time just flew by.

'If you suspected I might turn it down, there must be more to inviting me here,' I said.

There was a knock at the door and Thomas came in with a tray of tea.

'Thank you,' Janine told him. 'I'll let you know if we need anything else. Now where were we?' she said as he closed the door on his way out. 'How do you like it by the way?'

'Sorry?'

'Your tea!'

'Oh! Uh . . . milk no sugar please.'

She talked as she poured then handed me a tea and retook her seat. I thanked her. Janine picked up her own cup and thought for a moment.

'I once told you I'd read your tarot cards for you. I still stand by that if you're interested. You've got a fascinating life and I don't think the adventure's over yet.'

'I hope it isn't. At twenty I feel like I'm just getting started. It could be interesting, though. Just don't tell Linda; you know what she's like about that sort of thing.'

Janine laughed and turned her cup ready to hook her finger through the handle.

'Yes, I do. That's a long-standing joke. In fact, it's

part of the reason I didn't contact you through Linda; she wouldn't understand.' She took a sip of tea, looking thoughtful. 'Actually, I have a confession to make. I've already done a reading with you in mind; that's why I wanted to get hold of you with some urgency. There were certain cards that worried me.'

'Go on.' I thought I might as well hear her out on this one.

Janine took a moment, choosing her words carefully.

'I think you need to be very careful of selfishness and short-sighted greed in some people. Everything comes at a price, and the price of being where you are right now is betrayal, especially by people on whom you might otherwise rely.'

'Any idea who?'

She shook her head.

'Not at the moment. I wish I could tell you more about where it will come from but the cards are rarely that specific. They illuminate situations, rather than give details. Like I said, though, I felt the need to warn you. Some people might not be everything they seem, and I would have felt bad about it if I let it slide without saying anything.'

In my position, it wasn't exactly news that other people might have their own agenda. Janine seemed genuine and she obviously set great store by this stuff. I thanked her for her concern, although I couldn't think of anyone I knew who might let me down like that. She was as complex as Linda, in her own way, and despite her apparent openness, equally mysterious, yet so utterly different.

I already knew what a sensual creature she was, and the confident allure she radiated was irresistible. If she'd opened her arms to me there and then I would have fallen into them. I could imagine the feel of her lips on my skin, losing myself in the fabulous pillows of her breasts or delving between those wonderful thighs.

Oh, Linda! What have you started?

Let's face it, it wasn't as if I had the time for much of a private life these days, and dating other celebrities as a publicity stunt in order to splash it all over social media might have been a common promotional tactic but it just wasn't my style, so the thought of getting better acquainted was quite appealing, as a friend, a lover, or both.

Ultimately I wasn't sure what to believe about the tarot cards, but whether Janine was right or wrong in her predictions, I liked her. She was content to be herself without any apology and had the courage of her convictions. I admired that.

By the time my driver took me home, we had rekindled the flame of something I never realised had gone out. I felt like I'd rediscovered an old friend, and that meant more to me than anything else.

CHAPTER TWENTY-THREE

The driver pulled up outside the hotel, opened the door for us and went round the back of the car to retrieve our overnight bags from the boot. We stepped out into the bracing November wind that was sweeping down the street, whipping up the litter and the leaves.

Jayne and Sophie, our old friends from school, had come with me to join in Linda's twenty-first birthday celebrations at Rush, one of London's top nightclubs. It was only a few doors down the street from where we were staying, so at least it wouldn't be too far to crawl at the end of the night. A group of Linda's university friends were coming down to join us, and as well as reserving a VIP area in the club I had also booked rooms at the hotel for Linda, Jayne, Sophie and myself.

The receptionist smiled politely when I went to the front desk. I recognised her from previous visits.

'Good afternoon, Miss Taylor. I've been asked to let you know that Miss Maloney is here. She checked into her room about half an hour ago. I've put you all on the same corridor, as close together as possible. We have rooms 204, 205 and you're in 207, your usual suite.'

'Thank you. Which room is Linda, um . . . Miss

Maloney in?'

'She's in room 203,' said the receptionist, handing us the key cards. 'Enjoy your stay.'

We thanked her and made our way over to the lift.

I was glad to leave behind the ever-growing entourage of people that followed me everywhere I went for once and have a weekend off. Mitchell's people often ended up having to book an entire floor to accommodate everybody. I needed a bit of me time, to just be with friends and reconnect.

'Devil on my Shoulder' was already turning out to be another massive hit. It followed me around just like the PR representative, the stylist, the security guys and all the others. The song and its video were everywhere I went.

Linda was now in the final year of her Psychology degree and we were back to seeing each other when we could. I missed her. I had thought of going to see her at university when I had a day or two here and there, but I couldn't have turned up on campus without drawing attention to myself; we wouldn't have had a moment's peace. Jeff had warned me long ago how lonely it could be at the top and now the full extent of what he meant was finally sinking in. At least I had found a new friend in Janine.

The lift doors opened onto the second-floor landing and we made our way down the corridor to our rooms.

'I'm going to catch up with Linda then get ready,' I said.

'What time does the club open?' asked Sophie.

Jayne chipped in.

'About eleven, isn't it?'

I nodded.

'Yeah. That should give us plenty of time to have a chat in the bar before going to the restaurant and on to the club. I'll see you in the bar at six.'

'See you then,' they chimed almost in unison before disappearing into their rooms. The two of them always seemed to come as a package, but then to the untrained observer, so did Linda and I.

I placed my overnight case on the stand in my room, took out the gift bag with Linda's presents in it and made straight down the corridor to room 203. I knocked.

'Who is it?' called a muffled but familiar voice.

'Room service!'

There was the padding of feet and a pause. A shadow moved across the security viewer in the door and it opened.

'Room service my arse! I didn't think I'd ordered anything.' Linda tightened the towel around her body and still dripping from the shower, wrapped her arms around me before remembering where we were. 'Oh, you'd better come in. I'm not decent.'

'You're never decent you kinky bitch,' I assured her. 'What difference does clothing make?'

Linda blew me a raspberry.

'Slut!'

I followed her into the room. It was smaller than the more generous suites I was becoming used to, but in a similar style and just as comfortable.

'Happy birthday,' I said, holding out the bag. 'I know it's not actually today but I couldn't wait and I don't think I'll get to see you on the day.'

'You didn't have to do that. Arranging all this was more than enough, and I know you're run off your feet most of the time.'

'Yes. Unfortunately, I'm run off them, not swept off them.'

'I think I can remedy that. There's a 'do' on in a couple of weeks. Fancy a night out getting reacquainted with some old friends and making a few new ones? Janine and Alan will be there too. I gather she's been in touch.'

'Yeah, she has. I saw the message about the next event but I wasn't sure if you'd be there or not. It just seemed a bit odd going on my own; after all, they're more your group of people than mine.'

The thought of getting closer to the voluptuously appealing Janine did grab my interest, though. I checked the diary on my phone.

'Remind me again. What night is it?'

'It's the Saturday, two weeks today.'

'It's free at the moment. I'll block it out so Mitchell doesn't throw a spanner in the works with another telly appearance.'

She looked at me and sighed.

'You work too hard.'

I shrugged my shoulders.

We had visited most of Europe in the last few months as well as making three trips to the United States. I didn't know what time zone I was in half the time. We were looking to do a handful of dates the following year, including playing a couple of festivals, before hopefully starting work on a third album. Meanwhile, we were also finalising plans for the video that would go with the next single.

'We have to make hay while the sun shines,' I said. 'You never know when the bubble will burst.'

Linda put up her hand.

'Okay, that's enough metaphors for one afternoon. We're off duty, remember?'

'Come on then! Open up!' I held out the bag again and this time Linda took it.

'Ooh,' she cooed, 'lingerie! The good stuff too! Is that for my benefit, or your brother's, or yours?' Her sea-green eyes met mine in a moment of unspoken understanding.

'It's for you and whoever you want to wear it for, although I wouldn't mind seeing you in it. So do you still get together with Rob, then?' I asked.

'Sometimes, holidays mostly. I'm away most of the time of course, and he seems to be playing more and more matches.'

'Yes, he reckons he might even be on the first team squad in the next year or so.'

Linda ran her fingers through her damp hair.

'What a successful family you're all turning out to be.'

'It's like you once said: we're fortunate to be blessed the way we are. The rest is about making the most of things without falling into the shark tank. Even when things were hard for us as a family Mum never lost sight of herself, so we had a good role model. Speaking of success, what's happening with your plans for the future?'

'Ah!' There was a sparkle in Linda's eyes. 'I've got something to show you. It's more than just ideas now. Ryan's been helping me with the business plan and crunching all the numbers. He's been on board with a lot of it actually. In fact, he's pretty much a fifty percent partner. Half our initial client base looks set to be wealthy bankers and business people he knows. We're both pretty good at networking.'

'It'll be alright just as long as they're not like that vile creature, Samantha. What happened to her in the end?'

Linda looked at me questioningly for a moment then waved her hands dismissively.

'Oh, her! Ryan dropped her like a hot potato. She was history by the time he'd driven her back to London. She's old news.'

Inwardly I breathed a sigh of relief.

'So what were you going to show me?'

Linda opened up her purse and pulled out a small, metal case. She flipped it open and handed me a business card. It felt luxurious to the touch, almost like velvet, and had a purple background with a black lacy pattern over the top. There were gold letters embossed on its surface which read simply:

Passion Flower

Entertainment services for the

discerning hedonist

On the other side were printed a web address, a mobile telephone number, and an email address.

'The web site's almost finished,' she said. 'We've had someone working on it for the last couple of months. It should be going live early next spring.'

'You don't mess about, do you?'

'Nope! Like I said before, this has been a long time coming.'

'Well, let's just hope your clients aren't.' I sniggered. 'So how does it all work?'

Linda smiled at my double entendre and carried on with her explanation, trying to keep a straight face.

'Basically, we organise events to order. Guests are strictly vetted and we put people together with similar tastes so they all want the same kind of thing. We rent the plushest, most exclusive, private venues for one-off events then move on to somewhere else for the next one. Apart from the staff, who are, of course, non-participating, there are potentially three types of guest: paying guests, paid guests, and invited guests.'

'So what's the difference and how does all that make money?'

'Well, it's the paying guests who the parties are organised around. The more they pay, the more say they have in what the event involves, and believe me, some people will pay extraordinary amounts of money to get exactly what they want. Paid guests are basically escorts, male and female, who are carefully chosen for their suitability and their . . . let's call it 'sense of adventure'. The third category, invited guests, would be someone like you for instance, who is welcome to come and join in but doesn't pay. There are only ever likely to be a handful of those at any one time.'

'So what does it cost people to be there?'

'Anything from a few hundred pounds upwards, depending on the nature of the event and to what extent things have been organised around their personal tastes. The idea is we make their wildest fantasies come true, safely, consensually and discreetly.'

'Wow!' I was gobsmacked. 'And there's a big market for this?'

'Huge! And it's expanding rapidly. There are people out there doing similar things already, but not quite like us. We offer events that are tailor made and unique.'

'So, how long has Ryan been involved in this?'

'Oh, about two years, on and off,' she said, nonchalantly.

I didn't know what else to say. I was speechless.

It was Linda who spoke first.

'You said you wanted to see what the lingerie looked like on me.'

'Oh, yes. Try it on.'

She took another peek inside the bag.

'These look gorgeous. I'll be right back,' she said and disappeared into the bathroom.

I sat back on the bed and waited, listening to the sound of the hairdryer for a couple of minutes before everything went quiet. I checked my phone. Four thirty-eight. It was time to show Linda my little surprise. I slipped out of my jeans and hid my legs under the bedcovers, sitting up against the headboard in my tee-shirt and underwear.

Another minute later, the bathroom door opened and Linda reappeared, a vision of loveliness in her silvery grey, front-fastening corset with panels of deep blue lace and matching briefs.

'Well?' she asked, parading herself in the doorway. 'What do you think?'

I patted the bed next to me, giving her my best come-hither stare.

'You look good enough to eat. Come here, I've got something to show you.'

Intrigued, Linda did as I asked and I slipped my right leg out from under the covers, turning the outside of my calf towards her.

She glanced up at my expectant face.

'Nice ink! When did you get that done?'

'A few weeks ago, while we were in LA. Do you like it?'

Linda ran her fingers down my calf and across the tattoo of a prowling tiger, just above the anklet and its string of golden stars, stroking my skin.

'Looks great! They've done a lovely job too. It was bound to happen eventually; she's practically your mascot.'

I nodded.

'Sadie's done me proud alright.'

'How long before we meet up with the others?' she said, looking up at me.

'Long enough,' I purred.

Linda's eyes met mine and I hooked my fingers under the laces on the corset, pulling her towards me. I ran the edge of one foot slowly all the way up her thigh, fixing her with a penetrating stare.

'Long enough!'

CHAPTER TWENTY-FOUR

Jayne and Sophie were well into their first drinks by the time Linda and I made it down to the bar. We were almost twenty minutes late.

Sophie looked at Linda, then at me.

'We were starting to worry. What kept you?'

'Blame me.' I held my hands up. 'It took me ages to get ready.'

In actual fact, after Linda and I dragged ourselves out of bed, I had dashed back to my room for a quick shower, dressed and done my hair and makeup in record time. Despite that, all four of us looked ready to make a killing. Even the quiet and normally conservatively dressed Jayne had gone the extra mile.

I ordered a bottle of champagne and we drank a toast to Linda. She would be the first of us to turn twenty-one. I would be the last, but only a few days after Jayne.

The meal at the rather upmarket Chinese restaurant across the road from the club was nice too. I'd booked us a table in a quiet corner hidden from public view by a red and gold latticework screen, and the staff there could be counted on to be discreet. The band and our entourage had filled the entire place when we went there before, so I knew they would be alright. I had to be careful, otherwise we would have no peace once I'd been recognised and that wouldn't be fair on the others, especially Linda.

We left at ten forty-five and crossed over again to the club's private entrance. Even so, we had to pass by the main door. A line of expectant revellers was already forming underneath the sign where 'RUSH' had been spelt out in large, backlit, polished metal block letters. Despite being flanked by three friends, I knew I'd been spotted by the expressions on the faces in the queue. Tonight of all nights I could do without the intrusion of being approached all the time but I would have to be gracious about it. These days I always carried a pen in my clutch bag for autographs.

A bouncer opened the private door to let us in and acknowledged us as we came through, closing it behind us again while a young girl issued us with our VIP wristbands. Linda and I checked the guest list was up to date. I was pleased to see that Ryan would be there. After all, why wouldn't he turn up for his sister's twenty-first birthday celebrations? I was curious about his 'plus one', though. Linda hadn't met her either. Hopefully, she would be nicer than the last one that crossed my path.

'Ryan changes girlfriends more often than I change my underwear,' Linda admitted on the way upstairs. 'He's a bit of a serial monogamist, to be honest, and there are women falling over themselves to go out with him. I think there must be a queuing system.'

'Why don't any of them last? He's so nice.'

'Beats me!'

As usual, I had a sneaking feeling she knew more than she was letting on.

To the right of the landing, we passed the stairs that led down to the main area of the club and flashed our wristbands to the bouncer at the entrance to the VIP room. He opened the door to let us through. Large, semi-circular sofas wrapped themselves around a series of tables and there was a private bar at the far end. Steps led down to a viewing area in front of the glass wall that overlooked the main dance floor.

We settled ourselves down on one of the curved sofas and a waitress brought our second bottle of champagne of the night over to us.

'This is the life. I could get used to this,' said Sophie, leaning back on the sofa, glass in hand, as the music from downstairs began to pump out of the speakers in the private room.

Jayne agreed.

We didn't have to wait long before Linda's university friends began to appear. Linda went to greet the steady trickle of people that were now arriving, some bearing gifts and cards. I could see many of them doing a double take when they saw me sitting with Sophie and Jayne. One of them even pointed in my direction and asked Linda straight out: 'Is that Rebecca Taylor?' Linda nodded. I could just make out her words as she told them I was an old school friend and it was me they should thank for laying on the party.

The door opened again and Ryan appeared with a pretty, short-haired, blonde girl next to him. Although she was dressed up to the nines, something about her body language and her effusive smile told me she would at least be genuine. Once he had greeted Linda, he brought her straight over to meet us. Both Jayne and

Sophie looked at him doe-eyed but it was me he approached first.

'Rebecca, I'd like to introduce Adrianne.'

'It's nice to meet you,' I said, extending a hand as I stood up.

Instead of taking it she put her arms around me, practically jumping up and down in her excitement.

'Ryan's told me so much about you,' she gushed. 'In fact, sometimes he just won't shut up. Will you, Ryan?'

He smiled at her and rolled his eyes in amusement. I had a feeling it was probably her that never shut up. Despite that, Adrianne was a vast improvement on the 'Wicked Bitch of the West'. I smiled inwardly at the thought of landing a house on the evil Samantha's head, or maybe she'd melt if someone threw a bucket of water over her.

'Would you like to join us?' I said. 'We're just having some bubbly but they've got everything you can imagine up at the bar.'

They sat down and made themselves at home while the room filled up. Down below us, the club was getting busier and there were queues forming at the bar. Not many people had braved the dance floor yet, but the constantly shifting lights already created a sense of movement. Now the crowd was building up it wouldn't be long before people spilt onto the dance floor just to find some space.

As the party got into full swing, it was good to see Linda relaxed and happy, mixing with everyone around the room. Adrianne was monopolising Ryan so there wasn't much chance to talk. I would have liked to ask him more about Passion Flower but maybe this was not the time or place and besides, the volume of the music didn't make for easy conversation.

Linda, Sophie, Jayne and a group of others wanted to go down to the main dance floor. I had a feeling I would attract too much attention and I didn't want to spoil things for Linda but she was adamant, grabbing me by the hand and practically dragging me out of the door and down the staircase to the main part of the club.

'Come on! Don't be a party pooper.'

By this stage, she was quite tipsy. We were all feeling it a bit, but she had downed a little more of the champagne than the rest of us; it was her birthday after all.

'It's about time we got out there on the pull,' she insisted.

I gave in. Hopefully, due to the flashing lights, I would remain fairly anonymous in the middle of the crowd.

We made our way down into the throng and bounced our way onto the dance floor forming a gaggle of moving bodies, arms in the air, hips swaying to the insistent beat. It wasn't really my kind of music, but at that moment I didn't care. I felt free and liberated; glad to be among friends. The record segued into another and we danced on, writhing and turning in what space we had among the crush.

I needed to pee.

Bollocks!

Now I'd have to fight my way to the ladies room and probably be recognised in the process. I leant in to shout in Linda's ear, gesturing as I did so.

'I'm just going to the loo. See you in a minute.'

She nodded and carried on dancing, carried away by

the pounding beat, and I turned towards the edge of the dance floor, easing my way forwards through the sea of moving bodies.

I'd not gone more than a few yards before there was a tap on my shoulder.

Oh, here we go! Another autograph hunter!

I turned to face them wearing the benign expression I saved for insistent members of the public. Nothing could have prepared me for the shock. I looked up into a pearly smile beaming at me from out of the dark face of my angel of ecstasy.

'Lee! What are you doing here?'

'The same thing you are, I hope,' he shouted above the music, 'having a good time. You remembered me. I'm impressed.'

'I have to admit I hardly recognised you with clothes on and without your wings.' I gestured towards the restrooms. 'I was just trying to get to the loo.'

'Allow me,' he said, clearing a path with his tall, muscular frame and escorting me off the dance floor.

'I won't be a minute. Wait here,' I told him.

He was still there when I got back, despite my having been recognised twice in the queue for the cubicles.

Why is there always a queue for the ladies while the gents seem to go straight in?

'Come with me,' I shouted. 'I know where it's easier to talk.'

I led him up the staircase to the VIP room. The bouncer held the door open for me then noticed that Lee didn't have the right wristband on and put his arm out.

'I'm sorry, sir; you're not on the guest list.'

For once in my life, I pulled rank.

'Do you know who paid for this private room?'

'Yes, Miss Taylor.'

'Good! Then I'm inviting him.'

He opened his mouth to say something but thought better of it. His arm pulled back and he held the door open again.

'Thank you,' I said sweetly, and we walked in.

The music was still loud upstairs, but nowhere near as pounding as down on the dance floor. At least we didn't have to struggle as much to hear each other now. There were still quite a few people in the VIP area, including Ryan and his girlfriend who were busy chatting over cocktails.

Lee and I sat down on one of the free sofas, as far away from the speakers as we could.

'So how's life?' I asked him.

'Busy sometimes, you know. The dancing's either all go or nothing. What about you? Your career's certainly taken off since we made the video.'

'It keeps me out of trouble, more's the pity. It's been nice to catch up with friends. We're here for my friend's twenty-first.'

'So where's the birthday girl?'

'Down there,' I said, pointing through the glass. 'She's probably going to send out a search party if I take too long getting back. It's so nice to see you, though. You look well.'

In fact, he looked very well. My mind was racing about ten steps ahead of our conversation and had skipped straight to the part where I tore his top off and Sadie sank her teeth into him.

'I try to look after myself.'

And you've been making a good job of it.

'In my line of work it's pretty much essential,' he added. 'You must get recognised everywhere you go now. Even I get stopped sometimes.'

'Yeah. Fame's not necessarily all it's cracked up to be. It was never the reason I do what I do. Dancing must be much the same.'

'True, I suppose. I do it because I love it. It's certainly not the most reliable thing to do for a living.'

We had been talking for about ten minutes, leaning in close so we could hear each other properly before I realised Ryan was looking across at us. He smiled when I caught his eye and took Adrianne's hand. They stood up, ready to go downstairs and join in the dancing.

'Shit, we'd better go downstairs as well. Linda's going to think I've been abducted by aliens.'

'Come on then,' he said, taking my hand too. It felt comforting.

We descended the stairs and threaded back through the crowds until we eventually found Linda and the others.

'Where the heck have you b . . . ? Oh, hello!' Linda's eyes lit up. 'Are you going to introduce me?'

'This is Lee,' I shouted above the music. He was one of the dancers on the 'Come Inside' video. We bumped into each other a few minutes ago.'

Recognition dawned, despite the champagne.

'Oh, I know! He's the one who was . . .' she made a thrusting movement with her hips, 'while you were on the swing. Aren't you lucky to get reacquainted?' She flashed me an appreciative look.

Lee obviously got the gist of what Linda was saying

and grinned, joining in with the dancing. He could probably have put us all to shame but avoided fancy moves, resisting the temptation to show off. Nevertheless, he moved with an effortless ease that caught the attention of all the girls in our group. Sophie was practically frothing at the mouth, but he barely noticed. He only had eyes for me while we danced.

When he put his hands on my hips I melted against his body, falling into rhythm with him, grinding away to the incessant beat and tucking my head in against his chest. He lifted my face and kissed me momentarily.

'I'm sorry, I . . .'

'It's okay,' I said, looking into his eyes. 'You can do it again if you like.'

This time he lingered on my lips which parted to meet his.

There was a loud 'Wooh!' from the assembly of friends around us and the rest of the world faded away into the distance: the music, the crowds, everything.

He wants me too.

Sadie leapt into the air and did a back flip, whether that's something tigers are actually capable of or not.

We lasted another half hour on the dance floor before I couldn't stand the waiting any longer.

Enough foreplay!

'We're going to slope off to somewhere more comfortable,' I said to Linda. 'You're alright with that aren't you?'

'Listen if it wasn't my party and I might be missed, I'd be tempted to join you, sweetie.'

'Maybe next time,' I promised, kissing her cheek and patting her on the shoulder. 'See you at breakfast.'

I turned to Jayne and Sophie who were still dancing together.

'Take good care of Linda, will you? She might need it by the end of the night.'

Sophie looked at me, trying not to let the jealousy show.

'Don't worry. We've got it.'

Lee and I weaved through the bodies, stopping to pick up my clutch bag from upstairs on the way, and stepped out of the hot club into the chill night air. It was two am, and the street was empty except for a handful of parked cars. We walked the short distance between the club and the hotel, snuggling into each other to keep out the cold wind. At the entrance, I wrapped my arms around his neck and pulled him in close, kissing him. He returned my attention with increasing fervour, hands firmly gripping the cheeks of my behind and pulling me against the heat and stiffness of his erection.

'Mm!' I purred deep in my throat. 'I think we need to take this inside, don't you?'

'That sounds good to me.' His voice was like molasses to my honey.

We tried to maintain our composure on the way through the hotel lobby, but as soon as the lift doors closed we fell on each other, hands exploring, tongues entwined.

With a ping, the doors opened again and we tumbled out into the empty corridor.

'This way,' I said, leading him by the hand to the door of suite 207. I fetched the key card out of my clutch purse. Once we were inside and the door had closed behind us he picked me up, giggling with surprise, with his hands underneath me and my legs around his waist, and carried me through to the bedroom. He put me down gently and lay beside me, propped up on his elbow.

'I still don't understand why you'd be interested in someone like me. You're a big star now and I thought you were out of my league back when we first met.' He looked puzzled.

'Don't be daft. What makes you think I'm any different to the girl you met on a video shoot? I'm a musician, you're a dancer. What's the problem?'

'I guess when you put it that way: nothing.'

'Well then.' I sat up, sliding my hands underneath his top and lifting it up to kiss the smooth skin across his midriff. Whatever he'd used in the shower gave the aroma of his skin a deep, woody resonance. 'What say . . . we have ourselves,' I worked my way downwards, reaching to unbuckle his belt and sliding his trousers down his thighs, '. . . some fun?'

Jesus!

I ran my fingers across the bulge in his hipsters, eased them down over his erection and looked up at him, eyes wide with disbelief.

'Bloody hell, Lee! Is all that for little old, innocent me?'

'You're not old and I doubt you're completely innocent. As for little, what are you, five foot four?'

'About that, yes. I'm little compared to you. How tall are you, six foot two?'

'And a half! The extra makes all the difference, you know!' Lee's eyes shone with humour.

I glanced down at my fingers struggling to wrap themselves around his cock and lifted him towards me so that the dark, swollen head almost brushed my face.

Biting softly into my lower lip I looked up again into his eyes. He had an expression of expectant longing.

'Yes.' My mouth was watering. 'Apparently, it does.'

Cradling him against my palm I leant forwards and gently took one of his balls into my mouth then languidly ran my tongue up the ridge of his cock before dripping saliva onto the head and spreading it over the swollen glans with my fingertips. I teased around the corona before opening my mouth wide and slipping my lips around him. He exhaled sharply when I lowered my head to engulf as much of him as I could.

It was a struggle, even for me. I needed to find some bigger bananas to practise on. He groaned loudly and tipped his head back while I went to work, sucking hard and circling with my tongue before I slipped him slowly from my mouth and gently kissed the end.

'So.' I said, stroking his shaft with my finger. 'Is it?'

'Is it what?' His muscular chest was heaving. His eyes burned with dark desire.

'All for me,' I teased.

The intensity of his expression gave me my answer anyway but when he spoke his voice was weighty and resonant.

'Oh, yeah! Believe me; you can have as much as you want.'

CHAPTER TWENTY-FIVE

Half in and half out of sleep, I could feel his Lee's generous lips softly brushing my shoulder blade.

'How long have you been awake?' I asked, letting out a gentle sigh.

'Not long, but why would I want to waste too much time sleeping when I've got you next to me?'

I rolled over to face him.

'Didn't you say you have somewhere to go today?'

'Later on this morning, yes. I'm going with my family to see my sister's new baby. What time is it now?'

I stretched and checked my phone, feeling surprisingly energised considering how little sleep we'd had.

'Just gone eight. I'm supposed to be meeting the others for breakfast at nine thirty.'

It was a good bet Linda and Co. weren't going to be quite as bright and breezy. They had been planning to hit the bar upstairs for shots when they came off the dance floor and the club didn't shut until five am, if they'd actually managed to last that long.

'Would it be alright to have a shower while you're at breakfast?' he asked. 'I'll probably have to go home and get everything sorted out before you get back, though.'

'Well make sure we swap numbers first! Don't think I'm going to let you slip through my fingers a second time. Call me later, okay?'

'Just try and stop me. You're going to think I'm a pain in the arse before long.'

'Oh, I don't know.' I chewed the inside of my cheek and raised my eyebrows. 'Things have worked out alright so far.'

Only a few hours before, I'd had my doubts I'd be able to cope, but I needn't have worried. To my surprise and both our delight he fitted beautifully . . . everywhere.

'I'm going to need a shower too before I go downstairs, but I reckon,' I ran the fingertips of one hand across his smooth chest, doing my best to look coy, 'that gives us long enough for a little appetiser to start the day.'

'Does it, now?'

Judging by the sparkle in his eyes and the growing stiffness that pressed up against me, Lee was now wide awake and in full agreement. *Choices, choices!* The tough part was deciding what best to do with the time that we had.

I sat up and straddled his chest, preparing to work my way down his body but his hands clamped across my buttocks, pulling me towards him instead.

'How about you bring some of that sweetness up here first?' he asked with a glint in his eye.

'Well since you ask so nicely,' I began to sidle up his body instead, 'then how can I refuse?'

He guided me until I was poised right above him, steadying myself against the headboard, then wrapping his hands around my thighs he lifted his head to meet me. Looking down my body I watched as his lips closed around my pussy and I could feel his eager tongue working its way inside me. I began a little rolling motion with my hips, gripping the headboard tightly, my mouth falling open as he went to work. He seemed to be enjoying himself just as much as I was.

'Oh Jesus, Lee! That's good.'

He stopped for a moment and lowered his head.

'After last night, returning the compliment seems like the least I could do.'

'You're very welcome, but don't stop,' I panted. 'I was just getting into that.'

His willing tongue made contact with me again, swirling and probing, his mouth pressing against me. I bit my lip, looking down into the deep brown eyes of my angel and melted like warm butter onto hot, fresh toast.

-0-

When I strolled into the dining room just after half nine, humming a little tune to myself, Linda, Jayne and Sophie were already sitting at a table with coffee and fruit juice in front of them, looking a bit grey. They perked up when they saw me but there was no hiding the collective hangover they were nursing.

'Here she comes,' announced Linda, 'doing the walk of shame.'

'I don't know what you mean,' I protested.

Linda continued, undeterred.

'So, how do you feel now you've gone over to the dark side of the force? Is it true what they say?'

'As if you haven't found out for yourself at some point!' I snorted. 'Anyway, that would be telling,' I said with a grin, putting my hands out in front of me and moving them further and further apart.

'Oh, you lucky cow!' piped up Sophie. 'He was dreamy too.'

'Yes, he was. I could tell you fancied him, but in all fairness, I saw him first. We met on a video shoot but lost touch. So how was the rest of your night?'

'Good, I think,' said Jayne, trying to keep a mouthful of coffee down. 'I don't really remember much after about half three. I swear I'm never touching tequila again for as long as I live.'

I winced on their behalf.

'Ouch! Tequila and Champagne: that's not a good combo.'

Linda looked at me out of one eye, screwing up the other side of her face.

'No. It bloody well isn't.'

Still chuckling, I went over to the food counter and filled a plate up with a full English breakfast: sausages, bacon, scrambled eggs, black pudding, beans, mushrooms, tomatoes, hash browns and two slices of toast. They all shot me a filthy look when I took it back over to the table and sat down.

'What? I'm hungry. Don't look at me like that.'

'You mean you haven't had enough black pudding already?' asked Sophie.

'Well,' I pouted, 'there's always room for a little more.'

Linda sniggered.

'Fuck it! If you can't beat them, join them,' she said, getting up to fetch a plate and leaving the other two shaking their heads in disbelief. 'Best hangover cure there is if you can keep it down.'

A waitress came over and I ordered a pot of tea just for good measure. All told, it had been one hell of a night but since we had to vacate our rooms before midday, I was looking forward to going home and getting some sleep. Although I definitely had the advantage over the rest of them, the tiredness would catch up with me sooner rather than later and I was already starting to ache in an assortment of places. I hadn't had a night like that in a long time and hopefully, it wasn't going to be the last.

When I got back up to my room there was a note propped up against the pillow, written on hotel stationery.

> Rebecca,
>
> Thank you for a wonderful and totally unexpected night. I can't wait to see you again. I'll call you later, when we get back from the hospital.
>
> Lee xxx

Life felt good.

I arranged for the driver to pick us up at half eleven

and danced around the room, clearing up my stuff and humming to myself. It had been ages since I'd felt as light of heart and nimble on my feet.

Once a cheerful but still bleary-eyed Linda had been dropped off, I was the last of us to make it back home. Mum was busy making Sunday lunch when I came into the kitchen.

'Good afternoon,' she said, looking at her watch. 'Big night, was it?'

'You could say that.'

'There's going to be plenty of food. Do you want to join us?'

'Actually, I had a massive breakfast not that long ago, so I'm good. Thanks anyway. I'm just going to chill and recuperate if that's alright.'

'No problem, sweetheart.'

I put the TV on in my room and watched it from the bed, checking my phone periodically to see if Lee had left a message.

Nothing yet.

By late afternoon I was getting a bit concerned. Maybe there'd been complications at the hospital. Maybe he'd changed his mind about seeing me. I tried to convince myself it was just tiredness and paranoia and resisted the temptation to call him. I didn't want to scare him off by appearing needy and he did say he would call when he could.

The last twenty-four hours were finally starting to catch up with me. By early evening my eyes were becoming heavy and still fully dressed I drifted off into a deep and dreamless sleep.

CHAPTER TWENTY-SIX

I opened my eyes to the sound of my mobile phone ringing. The light of a clear, autumn morning streamed into the room.

Oh good! It must be Lee. I wonder what kept him.

It wasn't. It was Mitchell.

'Rebecca, have you seen the papers?' He sounded concerned.

'What? No. What time is it?'

'I suggest you check out the tabloids. I know you don't normally read the papers, but I think on this occasion you're going to need to. Don't get them yourself, though; send somebody else. Call me back.'

And then he was gone. I didn't get a chance to ask him anything else before he rang off.

What the fuck?

I went down to the kitchen where Mum and Jeff were eating breakfast.

'Morning, Rebecca. You looked so tired yesterday I decided to let you sl . . . What is it? You look like you've seen a ghost.'

'I've just had this really weird call from Mitchell. He says we need to check out the papers but I'm not to go out to get them myself.'

'I'm on it,' said Jeff, grabbing his jacket and his keys. 'It's only five minutes to the shop and back.'

Fifteen minutes later he returned with a worried expression on his face.

'I've just had to run the gauntlet of half a dozen cars full of photographers and reporters parked in the road outside the house. I think you ought to look at this, Rebecca: page five.'

He slid the paper across the breakfast bar towards me.

I turned the first couple of pages over and froze. There were pictures of myself and Lee snuggling together on our way down the street and locked in a kiss by the entrance to the hotel underneath the headline 'My Nights of Passion with Rebecca Taylor'.

My brain raced, trying to process everything, but didn't know where to start.

First, there was confusion. Where had the photographer been? The street was empty except . . .

Shit! They must have been waiting for us in one of the parked cars!

How did they know where I'd be? Was Lee involved? He'd obviously talked to reporters, but when? Was this whole thing a set-up?

Then there was righteous indignation. What business did the photographers have following me to my friend's birthday party? How dare Lee talk to the papers, whether it was a set-up or not. And it was one night, not several; they couldn't even get that bit right.

Mum came round and looked over my shoulder at the open paper.

'Oh, Rebecca, sweetheart! Who is he anyway?'

'He's someone I bumped into at Linda's party. We'd met before. He was in the 'Come Inside' video.'

'Well, it was only a matter of time before they managed to catch you out having some sort of private life. They've been gunning for you ever since the song came out. It's not as if you were doing anything so terrible is it? 'Twenty-year-old woman cops off with young man at nightclub'. Big deal! If you weren't famous it wouldn't exactly be newsworthy, would it?'

'I know that. It's more Lee's role in this that bothers me. They can print what they like. Most of it is probably crap anyway; it usually is.'

'What have they said?'

I read the article out loud.

'Our enterprising photographer snapped sexpot superstar Rebecca Taylor (21) in a hot clinch with hunky dancer Lee Daniels (24) outside a famous West London hotel. When our reporters spoke to him he confessed to having steamy all night sessions with the gorgeous singer, known for the sexy singles 'Come Inside' and 'Devil on my Shoulder' and their now infamous, raunchy videos which have caused an internet sensation.'

I put the paper back down on the breakfast bar. I couldn't stand to read any more.

'This is such bullshit. They're making a story out of nothing just so they can push people's buttons and sell their tawdry little rag. They couldn't even get my age right; I'm not twenty-one yet. I need to hear Lee's side of this, but right now I'm so fucking angry with him for talking to the papers. Whatever happened between us is nobody else's business.'

Jeff had been checking the other paper he'd brought

with him.

'What does that one say?' I asked.

'Pretty much the same.' He opened it up at page seven. 'It looks like the photographer was a freelancer who sold the shots to as many papers as possible. They all seem to have been taken from the same viewpoint.'

'I'd better ring Mitchell back. He'll want to know what I think.'

I picked up my phone. There was still nothing from Lee. He was probably too ashamed to ring me. I wanted to speak to him, but first I needed Mitchell's input. I dialled, pacing up and down the kitchen floor.

'Mitchell? Hi, it's Rebecca.'

'Have you seen the papers yet?' He sounded relieved to hear my voice.

'Yes. It's a whole lot of nothing really. I hooked up with someone at a party, so what? What hurts the most is he seems to have gone to the press, so I do need to speak to him.'

'I agree. From the point of view of your career, it will do no harm at all. You're not trying to project a squeaky clean image so they've got nothing on you there.'

'There are reporters camped out at the end of the drive, though.'

'I thought they might do that. Media exposure is a two-edged sword; you live and you die by it. The crucial thing is not to fall on it. Don't attempt to speak to them; in fact, don't go outside at all. Just lay low until they eventually go away.'

'Oh great! So basically I'm a prisoner here for the moment.'

'I'm afraid that's about the size of it. What they want is

to provoke a reaction so they can get more news out of it. Don't let them wind you up to the point where you do anything foolish because they'll keep going until you snap and then you'll get the blame. This is what the tabloids do; they build up your profile so they can knock you down again. It's like a game of skittles to them.'

I exhaled slowly.

'Wonderful! This just keeps getting better and better.'

Mitchell remained insistent.

'Just whatever you do don't engage them, any of you. Stay inside and out of sight.'

Our home, my family's home, had been turned from a place of refuge to a prison without bars. We were basically under house arrest. Rob had gone out early enough to have missed everything, so we would have to warn him before he became embroiled in the cordon of waiting reporters and photographers at the end of the drive when he returned. The last thing we needed was him losing his cool and thumping one of them when they goaded him.

By the afternoon, the circling vultures had become impatient at the lack of carrion to pick. We were having a cup of tea and trying to relax when we heard a tap at the window. The moment we looked around to see what it was, a flash lit up the room as a photographer began taking pictures through the glass, then another through the side window, followed by another.

We retreated to the snug.

'This is ridiculous!' Mum was fuming. 'Sitting at the end of the drive is one thing, but surely they can't come up to the house like this.'

She telephoned the police and explained the situation,

only to be asked if our gate was closed.

'No,' she said. 'We never close the gate at the end of the drive. Why?'

I could just make out the tinny babble of a voice on the other end of the line.

'So you mean to tell me that unless we close the gate, anybody can come up to the house and they're not trespassing, is that it?' She shook her head in disbelief. 'But what about our eighteen-year-old son? He'll have to fight his way through the press outside then get out of the car to open it up again. He'll be mobbed.'

Once again the voice on the other end of the line droned away.

'So there's nothing you can do. Well, thanks for your help.' The incredulity in her voice had been replaced by resignation and finally by sarcasm. She put the phone down.

'It seems that there's nothing we can do beyond asking them to leave which, let's face it, they're not going to do because they've got the scent of blood in their nostrils.'

'Doing that would just leave us exposed anyway,' added Jeff, trying to stay strong for all our sakes. He couldn't hide the note of despondency in his voice, though.

'True,' I said. 'Mitchell was very clear about keeping our heads down.'

I'd never really seen the point of electric gates. They always seemed a bit flashy and unnecessary to me, but now I was beginning to appreciate the advantages. Mum phoned Rob to warn him about the situation while I took the remainder of my tea upstairs for some solace. If he had any sense, he would go to Nanna and Pappy's place instead of coming home.

I rang Linda's mobile. It went straight to voicemail so I left a message for her not to talk to anyone about me if they approached her and to call me when she got the chance. Still there was no word from Lee, but I was damned if I was going to be the one to call him. I sat back on the bed with my tea, staring up at the ceiling.

Another half hour passed before my phone rang. It was Linda.

'Hey sweetie, what's going on? I picked up your message and somebody just said there was some shit going on in the papers today.'

'Where are you?'

'Back at university: I've just come out of a lecture. Why?'

I told her about the article and the pictures, explained the situation with the reporters and what Lee appeared to have done. She was better off out of it.

'The absolute fucker! Just wait till I get my hands on him.' Linda sounded furious.

'Let's not jump to any conclusions until I've heard his side of the story, okay? The trouble is the longer this goes on, the harder it's going to be getting straight answers.'

'Well if you need me, call me. I'm just on my way back to digs now to finish an assignment so I'm there if you want to talk.'

'Thank you. You're a true friend. I could certainly use that kind of friendship right now.'

'You're welcome. Catch you later, sweetie.'

Even though I knew what the answer would be, I checked my phone again for any incoming calls or messages. Still, there was nothing.

I was close to giving in and ringing Lee myself when a call came in from an unknown land line. I recognised the deep voice on the other end, even though he sounded nervous.

'Rebecca?'

I stood up to speak to him.

'Hello, Lee. I think you've got some explaining to do.'

'Yes. I guess I have, but it's not what you think.'

'Go on then; tell me what I'm thinking.' My tone remained sharp.

'It wasn't a set-up, I promise you. I was as surprised as you were when we bumped into each other.'

If that was true, then either we were followed or someone else tipped off the photographer. Finding out the truth behind that would be another matter.

'So what happened, then?'

'When I got back from seeing my sister and the new baby, they were waiting for me outside the house. They knew my name; they knew all about me. Then they started asking me all these questions about you and they wouldn't shut up or go away. They wouldn't take no for an answer. I couldn't even get to the front door.'

'What did you tell them?'

'Hardly anything.' It was a strange choice of words. What was that supposed to mean?

'But you didn't deny it, though. That told them everything they needed to know. They were bluffing you.'

'I . . . I'm so sorry. I'm not used to handling this sort of thing.'

I started to ease up on him a little. No matter how stupid he'd been, naivety was a forgivable sin.

'I don't personally care who knows I have a sex life. It's not me that's been hit hardest, it's my family. We're all under siege right now. I get the impression you're close to your family.'

'Yes. I am.'

'Then maybe you can understand how hurt I am by this. It's turning their lives upside down, that's what's really unfair.'

A thought crossed my mind and I had to ask the question.

'Did they pay you?'

He went quiet and my stomach hit the floor.

'Lee, did they pay you for talking to them?' This time there was greater urgency in my voice. There was another pause before he answered.

'What you've got to understand is the dancing jobs have been few and far between and I'm behind on the rent and . . .'

'You bastard, Lee!' The words came out in a kind of explosive whisper as I choked back tears of outrage that welled up from somewhere deep inside. I found my voice again.

'I don't have to understand anything. None of that shit would have mattered if you played your cards right. I really liked you. I thought we were at the start of something good. Any debts you owe, whatever hole you'd dug yourself into, they wouldn't have mattered because I'd gladly share my good fortune with you. It would be a drop in the ocean. All you had to do was stand by me but you've blown that now; you've blown everything.'

'I didn't want you for your money. I wasn't going to

count on you for that. How could I? What I wanted was you.'

'But it didn't stop you caving in at the first sign of temptation, did it?'

Apart from the sound of his breathing, he remained very quiet on the other end of the line. I guess he didn't know what else to say in his defence.

'The thing is,' I said, discovering a new reserve of calm, 'there are people out there with far more dirt to dish on me than you could imagine, and you know something? None of them has ever breathed a word, not one person, despite the fact that some of them have lifestyles others might make all sorts of moral judgements about. They've still got something you don't: integrity. You can't put a price tag on that, no matter how you try to justify it to yourself.'

'I'm sorry,' he repeated, probably more cowed by my cool rationality than if I'd actually lost my temper. While everything in life whirled around me in chaos, at the eye of the storm everything remained momentarily still.

'Sorry won't cut it, Lee; it's too late for that. You can't undo what's been done. It's not just me, you sold my whole family out and I won't ever be able to get past that. Some things might be forgiven, but they're never forgotten.'

'I didn't mean to hurt you, Rebecca,' He sounded like he meant it but I wasn't about to relent; I couldn't. Without trust, what did we have left to base a relationship on?

'You know, you're not the first person to ever say that to me, but the difference is they were only trying to do the right thing. On the other hand, you were too short-sighted and selfish to know what the right thing was. Whatever they paid you, I hope it was worth it.'

'Rebecca, if I could take it back and do things differently, I would.'

But it really was too late for that; he knew it too. He sounded broken.

Anger reared its head again: a spitting cobra, poised, waiting to strike. I did my best to quell it, but alongside the anger lay the sense of loss and sadness at what might have been. I wasn't sure which was worse. If I was honest with myself I wasn't even sure whether the anger was all directed at Lee, or whether some of it belonged to me for allowing this to happen, for being foolish enough to think that I could have a normal life. I could feel my self-control slipping away and I was damned if I was going to show him any weakness. Why prolong the agony?

Taking a deep breath I levelled my voice, trying to keep the bitterness at bay but failing.

'Goodbye, Lee. Take your thirty pieces of silver and have a nice life. I hope you and the money are very happy together.'

I pressed 'End Call' on the screen and stared at it for a moment with my hand over my mouth, hoping to steady my breathing and hold on to some shred of dignity, but the cobra bared its fangs and lunged. Venting all my venomous fury I hurled the phone at the door, shattering it into a dozen pieces, and slumped onto the edge of the bed with my head in my hands.

ABOUT THE AUTHOR

D.V. Williams was born and grew up (sort of) in the southeast of England. After eminently sensible careers in industry and teaching while spending any free time writing songs and poetry and performing in bands, he finally carried out a lifelong threat to do something life-affirmingly un-sensible and write a book. The creative urge had finally taken over. There was a story to be told that refused to go away.

Two years on, and the first three books about Rebecca's life and loves had been completed. All that was needed now was to get them published, and that, as anybody who's ever tried it knows, is another journey altogether.

The author is married with two teenage sons and lives in southwest Wales. They share their home with two cats, a neurotic collie, and an ever-growing collection of musical instruments.

www.dominic-williams.co.uk

www.facebook.com/DVWilliamsAuthor

www.twitter.com/DomVWilliams

COMING NEXT . . .

THE GILDED TOWER

D.V. WILLIAMS

It's lonely being famous. What chance is there for love?

Hounded by the paparazzi, Rebecca Taylor moves into a large house and grounds, protected from prying eyes by a high wall and electric gates. Her only regular company around the house is her housekeeper, Francesca. Publicly she is now a big star living the dream, but privately she is still haunted by her lover Lee's betrayal and longs for the affection and adventure she once shared with Steve.

But a nomination at the UK Music Awards is about to change everything for the better again and maybe love is finally on the cards. Her best friend Linda Maloney's business plans are at last becoming a reality too, catapulting Rebecca, not for the first time, into a secret world of decadent and forbidden pleasures.

As Rebecca is about to discover, when you appear to have it all there is a lot to lose.

Tigers Book Three

Lightning Source UK Ltd.
Milton Keynes UK
UKHW03f0335310318
320333UK00002B/92/P

9 780995 771529